Buried Truths

Book Two of the Tales from Edovia Series

Copyright © May 2016 Nicky James

This is a work of fiction. Names, characters, places, and incidents are the product of the author's imagination. Any resemblance to actual persons, living or dead, events or locations is entirely coincidental.

Cover Art provided by Jay Aheer of Simply Defined Art

Editing provided by Pam Ebeler of Undivided Editing

All rights reserved. This book is licensed to the original publisher only. No part of this book may be reproduced, scanned or distributed.

This book contains mature content and is only intended for adult readers over the age of 18.

TRIGGER WARNING

This book contains scenes of self harm that may act as triggers for some people.

Also from this Author

Tales from Edovia

Something from Nothing

Buried Truths

Secrets Best Untold (Coming August 2016)

Acknowledgments

Where to begin? Writing and publishing has been my dream come true and without the help of certain people I could never have made it happen.

Thank you Pam Ebeler. You have been more than an editor; you have been a friend. You helped me believe in my boys and bring their stories life. Your encouragement and kind words always make me soar while your hidden comments in the margins make me smile and laugh.

Thank you Jay Aheer for making such incredible covers for my stories. I stare at them for hours admiring their beauty. You have a gift and I'm grateful you were willing to grace my work with it.

Lastly, thank you to my husband and my rock, Jamie. You put up with all my craziness and listen to me when the voices pop out of my head unannounced…Even if it's at the supermarket. You have been my biggest supporter and I could never have made this journey without you.

Dedication

This one is for all the people out there who picked up my books and gave them a chance. Thank you!

Buried Truths

Tales from Edovia: Book Two

Nicky James

Jay:
Thank you for your time, love and patience. I hope you enjoy this journey
Nicky James
xoxo

Chapter One

Aaron

"Do it! I don't care where. I'm going to close my eyes and just cut me, all right?"

I stand with my eyes squeezed shut before my best friend Caleb, and wait for the familiar sting of flesh being pierced. Yes, familiar…Don't judge me.

"This is getting out of hand, Aaron. You know you shouldn't be doing this. You'll end up with a festering wound if you're not careful. People have died from lesser things."

"I'm counting on it. Then I'll get to see him even more. Now do it for crying out loud, before Leeson looks over here and catches us."

Too late.

Captain Leeson's voice booms across the training field as he stands with his arms crossed over his chest, glaring at us with steel gray eyes. His darker blond hair dances in the warm summer breeze across his tanned skin, causing a few sun bleached pieces to catch the light and reflect them back to the eye, a symptom of having spent many long days in the outdoors.

"This doesn't look like drills, boys. This looks like messing around. If I don't see something productive from you soon you'll be spending extra time with me after everyone else gets dismissed."

"Way to go," I say, glaring Caleb's way, "I told you to hurry up."

"Good grief, Aaron. If you want this guy that bad there are other ways to go about getting him, better ways that don't end with you bleeding all over his floor. I shouldn't even be condoning this. Now come on, you take offense and let's get to work before we end up having to be here all day." Caleb's hazel eyes are filled with annoyance. "I don't know about you, but I have better things to do than spend my day here."

"I *had* better things to do as well, but it was all based around this and you're too busy deciding what's best for me or not."

"Because it's wrong on so many levels, Aaron. Wake up."

I hold my sword at the ready and wait for Caleb to do the same. Glancing back over to the captain, I see he hasn't taken his eyes off of us.

Damn. I'll have to convince Caleb to work it into our drill somehow. Once Leeson thinks any of his men aren't working hard enough, his hawk eyes never stray far. He's a hard ass on the field and doesn't tolerate slackers. He works his men to the bone and has a keen eye for those who don't take training seriously. He's a well-respected man, but sometimes I wish his attention to detail and scrutinizing glare would take a break.

Caleb nods his head, indicating he's ready for me to begin.

We were both recruited at the same time; just after one of the biggest trails ever recorded. The King himself and our own Captain Leeson were tried for the crime of sodomy this past winter. There probably isn't a single person in Edovia who hasn't heard about it by now. It was a turning point in history, and my life. The King fought the law and won and in turn had the law abolished. It was hands down the greatest day, for me and everyone like me who have been hiding their sexuality all their lives.

Caleb has always known where my preferences in life lie and he never makes me feel ashamed for them. Even before the law was lifted, I never had to hide who I was from him. We've been best friends since childhood and we keep no secrets from each other. He accepts me for who I am and always has my back, no matter what.

Refocusing back on drills, I do my part by trying to land a hit on Caleb, while he does his best to try to defend my every effort. After the captain sees we have thrown ourselves back into our work and are no longer goofing around, I notice him turn his attention back to the lessons he was giving a few other men. I'm not stupid though, I know he hasn't forgot about our inattention and will check back in at any moment.

Having landed a few lucky hits on Caleb, I lower my sword to take a breather.

"Let's switch out." I say. "Work through the drill as usual, but when I give the word, I'm going to stop deflecting and you cut me. Got it?"

"Aaron! Seriously, knock this shit off-"

"Do it, Caleb. You said you'd help me. I'm begging you. Just don't tell me where. I don't want to know."

Caleb sighs and runs a hand through his shaggy blond hair, "You don't need a wound to see the doctor. You're sick enough in the head. You know that, right?"

Despite his insistence that I'm crazy and his hesitancy about helping me, I know Caleb won't let me down. He hasn't yet and he knows it's important to me. We begin our next round with me taking defense this time. I play along as Caleb makes easy, even hits at me. I can tell he is just making it look like we are hard at work for the captain's sake, but in truth, he is waiting for me to give the word.

I kept one eye on Caleb's sword and the other on Leeson. The instant Leeson's back is turned to us again; I meet Caleb's eyes.

"Now," I say, lowering my sword and squeezing my eyes closed again.

I know it is coming, but the moment the cold steel sinks into my skin, I reel back nearly falling on my ass. A warm rush of blood pours out of the wound and runs flowing down my face. The stupid, bloody shit sliced me across the forehead. My hands reflexively fly to the gaping wound as I hunch over trying to keep my feet beneath me.

"What the hell, Caleb?!? You cut me in the head!"

My head throbs and the more it does, the more the wound pours down the front of me. Using both hands, I try to contain the flow, but it seeps around my fingers, blinding me as it runs into my eyes.

"You cut my head? What is the matter with you?"

Caleb is at my side and grabs my arm, trying to steady me, I release my head and look up at him, shooting daggers his way and see the concern etched in his hazel eyes.

"Holy shit, that's a lot of blood. I didn't think I got you that bad."

"You cut my head!"

I know I asked him to cut me and I know I told him to not let me know where. But my head?!?

I can hear a commotion being to brew around me and I know Leeson is probably nearby. Groaning to myself, I shuffle back upright. *Here we go.* I'm so angry with Caleb right now, but I know I need to put it aside and pretend this was all an accident for both our sakes or we might be dismissed from the King's men for good. However, make no mistake, the man is going to hear an earful later. You don't just go around marking up a guy's face.

"What the hell is happening over here?" Leeson has approached and I can tell by his voice, he is far from impressed with us.

"It was an accident, Sir." Caleb tries to explain what happened, but seems to be having difficulty coming up with a good reason for his blade to have been striking at my face.

"You alright, Pryor?" Leeson asks me.

I'm thoroughly saturated with my own blood at this point and am fuming mad at my so called best friend, but I nod. "It doesn't hurt too much, Sir. Just a lot of blood."

"You'll need that sewn up. Mathers, take him to see Dr. Schuyler immediately, then report back here. We need to have a little chat."

"Yes, Sir." Caleb says. Despite the waves of blood obscuring my vision, I don't miss the sneer Caleb aims in my direction.

As we make our way through the city, my forehead continues to bleed everywhere. Concern that I may be losing too much blood quickens my pace. The damn thing won't stop. At this rate, I may bleed myself dry before I even get there.

"Why the hell did you cut my face?" I ask.

"You said to cut you, you didn't specify where. Anyway, I was thinking of you when I did it."

I glare at my best friend.

"You think I wanted to be sliced in the head? What kind of sicko wants to be cut in the head?"

"What kind of sicko wants to be cut period, Aaron? I'm not the one with the problem. Anyway, I did you a favor. Think about it. Now you'll get to stare into his face as he sews you back up. Dreamy right?" Caleb waggles his eyebrows at me.

"I hate you."

"No you don't. You'll thank me once you're in front of him, staring into his eyes."

"I'm going to have a scar on my face now. I will not thank you for that."

Caleb shrugs, "Maybe next time you'll come up with a better plan to see the guy then."

Standing in front of the surgery, my heart begins to pound a little harder in my chest - which isn't helping my bleeding predicament I might add. I'm moments away from seeing him again and am feeling lightheaded and increasingly nervous. I turn to Caleb, swipe my nearly black hair to the side and hold a hand to my head to redirect the blood flow so it won't blind me. "How do I look?"

Caleb rolls his eyes. "Like an idiot." He says as he knocks on the door.

When the doctor opens it, my breath is momentarily knocked out of me as I stare into the most beautiful face I have ever seen. Yup, totally worth it. His chestnut brown hair is tied back in a tie behind his head, but a few wavy strands that aren't quite long enough fall forward into his face. I want to reach out and tuck them behind his ear, like I've seen him do a million times before. He is several inches shorter than my six foot two frame, so his emerald green eyes need to climb up to meet my own. I must be quite the sight, because even being a doctor, his jaw falls open when he sees my blood soaked face.

"Good grief, Aaron. What have you done now?"

"Hi, Chase." I say lowering my eyes in shame and hoping my blood stained cheeks hide the flush creeping into my face.

"The idiot took a sword to the face, Doc. Needs you to work your magic yet again."

Dr. Schuyler, or Chase as I've come to know him, holds the door open for us to enter. I make my way into a little side room where he sees most of his patients and sit down on what is beginning to feel like my own personal stool. Beside me, a large wooden table sits empty, waiting for the necessary tools Chase will use to mend me up. I know the drill. A small table against the far wall is bursting with various supplies, all with their own specific use, many of them foreign to me. A collection of vials clutter the shelves above it, filled with more items whose uses are also unknown.

I'm embarrassed to admit this is my fourth, self-inflicted - or rather, Caleb inflicted - injury and fifth visit to see Chase since our arrival in the city this past spring. The first time I came for doctoring was for legitimate reasons. I fell during practice and thought I had broken my arm. Turns out, I just strained the muscle, but the visit was not in vain. One look at the city doctor and I knew my life would never be the same.

Chase flies in the door behind us and wastes no time getting to work. He grabs a clean strip of cloth from a pile, wads it up and jams it hard against my forehead.

"Hold this for me, good and tight, while I get some things together." He instructs.

Doing as I'm told, I hold the cloth to my head as I watch Chase gathering supplies. His back is turned to me and I have an excellent view of his perfect, round ass sitting snug inside his tight fitting breeches.

Holy hell you're gorgeous.

His crisp white shirt has the sleeves rolled up to the elbows and his slight, tanned arms work hard to prepare what he needs. He isn't built like the men I work with day in and day out on the field, he has a much smaller frame that I could easily wrap up in my arms if I wanted to…and I want to. Where soldiers have heavy, thick muscles from swinging swords all day long, his are lithe and lean, perfectly toned to suit his body.

Chase spins around, breaking me out of my daze, and comes to set some things down on his work table beside me.

"Okay, let's have a look at what you've done."

He peels the cloth off my head and the blood continues to pour as it did before.

"Why is it bleeding so much? Is it that deep?" I ask.

Chase replaces the dressing, puts one hand behind my head, and applies pressure with the other; pressing tight as he tries to control the blood flow. His face is close to my own and his eyes fall from my forehead to meet my gaze. Like a lush forest, holding mysteries waiting to be discovered, they beckon me and I lose myself in their green depths. Everything around me is forgotten. I probably couldn't remember my name at this point if someone asked. Stupid Caleb was right, it's the perfect place to be cut. Not only am I swooning, but apparently I'm a bloody poet now...*Lush forests? Mysteries waiting to be discovered? What the hell?*

"It's probably not so bad, the forehead bleeds a lot is all. Once I can get some control over it, I'll sew you back up and you should be good as new."

"Uh-huh." I can't even remember the question I asked.

"Well if you think he's going to live, Doc, I'm going to head back to the field. The captain needs to have a word with me now. I'll catch up with you later, Aaron."

Reluctantly, breaking my eyes away from Chase's flawless, jade gemstones, I glance over to Caleb. He brings a hand up to cover his heart and mimics the pitter patter he knows I'm feeling in my chest right now. He bats his eyes in a love sick manner and makes kissy lips, teasing me. I dart a glance to Chase, but he is occupied with my forehead and is oblivious to Caleb's mocking. I give my friend a quick grin.

"Thank you, Caleb. You were right." I add, giving credit where it is due.

Caleb gives me wink, "You are very welcome."

Removing the cloth again, satisfied the bleeding is somewhat under control, Chase starts to work at sewing me back together. Bringing his face even closer to my own, he works at making an even job of each suture. I inadvertently flinch each time he pierces my skin, but do my best to sit still. His tongue sticks out of his mouth a little bit while he concentrates, toying with the upper corner of his full, pink lips. It's a habit I've seen him do on a few occasions now, but never so close. I have to fight the urge to lean in and kiss the man right there. Take those lush lips, taste their essence, and feel that teasing tongue tangled up with mine.

"Have you ever considered a different job, Aaron? I'm not sure you're really cut out to be a soldier."

Ouch. That is the downfall to my plan. Chase is beginning to think I can't handle myself on the field, when in truth, I really am a decent swordsman. Not the best by any means, but I can certainly hold my own.

"I'm not that bad. Truly."

Chase looks down into my eyes to assess my honesty.

"Well if that's the case, then I'm starting to think you're getting hurt on purpose."

"W-why would I do that?" I stammer.

"Either you have a strange obsession with your own blood or," Chase pauses regarding me, "you're trying to make excuses to come see me."

I swallow the newly formed lump in my throat. Well, I guess I've crossed the line into obvious obsession. Now all I need to do is own it. My heart hammers in my chest as his beautiful eyes wait to hear which it is.

Just tell him how you feel. Ask him to dinner maybe. Drinks. Ask him out for a drink. That's a nice casual outing. Okay, I can do this. I'm going to ask him to go have a drink with me.

"You have to admit; blood has strange qualities. Like how it's warm and wet when it flows from a cut…and then, when it dries, it gets all sticky and gooey. Haven't you ever wondered why it does that? I have, it's so weird."

…and now I want to die.

Okay, I admit, I have a serious problem and it is called, "whenever the heat is on, make a joke, any joke. Lighten the mood". Which is exactly what's happening.

There is a lull in the moment before Chase starts laughing so hard he is unable to continue sewing up my face, which in turn makes me laugh too. A huge sense of relief washes over me, but do I stop? No, his laugher eggs me on.

"See, look," I say, showing him my blood coated fingers and how they have begun to stick to one another as the blood dries, "Sticky."

This only encourages more fits of laughter between us. He has the most incredible laugh. I could listen to it all day. When Chase finally catches his breath, and is able start resewing, he shakes his head at me in disbelief.

"I guess you kind of need cleaned up. You're quite the mess this time."

"Yeah, turns out I can't hold blood in with just my hands. Not for lack of trying though, I might add."

Finished with the last few sutures, Chase gets up and wets a strip of clean cloth in a basin of water on the far table. Instead of handing it to me to clean myself up, he makes work of doing it for me. He wipes across my cheeks and over my nose, taking special care around my eyes. His face is so close to mine, I can smell his sweet scent. I inhale a mixture of lavender, wood smoke, and a trace of earthy pine. It's intoxicating. I find myself lost again in his eyes as he works. He stands closer to me than I think a doctor might normally stand while working on a patient and I wonder if he feels the connection between us too. His eyes dart around while he works, but every now and then, they meet mine and a soft smile is exchanged. I don't hear him the first time he speaks, being so caught up in admiring the delicate way his fingers work to clean me up.

"Sorry, what was that?"

"You can wash your hands in the basin if you'd like. Your face is clean."

"Oh, thank you."

I make my way to the basin and scrub the drying blood away into the water. I'm reluctant to be leaving already and have become anxious at the fact that I still haven't found enough nerve to ask the man to have drinks with me. Why is this so difficult?

It has never been a question of whether or not Chase shares my same preferences for men. I know he does, or at least I put a lot of faith in the things I've heard. When the infamous trial finished, the city was flooded with all kinds of rumors surrounding the King's relationship with Captain Leeson. One of those rumors was that Leeson had been in a past relationship, years ago, with Chase. I guess I don't have any solid confirmation that it's true, but call it a hunch, I feel in my bones it is.

Chase offers me a towel and I accept it gratefully. I want to say something and I don't want it to be stupid. I shuffle on my feet trying to find a reason to stay longer as I take my time drying my hands. I have done this same song and dance so many times, I want this to be the last. Chase watches me and I get the sense he knows why I'm lingering. I don't know what holds me back every time. Fear of rejection maybe? Whatever it is, my nerve slips away and I slump my shoulders in defeat, finding nothing to say. I turn to the door to leave, cursing myself yet again.

"Thanks again, Chase. I'll try to be more careful," Lies. I know by the time I'm halfway through the city I will already be conjuring up another way to find myself back here. Caleb will tear a strip off me and might just refuse to help me again, leaving me no choice but to do it myself, something I've been avoiding at all costs. I have my reasons.

"Oh. Just for the record." I say as an afterthought, turning back to him. "I really don't have a sick obsession with my own blood."

Chase's face lights up into a warm smile and his eyes shift to the ground, almost like he is struggling to hold my gaze.

"You know, Aaron. You should probably stop by in a couple days and let me check on those sutures. You know, make sure their holding up."

My heart speeds up in my chest, "I can do that...Umm...Okay. See you in a couple days."

Chapter Two

Chase

When Aaron walks out of the surgery, I bar the door and lean hard against it, letting out a rush of breath. It's all the confirmation I need. The man has been showing up at my door about every seven to ten days with a new injury since he was recruited and I have been trying to puzzle out why.

At first, I was skeptical about his ability as a soldier. I've seen many injuries from field training over the years, but never so many from the same person. Today's injury caught my attention more so than all the rest.

I spent three years as a soldier before my parents insisted I walk away with my dignity and start studying to be a doctor. I was horrible at it. No matter how much effort I exhausted into my training, I couldn't wrap my head around anything I was taught. No coordination and no skill. I hurt myself more times than I can count, but never once, did I ever take a sword to the head. It's the most absurd place to take a hit. First of all, when it comes to practicing on the field, you are never supposed to make shots at an opponent's head. It's a strict rule that is observed across the realm for safety reasons and unless things have changed in the five years since I swung a sword, Aaron's injury today makes no sense. Additionally, it's hard to disregard the smug smile on his friend's face every time he's brought in. It's not the look of a person who feels bad for what's happened.

I deduced Aaron is either a worse swordsman than me, supremely clumsy, or is trying to get my attention. I admit, I was a little afraid it might be the latter and was hoping I was wrong. His final remark all out answered my question. He's not obsessed with his own blood - thank the Maker, because that's just weird - which means only one thing; he's obsessed with me. I should be flattered and if things were different I might be. I don't even know why I suggested he come back to see me in a couple days. His sutures won't need my attention and I certainly don't want to give him the wrong impression. I can't become involved with anyone right now - well, probably ever - despite the fact that the mere sight of him makes my blood run warm and makes me forget all my rules.

When Aaron isn't showing up at my door, drowning in his own blood like today, he is quite an attractive man. His hair is such a dark shade of brown it is nearly black and falls in an uncontrolled, yet somehow orderly, arrangement wherever it pleases on his head. On more than one occasion I have wanted to reach out and run my fingers through it to see if it truly is as soft as it looks. Not being long enough to be tied back, Aaron makes a nervous habit of always swiping it out of his eyes, where it likes to fall. His eyes are such an interesting shade of brown that I notice they change shades, depending on how the light catches them. Under his armor, the skin covering his well-defined, muscular, soldiering body is marked with countless scars, an observation I made when I mended his last injury less than a fortnight ago. Scars that are the reason I have questioned and re-questioned my theory of his constant visits to the surgery. Scarred, but remarkably toned and attractive nonetheless. Just touching his skin gives me an acute awareness of all my senses and sets my heart to find a faster rhythm than its usual steady pace.

Regardless of my intense, internal lectures, I inevitably forget myself in his presence and find myself acting in ways I shouldn't and inviting him back to the surgery unnecessarily. However, if I'm being honest, I'm somewhat concerned what he might do to himself next if I didn't, considering he's now marking up his face. Would he lop off an ear? I really hate to see him damaging himself. So, maybe it's a little selfish, but I want to make sure he doesn't do any more damage to his beautiful face. Okay, so maybe I can't get involved with somebody right now - or ever - but a man can look can't he? And Aaron is certainly not hard on the eyes.

* * *

Three days later, just past midday, I'm finishing wrapping up a young boy's arm after having treated a minor scrape. Truly, it didn't need my attention, but the mother insisted I look at him. I try hard to appease the people of the city and the poor woman seems irrationally worried. The child plays along well with his mother's concern of course, whimpering and crying dramatically, making me have to fight not to roll my eyes.

A knock at the door makes me pause mid wrapping and I rest the boy's elbow, along with the remaining cloth, on my work table.

"If you'll excuse me a moment?" I say to the mother who is crowding my space, shadowing my every move. I shuffle around her and go to answer the door.

Swinging the door open, I suppress a grin that wants immediately to monopolize my face. Sun gleams off the dark, silky hair of a tall, gorgeous soldier whose sutured head will no doubt not need my attention today. Aaron grins warmly through his stubbly face, eyes squinting against the brightness of the day. Of course he looks downright adorable. He would.

"Good news, Doc." He says. "No new injuries. Just here to have the head looked at." He taps a finger beside his injury. "Although, Caleb tells me it will need more than just a few sutures to fix it…and on that note, I'm actively looking for new friends."

His uninhibited personality makes me smile despite myself and I hold the door for him to enter.

"I'm glad you're in one piece today. I'm just finishing up with a young boy. I'll be done soon if you don't mind waiting."

My eyes linger on his radiant smile and I have to force myself to tear them away so I can get back to work. Damn, every bloody time he's around, I feel my self-control slip and I find myself drawn toward places I promised myself I wouldn't go. Why did I insist he come back? What am I doing?

Returning to the other room and my waiting patient, I finish wrapping the boy's arm and explain to his mother that he will need to rest for a couple days and then he should be good as new. The mother seems appeased and I force a smile to my face. Her boy could run off with his friends right now and be completely fine, but there is no sense arguing with her over-protective ways.

Once my young, whiny patient and his smothering, bodyguard of a mother have left, I invite Aaron into the room. He fidgets and paces around instead of automatically finding his stool, like he normally does. I know I should invite him to sit, but seeing as I don't know what sort of doctoring I'm to administer to his already well-healing forehead, I join him in his awkward fidgeting.

"My sutures are fine aren't they?" He asks, as he picks up a few bottles of herbs sitting on a table by the wall. He refuses to look at me, but I can hear the underlying question in his tone. The one that wants to know the real reason I have asked him here. He's not been fooled by my invitation and is delicately dancing around the subject the only way Aaron knows how. It's kind of cute watching him flounder. He has a youthfulness to him that is terribly endearing even though I figure he's probably close to my own age.

"Most likely."

The heat in the room feels like it rises a few degrees and I pull at my shirt discreetly where it sticks to my body under my apron. I had no intention of leading him on. I try to sum up all the points to justify why I cannot pursue anything with him as I watch him fiddle with the items on the table. Although, as my eyes drift down over his body, I can't remember a single solitary reason why not. I feel like my body is pulling me in two, distinctly different directions, and the rules I have made for myself are drifting out the window.

"You probably thought I'd be clumsy and pull the sutures loose or something, right? That's why you wanted to see me again…Right?"

He's fishing for confirmation and all I see is a possible escape.

"Yeah," I say, straightening up, forcing my eyes off the rippling biceps that are so prominent through his shirt, "I was concerned. If they get pulled, they might come out. They might even bleed again. Bleeding would be bad. You saw how much it bled the first time. I just…Just wanted to be sure things were healing okay." Ugh…How lame was that?

Aaron turns to face me and I see disappointment saddening his features. It's not what he wanted to hear. I feel instantly guilty and in an effort to save the situation from falling apart, I grab the stool near me and yank it out, patting a hand on the top.

"Why don't you have a seat and I'll take a look." I say, trying to break the tension.

Aaron lowers his eyes and comes to sit on the stool. I pull my spare seat from across the room and shimmy it up beside it so I can sit in front of him, much closer than is necessary. He won't look up, the hurt on his face staying hidden behind downcast eyes. Brushing his hair back with one hand, threading my fingers through his thick locks. I'm rewarded with finding out it is exactly how I imagined it would feel; silky, smooth and feather soft. I tilt his face up with fingers of my other hand under his chin to get a better view of his forehead. The warmth of his skin and our close proximity sends a flutter to tickle my insides. I trace a finger over his sutures, not seeing them at all, my eyes are everywhere but on my work. His chiseled jaw, the rough day's growth of stubble on his cheeks, his slightly pouting bottom lip. Hesitantly, perhaps sensing my inattention to his injury, Aaron lifts his eyes to my own and the brown I see today is dark and rich, making his pupils almost none existent. I'm lost in their depths, forgetting not only what I'm doing, but my every intention of not allowing myself be become attracted to this man.

Moments pass and neither of us move. My heart beats harder against the inside of my chest with each passing instant and I become aware of a distinct pull between us, drawing us together. I see Aaron edging himself closer to me and realize I'm doing the same, our gap narrows. Time seems to be moving in slow motion and the tiniest movements seem to be happening over a large expanse of time. I see us coming together. I know what is happening. If I don't do something right now to break this trance we will end up somewhere I can't go. I need to stop it. Jerking back, I let my hands fall from his face.

"It's looking much better," the words croaking out of me are hoarse and broken, "I-I don't think it will scar too badly."

The pounding in my chest increases tenfold when Aaron doesn't respond immediately. He just stares into my face, eyebrows drawing together in confusion. Having released my hold on him, I spin on the stool to put myself at a safer distance, but Aaron's hands jump out and grab at mine. He stops me in my tracks, holding me tentatively. He's trembling. His thumbs trace over the tops of my hands making small circles and I watch them before looking back into his face. I realize then, I forgot to pull away. I should have pulled away. The energy drawing me toward him is back and it's stronger this time. Aaron increases the pressure on his grip preventing me from fleeing again.

"Have drinks with me? Dinner? Something? Chase, I don't want to have to hurt myself again just to see you. Please say yes."

There it is. Exactly what I didn't want to hear…Or did want to hear. I don't even know anymore.

"Aaron…" I lower my eyes from his intense stare and continue to watch his thumbs circling my hands. "I can't."

A knot pulls in my chest at hearing my own words.

"Oh." He pulls his hands back and goes to stand, but I shuffle my body back in close to him, so close he is trapped in front of me. I place a hand on his knee, stilling him.

"Aaron, wait."

"No…It's okay. I understand. I just thought…I was wrong."

He pushes my hand away and squirms out from in front of me, almost falling in an effort to get away as fast as he can. I know I should let him go. I know I should leave it at this and not turn back, but my heart and my head have two differing opinions on the matter and I seem to have lost the ability to control either.

"Aaron. Don't leave."

He halts at the door, hand on the knob, but doesn't turn back.

"Let me explain." I say.

"You don't have to explain. I put too much faith in rumors and I was an idiot, I'm really embarrassed right now. I just thought you were like me."

"I am."

My head is screaming for me to shut up and not lead him on, but my heart can't let him walk out that door…Doesn't want him to go.

I have his attention. Aaron turns and studies my face.

"You are?" He asks.

My biggest concern is giving any truth to the rumors that have been circulating the city since last winter's trial. I have gone to great lengths to deny them. I need them to die off and for people to forget what they've heard and hopefully never give them cause to think those things again. It's absolutely imperative. So, when I keep talking, I can't understand why I feel such a need to explain myself to this man in front of me. Why can't I just let him walk out the door?

"I am." I confirm.

"Then it's me."

"No…I-"

"Then why won't you let me buy you a drink?" He asks.

The hurt look in his eyes is enough for me to jump right off that precipice where I'm precariously dangling. I'd be kidding myself if I thought for a moment that I didn't want to see where this might take me. Aaron is gorgeous and funny, if not a little daring and stupid, having purposefully injured himself on numerous occasions just to get my attention. My head knows the risks, but my heart doesn't seem to care.

"I'd love to have drinks with you, Aaron."

His entire face lights up and I swear his eyes visibly lighten at my acceptance and I can't help but smile.

"That's great…Umm…Tonight maybe? How about we meet up at Statin's at sundown?"

A sense of panic ignites in my gut. Statin's is the busiest tavern in the city and if I'm to show up there to have drinks with Aaron it will no doubt give truth to those blasted rumors. I can't have that.

"Not Statin's. Maybe we can meet up somewhere a little quieter? Maybe Trixie's or something?"

Aaron raises an eyebrow and a queer look contorts his beautiful face. Trixie's is a low end tavern in the poorest end of the city where the scummiest people around might frequent if they can find enough coin to barter a drink out of the owner. I only suggested it because I know no one I know will ever step foot in that place.

"Cheap drinks. Quieter atmosphere." I offer with a shrug by way of explanation.

Aaron isn't fooled but he doesn't persist in trying to have me explain, for which I'm grateful.

"Okay," he says drawing out the word in hesitation, "Trixie's at sundown."

"I'll see you there." I say.

Once Aaron leaves, I sit down heavy on the stool he has recently vacated. My gut is turning with a sense of unease at what I have just agreed to do. Getting involved in any kind of relationship should have been off the table. I can't risk it and I know it will only end badly. It always does. Regardless, I caved into my ridiculous attraction to the man. Even now, I can't get out of my mind the way his warm skin and soft hair felt under my fingers and I close my eyes trying to relive those brief moments when he was trapped sitting in front of me. That instant when he was about to kiss me, I froze in front of him and waited; wanting it to happen, but let reason leak its way in and ruin the moment. Now, disappointed at having lost that kiss, I'm aching for it even more. I want to know if those pouting lips taste as good as they look.

    Breathing out a heavy sigh of defeat, I stand up and start organizing and putting things away. It has been a quiet afternoon and I have no wish to continue sticking around inside. The mid-summer day is hot and breezy and I want to go out and enjoy it. Maybe a good walk around the market will clear my head. I still have a while before sundown, so I head out to enjoy the day.

Chapter Three

Aaron

The last slivers of sunlight radiate across the horizon, leaving the sky various shades of pink and yellow before dipping out of sight. The shadows are dark and apart from the painted clouds stealing the remaining color from the day, the world has settled into a pallet of grays and blacks.

As I walk down one of the city's less travelled streets, dipping down decrepit alleyways, passing innumerable buildings with boarded up windows, and skipping over trash and broken furniture tossed into the road as unusable, I keep my eyes peeled, staying on alert. Once in the meager back end of Ludairium, a woman emerges from the shadows with a dirty face, yet painted in an attempt to accentuate her features and wearing a dark hooded cape. She rubs up against me, snagging at my sides, reaching for what I can only guess. Coin? My manhood? Does she want money or sex? I have no idea. Her touch sends goosebumps down my arms and before I can react her mouth is by my ear, whispering, slurring something unintelligible. A shudder runs over my body as I throw her off with ease and quicken my pace, keeping my head down. I can hear her curse me as I put distance between us.

I still can't understand why Chase insisted we meet at Trixie's. No one goes to Trixie's. Yes, the drinks are cheap, but there is a reason for that. They taste of puddle water and if you want something to eat, it is always less than edible.

I'm not even comfortable walking the streets to get to Trixie's and I'm a pretty big guy with a cocky soldier attitude that encourages most to stand back. Certain even I could end up being mugged, I keep one hand on my sword hilt while constantly surveying my surroundings with every step I take. I know Chase doesn't carry a weapon and it bothers me that he will be walking here alone. I should have offered to meet him at his place.

Once inside, I glance around to see if Chase has already arrived. It's gloomy and dark. Shadows spill into every corner hiding the view from most patrons, giving privacy for reasons I wish to not even guess upon. The tables are scattered at random around the room and are sticky with spilled food and drinks that have been left behind by past customers. I get the feeling the tables will remain uncleaned seeing as the lone, scruffy, toothless man behind the bar counter doesn't seem to have intention of rectifying the problem. The smell turns my nose and I take a few breaths through my mouth as I try to become accustomed to it. Stale piss and rotted food; a retched combination. I don't see Chase anywhere.

Making my way to one of the darker corners in the back, I plant myself down, hoping the seclusion takes us out of target range of any potential fights that may arise from drunken men. I position myself with my back to the wall so no one can sneak up on me and so I can keep an eye out for Chase's arrival. I don't like the vibe of this place and I don't think I'm going to be able to relax and enjoy a nice evening with Chase being here. Why couldn't we have just gone to Statin's?

Toothless wonder saunters over and offers to bring me a drink. I consider his offer. I'd like to encourage Chase to go somewhere else, but he seemed insistent earlier for whatever reason. Reluctantly, I order two mugs of ale and toss the man a couple coins as payment. The man sneers as he scoops up the coin and makes his way back to the bar.

This is just too damn creepy for my liking.

A short while later, Chase strolls through the door and scans the tavern with downcast eyes. Catching sight of me, he walks over to the back corner table and slumps down on the bench across from me.

"Can we go somewhere else?" I beg, before his ass even reaches his seat, "I feel like I'm going to be mugged, or raped, or stabbed, or something equally as bad. Maybe all three. This place gives me a bad vibe."

Chase smirks, "Tough guy Aaron is afraid of a scummy tavern, who would have thought? It's fine, relax."

"Okay…But for the record, when I invited you for a drink, this," I indicate with the twirl of my finger, "isn't what I had in mind."

Chase glances around the tavern and shrugs his shoulders. Looking to the wooden table, he draws circles on the surface, tracing along the cracks. "I have my reasons."

"Care to shed some light on those reasons, you know, since I'm risking my life over here."

Chase glances up at me shyly, a tentative smile curling the edges of his mouth. His fingers continue to dance around in a distracted manner on the table and I get the feeling he's uneasy and not because of where we are.

Just as I think Chase is going to say something, toothless wonder shoves two mugs of ale across the table toward us and turns with a grunt to head back to the bar. Chase's gaze follows after the man and for the first time I see what may be discomfort at our surroundings in his eyes.

"Why here, Chase?" I ask again, bringing him back to the conversation.

Chase breaths in a deep breath and I see him let it out slowly as he glances around us again, avoiding my eyes.

"I don't want people to see us together and get the wrong idea."

My eyebrows draw together. "Oh. Maybe I have the wrong idea." I lower my gaze to the table and unconsciously mimic his fidgeting. "I asked you for a drink, Chase, because…Umm…Because, I like you and I-"

"I know." Chase crawls his hand across the surface and lets his fingers graze against my own before pulling away. I lift my eyes and his emerald gemstones are looking at me intently. "I can't feed the rumors, Aaron. I need people to forget what they think they know about me. It's complicated."

I crawl my fingers after his and take hold of them. Panic rises in Chase's face and his eyes dart around the room as he yanks them out of my reach.

"The laws been dropped. Why does it matter what people think anymore? We don't have to hide, Chase."

Chase reaches for his drink and takes a long pull. His face contorts in disgust as the liquid hits his pallet and I can see him panic momentarily, unsure what to do. His eyes bulge wide and dart around looking for somewhere to spit it out. Resigning, he puts his mug to his mouth and spits it back inside.

"Holy hell! That's terrible." He says.

I take his mug and shove it aside before grasping for his hands again, holding them tight. He stiffens at my touch and stares down at the table.

"It's not that straight forward for me, Aaron. I wish it were."

"Why?" I ask.

"It's complicated."

"You said that already. I've got nowhere to be so why don't you fill me in, so I can understand."

Chase sighs and pulls against my grip, trying to dislodge his hands from mine. Taking the hint, I let them go with a sigh and rest my hands in my lap instead, trying to hide my disappointment.

"Well, long story short. It would be seen as a huge disgrace to my parents if they ever found out and I would probably lose my inheritance and probably be disowned. Not that I give a horse's ass about my inheritance, but the disgrace alone would be awful and I'm their only child. My duty is to the family name. I'm to take over the manor and lands when my father passes…I-I can't do that to them…I can't…So people can't know, because if they ever found out-"

"Whoa, whoa...Slow down." He is stumbling over his words trying to get them out and is speaking so fast I can hardly keep up. "Who the hell are your parents?"

It's just one of about a dozen questions that are now running around in my brain since Chase started talking.

"Lord and Lady Fredrick Schuyler of Saldrium." He says, his tone matter of fact.

"Are you serious?"

"Very."

"Don't they own the city or something like that?"

"They run it under the King and most of the surrounding lands."

"Wow! And you're their kid?"

Chase slumps forward and buries his face in his hands, elbows resting on the table. He blows a long breath past his lip. "The point is, if they were to ever find out, I would disgrace my family name and it could ruin them. They expect things from me and this is not one of those things."

Chase is consumed in paranoia as far as I see it. Why would it disgrace them? The laws are gone and the one man who stands in a position to strip Chase's father of lands, is the King himself, who keeps company with another man and is the prime reason we can be open and free right now. I'm about to put out this argument, but Chase lifts his head and my words are stopped when he speaks.

"My parents are old fashioned. Their circle of friends will shun them. It's not about losing title or lands, it's about their bloody position in society. Aaron, they can't know."

It's like he's inside my head, bashing my points before I even make them.

"So that's why we're sitting in the scummiest tavern in Ludairium, so no one knows you're having drinks with a man? We could be friends. Friends have drinks you know."

"They do. But you didn't ask me here as a friend, did you?"

"No." I risk inching my fingers across the table again. "Then why can't I touch you? We're hidden away…By your choice."

"I don't know…I just…" his voice trails off.

His emerald gaze is locked on me and I can see the intensity in his eyes, the same want and need I feel so badly is being reflected back at me. Forgetting all his adamant explanations about why no one can know, I feel the distinct pull between us again and I'm drawn into the heat radiating off his stare. I felt it in the surgery this morning and was sure Chase had too. How long did it take me to finally get the nerve to ask him for drinks? Too long. I'm not making that mistake again. His eyes are almost begging me to kiss him, just as they were in the surgery this morning. I can sense it. I know. Without a second thought, I lean into the table, never taking my eyes off him, and move closer to his lips, ready to capture their sweet essence in my own. Right as they are about to touch, I close my eyes and feel my skin prickle with anticipation. Out of nowhere, the wind is knocked out of my lungs as the edge of the table slams into my gut and I'm thrown backwards. Opening my eyes at the shock, I see Chase grasp the edge of the table to save himself from tumbling to the ground. The sheer force at which he threw his body against the table to get away from me in the first place has him dangling over the other end of his bench threatening to fall.

I look down at the feeling of a wetness leaking through my breeches and it's only then I realize our drinks have spilled in the process and are running over the table edge into my lap. Instead of moving out of their way, I study the mirrored shock in Chase's face.

Okay, so apparently I'm not as good at reading people as I thought. That went badly.

"Shit, Aaron. I'm sorry."

Chase is swiping the ale away, splashing it off the far edge onto the ground so it doesn't continue to soak me, because I still haven't bothered to move out of its way. I stare down at my wet breeches and back to the man in complete confusion.

"I'll get more drinks. I'm so sorry." He says before standing to walk away.

Clamping a hand around his wrist, I prevent his leaving.

"Don't. They aren't worth drinking anyway. I'm pretty sure it was sludge mixed with piss, at least by the look on your face when you sipped it earlier."

That got the intended smile out of him I was hoping for.

"It was pretty awful." He says sitting back down across from me. "I'm sorry, Aaron. I didn't mean to react like that."

"It's okay. Although, I'm going to stop trying to read that look on your face because apparently I don't speak that language. That's two times I swore it was telling me something else."

I know I'm not hiding my disappointment behind humor very well at all, considering the sympathetic look I'm getting in return. Chase glances around the tavern. There are few patrons this evening and the ones present are so far gone with drink or so accustomed to rowdy behavior they didn't even notice what just happened at our table. Chase meets my eyes again, only worry creases his forehead now and his brows are pulled together.

"Listen, I shouldn't have done that." I say, trying to soothe the tension. "Please, stay and…Well don't have another drink with me, because there is no way in hell I'm paying for more of that crap, but please just stay." I want to reach out for his hand, but I hold back not wanting to make him uncomfortable again. "I'd really like to get to know you, Chase, if that's okay?"

Chase nods his head and moves his hands close to mine again, but makes a point of not allowing them to touch. I don't pursue them. I'd like to think I've learned my lesson and I'm not that stupid.

"So, you have noble blood seeping through those veins then huh?" I ask, trying to keep the mood light.

Chase rolls his eyes. "Yeah, something like that."

"You don't give me the impression that it's a good thing."

"Well, when your parents sit in a high position, they impart high demands and I've spent a lifetime trying to live up to them."

"Did they make you become a doctor?"

"Yes. But not before I fought them tooth and nail. I wanted to be a soldier with the King's army."

"You don't strike me as the soldier type." I tease.

He chuckles a low, sexy rumble in his throat as the sides of his mouth turn up in a slight smile. "I'll try not to hold it against you that you are taking their side."

Chase runs his fingers over the cracks in the table top bringing them closer to my own, intentionally brushing them together a few times. He lifts his eyes to peer up at me and the warm smile grows. The mix messages he's sending are driving me crazy, but I'm not making the same mistake three times. I'd like to think I have half a brain to know when to keep a little distance.

"When I was ten, I wanted to be a soldier so bad I convinced my father to bring in a tutor to train me. Years he spent trying to mold me into a soldier. My father even pulled strings when I was sixteen and had me recruited in Prag. I was sent there and served with Jefferson's men for three years. I'm pretty sure I was the worst soldier in the realm." I laugh with him as he continues. "Well, my father kept tabs on my progress with Jefferson and when there was nothing good to report. Ever. My parents marched into Prag one evening and told me they were through with this ridiculous notion of mine and I was going to return with them to Saldrium and take up studies to become a doctor and learn to run my father's lands in the process. I was a disgrace to our name and my father said he would not have it tarnished with my foolery any longer. So that's what happened. I was taken by the collar and dragged from the city without another word that very night." He lowers his head in contemplation and a sadness takes over his beautiful features as he seems to be remembering something.

"Wow."

"Yup. The lectures I endured for the next four years after that always consisted of; 'Obey your parents', 'We know what's best for you', 'Remember what happened last time', 'You will not disgrace this name, young man'. So on that note, I'm finally free of their badgering and binds again and have no intention of giving them any reason to come back and lecture me for the next four years."

Chase goes quiet across from me and lowers his eyes to the table again.

"This isn't what you had in mind for tonight is it?" he says.

"It's not how I planned it, no." I say honestly. "But I'm getting to know you and I've been wanting to do that for a very long time."

I watch his eyes scan the tavern again before he slides his hands forward and interlocks his fingers with my own. It startles me and sends a warmth coursing over my body at his boldness.

"Let's get out of here." He says.

I can't agree with him more. The tavern has succeeded at keeping me on edge all night and I can't sort out what Chase wants when there is a constant possibility of onlookers. I need to take him somewhere and get him alone so I can judge what he wants properly. I stand from the table and Chase's eyes land on the crotch of my breeches.

Okay, this man is way too confusing. He can hardly hold my hand, won't kiss me, but is now staring at my crotch?!?

"Shit, Aaron! You're soaked. I had no idea." Chase says.

Oh…I forgot about that.

I run a hand over my breeches smoothing them out and laughing. "It's not a big deal. I'll dry."

We make our way through the rough area of Ludairium as quickly as we can. Neither of us saying a thing until we have put a safe distance between us and the last beggar we pass. Ensuring we stay somewhat secluded, I turn Chase toward the outskirts of the city and take him around the outside of the city wall as we continue to walk awhile in silence. Eventually, we ease into casual conversation. Chase reveals a little more about how it was growing up under the firm thumb of Lord and Lady Schuyler. I'm entranced just listening to him. He's more relaxed being in the shadows of the city than he has been all night and the warm tone of his voice draws me in. I could listen to him talk all night. As the moon rises high in the summer sky, Chase slowly brings our pace to a stop and turns to look at me. His eyes are dark in the moonlight and there is no more hint of their usual green. He rocks on his feet and looks up at me through his long lashes.

"I had a good time tonight, Aaron. I hope you can forgive my quirky behavior earlier."

I don't answer him, I just stare into the depths of those dark, wondrous spheres looking up at me. We are alone. Completely alone. Do I risk it again? If he throws me away now, then I'll know for sure. I have to risk it. Stepping forward, I close our gap, bringing my body to hover directly in front of him. His eyes never leave mine and he doesn't step away. I see that same look in his face that I saw at the tavern earlier and before at the surgery. Reaching out a tentative hand, I interlock our fingers together. He doesn't pull away. A flutter tickles in my belly and my heartbeat accelerates at the touch. I realize I'm more nervous now than I was both times before. The heat radiating in this moment has my blood running hot through my veins and I pray he doesn't push me away. I bring my forehead down to rest on his. He leans in toward me.

I didn't imagine that, did I? I don't want to be wrong again.

"I'm okay with keeping this a secret, Chase." I whisper, "I've had to hide my whole life until this past winter anyway, what difference does it make? If it means, you'll come out and do this again with me-"

"Are you going to kiss me or just stand there talking, Aaron?"

A smile breaks across my lips. "Oh, I see, those are 'kiss me' eyes you're giving me. All evening you've had me believing that-"

"So you're just going to talk." He smirks at me.

"I'm getting there. You've got me all nervous now."

I trace my thumbs along the top of his hands and step the last step closer to him so our bodies are touching. Bringing my face down to his, I brush my nose along his cheek and move my mouth closer to him. The smell of wood smoke and lavender mixed with a trace of pine and a unique smell that is all Chase invades my nose and I inhale deeply, breathing him in. My lips brush his scratchy stubble along his jaw as they move closer to their target. Closing my eyes, Chase turns his head and my mouth meets with soft, supple lips. Sparks ignite sending bursts of energy radiating all across my body. I want to taste more of him and I dance my tongue along the seam of his lips asking for entrance. Without hesitation, Chase parts his lips and in an instant our tongues are tangled together. I move my hands around his waist and hold him tighter to my body. Damn the man can kiss. I lean into him, pressing my lips harder to his, reveling in what my mind has imagined a million times before now. Only, my imagination did this no justice. It's so much better than anything I had conjured up before. I feel Chase rise up on his toes to get closer and his arms are around me as well, holding me to him, not pushing me away.

After what must have been quite a while, but what is nowhere near long enough, I pull back, releasing my lips reluctantly from Chase's and look deep into his emerald spheres.

"Damn. That was even better than I imagined." I say and nip at his bottom lip with my teeth. A smile radiates across his face as he pulls back to dodge my attack, laughing.

"And how long have you been imagining kissing me?"

"Longer than I'd like to admit." I say, taking Chase's hands back in my own, "Can I walk you home?" I ask.

Chase nods and allows me to continue to hold his hand until we enter the perimeters of the city, at which point he drops it. I'm okay with that, I understand now. We make our way through the city to Chase's residence in silence. Standing outside his door, I notice Chase will not make eye contact with me and is scanning up and down the empty streets instead. The night was a little odd at first, but ended on a definite high. I'm not sure what to say now. I want to kiss him again, but get the feeling that would be a bad move, so I resist. I want to see him again. I want to ask him if it's okay.

Ducking my head and kicking around a lose stone with my toe, I try to find something to say, a reason to come back to the surgery.

"So…Umm…When did you need to check these sutures again?" I say, knowing it's lame but hoping he picks up the hint.

Chase's eyes draw up to mine and he raises a brow. "How about you pop in if they start bothering you. I'd be happy to have a look any time."

I smile broad and give him a small wink.

"Thank you for tonight, Chase. I'll see you around."

Chapter Four

Chase

"We'll need to think about replenishing the supplies sometime soon, before winter settles in and the land is frozen over." Doctor Richard Greaves says as he lines up another half empty bottle with the others he has set aside.

"I'll get to work on that as soon as I can." I say.

Doctor Greaves has been Ludairium's city doctor for over three decades. For a man in his sixties, he still manages to keep up with the busy demands of running the surgery. Although over the summer, he has relaxed some in his dedication to patient care, having placed the majority of that responsibility on me, but he is always on top of keeping the books in order and ensuring we run a smooth practice.

Slicking a hand over his meticulously sleek and silvering hair, he leans over, resting his hands on the table.

"I don't know what I'd do without you, Chase. I might have to put my foot down if you're asked to accompany the soldiers again. I'm not sure I have it in me to do this full time anymore."

I came to the city last fall and took up an apprenticeship alongside Doctor Greaves. The apprenticeship was short lived when I was declared suitable enough to be titled a full fledge doctor soon after my arrival. Over the winter, I wound up on the road with the King's men travelling across Edovia, uniting armies from coast to coast as they prepared for the coming battle at the north border against our enemy, the Outsiders. There has been threat of them taking over our lands for the last couple years as they persist in their south-moving quest to own the entire continent.

The army of men only returned briefly to the city for the infamous trial of the century. After matters were settled, out we went again, tying up all loose ends. Arriving back in the late spring, I began taking over Doctors Greaves duties one by one until I was doing nearly all his work and allowing him most days to rest and take comfort in being an old man. He still likes to make his appearance at the surgery daily and dabbles in work here and there, but he seems much happier now that the pressures of the highly demanding work of doctoring an entire city are off of him.

Fall is around the corner and there is talk of the armies marching north soon to secure the border once and for all. I'm unsure how fast it will all come together, but I'm fairly certain I will be pulled along to join them. Having a healer on the road is only wise. I made comment on the matter to Doctor Greaves before, but he hadn't seem concerned until now. As summer fades and he is becoming more accustomed to not being front and center at the surgery, I can see the worry of my potential departure weighing heavily on him. I've considered taking the matter to the King himself, to encourage him to bring another doctor into the city, but have yet to act on it. The King and I aren't exactly best of friends - worst of enemies is more like it - and we have had words on more than one occasion. Nasty words. Considering I spent a good year sharing a bed with his lover long before they met, I suppose the man has good cause to not like me too much and I should just be happy he allows me to hold a job in his city.

Doctor Greaves rubs his eyes and sighs. "If you're okay here, Chase, I'm going to call it a night."

"I have everything under control. Get out of here, Doc."

The fading sunlight sets me in motion to light lanterns so I can continue to work. It has been two nights since Aaron and I got together for drinks and a late night stroll around the city limits. Two nights since I caved into my desires and allowed him to kiss me and I have thought of little else since.

I'd be lying through my teeth if I said I didn't enjoy the evening we had, as awkward as I made it. However, the idea of allowing this to turn into anything makes me leery. I'm only going to end up hurting him and it's the last thing I want to do. I have no business toying with his emotions and making him think this can be any more than a friendship, but the draw I feel toward him is so strong I can hardly ignore it. I don't know how I'm supposed to convince him this is a bad idea when I can't even seem to convince myself.

I sit down on the stool in front of the table and continue to take inventory on the dwindling herbs jarred up in front of me. I need to keep busy. I'm focusing on him again and I can't let my mind go there. I pull a few bottles forward and turn them around in my hand, examining the contents as my eyes lose focus on what they are doing nearly instantly.

I think I already crossed a line with him. I know I did. I invited him to kiss me, asked him to kiss me. That in itself all-out told him I was interested in pursuing something. Damn, but the way that kiss dominated my every sense was exhilarating. I felt it right down to my toes. A smile passes over my lips at the memory. His tongue, his hands wrapped so securely around me, his body blanketing me in his warmth. Even his attempts at humor when he was uncomfortable provoked me, urged me to want to make him nervous just so I could hear it again.

A commotion in the street startles me out of my daydream. A group of people pass the surgery, talking loud and laughing, it's only then that I realize I have been turning the same bottle of herbs around in my hand, not looking at it, for some time; staring off into my thoughts with a foolish grin on my face.

Dammit. I'm not doing a good job of turning these thoughts around. I'm supposed to be convincing myself not to do this, yet all I've succeeded in doing is make myself want him more. I have no backbone whatsoever. I will never come clean to my parents, so all I will do is hurt anyone I chose to be with. I have proven that already once in my life, and I swore I would never hurt anyone like that again. I still haven't forgiven myself and probably never will. I can't do this to Aaron. It's not fair. He's a really decent person and I don't want to hurt him just because I'm a coward. I have to turn this around before I get in too deep.

Placing the bottle of herbs back down on the table, deciding there is no way I'm going to be able to focus on the task any longer, I set to cleaning up and decide to head home for the night.

My rooms are in back of the surgery and are accessible only from an alleyway behind the building. The doctor was kind enough to allow me this living space as part of the agreement terms we set when I came to the city. Rounding the corner, I stop dead in my tracks as I nearly collide with a large man leaning against the wall outside my door. It's dark and when he stands up straight, towering over me, my heart jolts in my chest. Panic sets in and I stumble backward a few steps. I'm about to scream like a girl and run away when the man's face looks up and turns to me, smiling. It's then when I recognize him.

"Hell, Aaron. You scared the shit out of me."

Sucking in a few steadying breaths, my heartrate slowly returns to normal as I fight to regain my composure. Aaron brings a finger to his forehead and furrows his brow, running it over his sutures.

"These guys are itchy and poky. I think they need a doctor's touch. Can you help?" He says, smirking.

I roll my eyes and swat his finger away from his forehead, "They're healing, suck it up and be a man about it. And stop touching them."

Aaron pouts out his lip. "I thought you said to come by if they were bothering me."

I put my hands on my hips and cock my head to one side, raising a questioning eyebrow at him. "Are they bothering you?"

His pout turns into a grin and he steps closer to me, lowering his voice. "No, but not having seen you in two days is bothering me."

My brain is screaming to put more distance between us. Aaron has moved precariously close to me. I can't let him draw me in. I have to put a stop to this carefully, without hurting his feelings, before I make it worse.

Bringing a hand up, I place it on his chest to keep him a step back. The warmth of his skin through his shirt makes my brain stutter and my heart is quick to take over. At the same moment Aaron lifts his hand and laces his fingers into mine pressing it tighter into his chest. I forget to pull away…Again. The man's touch is hot against my skin. His soft fingers fit perfectly around my own and my breath catches in my throat as he leans in even closer, bringing his face within inches of my own. Memories of the last kiss we shared swim up to the surface and I find myself leaning in to him, waiting for more. My surroundings forgotten. He moves his face closer still, tracing his lips along my cheek up to my ear.

"Can I take you somewhere? It's private. No one will know. No one will see us and I promise you it'll be worth it." His breath whispers against me, sending shivers to race up my spine.

No, tell him no.

"Yes." I breathe.

And so the internal battle of heart vs. head continues. Only I'm fairly certain head has waved the white flag of surrender and heart is winning this battle.

Aaron pulls back and grins. He spins and makes his way down the road.

"Follow me." He says over his shoulder.

Now would be the time to call him back and tell him I changed my mind. Explain why this can't work and let him down gently, but my feet follow after him, eager to know where it is we are heading. It seems my body is teaming up with my heart and I find myself practically skipping down the road after him.

Aaron continues on ahead, checking periodically to ensure I'm still following him. Winding along the city streets, I start to wonder where in the world this man is taking me. Turning a final corner, Aaron comes to an abrupt halt and I have to dig my feet in so I don't trample over top of him. The city's old, abandoned, western watch tower stands in front of us. The towers haven't been used as watch towers for decades for whatever reason, I'm not too sure. The eastern tower inhabits the city's dungeon cells in its deep underground passageways, but the western one has not seen a single, solitary soul in years. The stone work climbing the side of the tower is well weathered and crumbling in places down its sides with chunks of rock having fallen away long ago. The stairs leading up to the large wooden door are pitted and cracked. Large amounts of them are missing and it looks like it would be an awkward climb up.

Aaron turns to me and glances quickly over my shoulder causing me to spin around to see if someone is there. The lone road leading back into the city is empty. The streets are dark, the sun having set long ago. Turning back to Aaron in confusion, I'm about to question him when he grabs my hand and pulls me up the broken stairs. It's as tricky a climb as it looks.

"What are we doing here?" I ask.

Aaron ignores me and drops my hand to approach the door. Pulling a dagger from a spot tucked in near his boot he proceeds to shimmy a nail loose on the board barring the door.

"Aaron, what are you doing?"

Evidently the nail wasn't snug in its hole and it falls to the ground after a few wiggles of Aaron's blade underneath it. He proceeds to do the same thing with each nail holding the board in place.

"Why do I get the feeling you've done this before."

Aaron gives me a wicked grin and waggles his eyebrows at me. "Keep watch and tell me if anyone is coming."

The man is off his tree. I glance behind me, keeping an eye out for anyone who might be approaching. The streets are still empty.

Letting the last nail fall to the ground, Aaron braces the large beam in his arms and lifts it down from its balanced position on two wooden supports. His muscles pull tight against his shirt at the effort and I forget my guard duty and stare at the gorgeous man in front of me. Aaron catches me watching him as he places the beam on the ground off to the side and stands up brushing his hands on his breeches with a knowing smile.

"Like what you see?" He says winking at me. *Cocky bastard.*

My gaze shoots from his arms and chest to his face and I can feel my cheeks flush. Not waiting for me to respond - thank goodness - Aaron grabs my hand again and pulls the door open, guiding me inside.

The air in the tower is cooler and damp. It smells musty and is infinitely dark. Aaron closes the door behind us and I'm blanketed in such absolute blackness, I freeze, afraid to move. I can't even see my own hand when I hold it inches in front of my eyes. Aaron grips onto my waist from behind and shimmies around me, moving his hand back into mine. I squeeze it tight, afraid he might let go of me and leave me lost in this abyss.

"Follow me, I'll guide you. Trust me." His voice comes from the darkness as his mouth brushes against my ear.

Feeling like I have no choice, knowing I don't want to stand here alone, I let Aaron take me into the nothingness.

After a few steps, Aaron stops abruptly and I bump into his back.

"There are stairs. We're going to climb them. They spiral up, so just keep your hand on my back and follow me. There will be a wall on your left to hold as we climb, I'll go slow. Are you okay?"

I nod then realize he can't see me. "Yeah, I'm okay."

Aaron continues forward at a gentle pace, allowing me to get better accustomed to the stairs and our climb. I grip a fist tight into his shirt, afraid I might lose him and be lost forever. As he feels me becoming more comfortable with the incline, he picks up the pace.

We continue curving up for what has to be a hundred steps or more before I see something that isn't complete darkness. A faint light is giving off a soft glow, allowing edges to become distinct and our journey up easier. Around the next bend, I see a door above us, opened to the night sky beyond. Climbing the last few steps, Aaron reaches again to take my hand. We are at the top of the tower, a small circular terrace only about four or five feet wide runs all the way around its circumference. Aaron take me to the edge where a stone wall stands waist high and we both peer over it into the night, clear across the top of the dark city below.

I'm speechless, I have never seen the city from such heights and the view is breathtaking. I only wish it was daylight so I could see even farther.

"Wow...It's incredible."

Running my hands along the stone wall, I walk the circle around the tower. On the opposite side, I'm disappointed that the forest beyond the city is even harder to make out in the darkness, but the coast and the Great Sea to the south stand out, reflecting the moonlight as it bounces off the surface of the waves making it look like it's sparkling.

"This is amazing, Aaron. Thank you for bringing me here."

I turn my head to see him smiling at me.

"This isn't what I brought you here to see." He says indicating to the coast with his thumb. "But I'm glad you like it. What I wanted to show you is higher up. Look." He says, pointing to the sky.

Tilting my head back, my breath catches in my throat and my jaw hangs open. The sky above is clear of clouds and there are billions of stars overhead. Clear of obstructing trees and buildings, there are stars as far as the eye can see and being so high up in the tower, I feel like I could reach out and touch the heavens.

"Have you ever seen anything more beautiful?" I ask.

"Yes." Aaron says. His voice whispers in my ear. He has moved behind me and his arms snake around my waist, pulling me closer to him. "You." My eyes fall from the sky as I turn in his arms to look at him.

"You are the most beautiful thing I've ever seen, Chase." He leans in and captures my mouth with his. His kiss radiates through my entire body, making me forget all my earlier arguments. Our tongues tease together as we explore each other's mouths. Aaron deepens the kiss and pulls my body tight against him, pinning me to the stone wall at my back. His hands move to the back of my head and he angles me enough so he can plunge farther into my mouth. My body's response is automatic and I run my hands up his back, gripping him around his strong shoulders. Everything around me becomes non-existent as I lose myself in this kiss.

What could have been an eternity, but is probably in actuality only a few moments, Aaron pulls back and rests his forehead to mine. His lips are swollen and red.

Being with Aaron is like being under a spell and I lose all sense of myself every time I'm in his presence. I need to break free now, before it's too late. This man has the power to undo me with a simple kiss and I know nothing good can come of this. I can't hurt him. I would hate myself even more.

"Aaron." I say. His warm gaze is making my knees weak. I pull back from his grasp and turn away, unsure if I will be able to say what I have to say while he looks at me like this.

"I…Umm…I don't think this is a good idea." My heart aches at having lost ground to my head and it fights to hold on, screaming at me to give it a try.

Aaron is silent behind me, but I resist the urge to turn around and keep fumbling to find the right words without hurting him.

"It's not about hiding…Which I appreciate that you will do for me…But…"

"But what?" Comes a suddenly serious voice behind me.

"I'll only end up hurting you. I don't want to, but it *will* happen. I can't give you what you need. I don't want to do this, Aaron. I don't want you to end up hurt."

The silence deepens and when Aaron says nothing after a few moments, I edge my body around to look at him. He's studying me with intense, dark eyes. His lips purse and he raises his head to the stars above.

The silence engulfing us makes me uncomfortable. I'm not sure what to do, so I just stand there watching him.

Eventually, Aaron lowers his head and the smile that forms on his mouth moves quickly to his eyes, lighting up all his features. It's not the reaction I expected and I'm confused. He turns to the stone wall at the edge of the terrace and proceeds to climb up to sit, straddling it, one leg dangling down toward the ground far below.

"I don't believe you." He says, grinning at me.

I'm not even sure what to say to that so I gawk at him, mouth open, but without words.

"You see," he says as he swings his legs up underneath him and kneels on the top of the wall, "your words are saying one thing, but the way you kiss me tells a whole other story."

Aaron gets both feet under him and with his hands out for balance, proceeds to stand on the wall. The width can't be more than a foot and my eyes go wide as he balances there.

"Aaron…What are you doing? Get down."

Ignoring me, Aaron peers down to the ground well over a hundred feet below and takes a few steady steps forward. I don't want to run at him and risk startling him, but a twisting in my gut at the thought of what he is doing makes me sick and I need him to get down.

"Aaron. Please. Get down."

Having walked a quarter circle around the tower wall he comes to a stop and looks down at me, the smile never having left his face.

"Am I scaring you?"

"Yes! Get down. You could fall."

"Then you can fix me up."

"It's over a hundred-foot drop. I can't fix dead. Get down." My voice has a sharp edge of panic to it and it sounds harsh and demanding to my own ears.

Shuffling his feet around, he turns to face me, back to the edge. He raises himself on his toes and rocks down again, up and down. My stomach drops and my heart hammers heavy against my ribs. Aaron goes still and then jumps down in front of me, eliciting a sigh of relief to pass my lips. I want to fall to the ground in relief. He closes the gap between us and takes my face in his hands. Determination darkening his already dark eyes.

"Don't play games with me and I won't play games with you. I know you want this, Chase. I can feel it in your kiss and the way your body responds to me. You aren't fooling me. Quit kidding yourself." He says.

"I'll only hurt you."

"I'm a big boy. You've warned me. Let me be the one to decide if it's a risk worth taking." His fingers trace along my jaw and I find myself nuzzling against them in response. No longer fearing Aaron will fall, I now fear the certainty in my heart. I know I want this, yet I know what will happen if I allow it.

"Now, are you done messing with me?" He asks in a whisper, brushing his lips against my forehead.

I nod. I've given my heart full rein. He's touching me and calling me out on everything I'm failing to hide. I can't say no. I can't even remember why I was trying to say no in the first place. I want him and this and I press into his body, raising myself on my toes to bring my lips closer to his.

"Kiss me, Aaron. Please."

As he lowers his lips to mine capturing them in an all-consuming, even deeper kiss that sings through my body, I know I'm in deep and I can't back out. I just hope I have the strength to do this without breaking this man's heart.

Chapter Five

Chase

The following days at the surgery pass in somewhat of a blur. One chore melds into the next, with me not paying much attention to what is going on. Every day is the same, every day my thoughts are elsewhere.

There has been a steady flow of patients in and out over the course of the morning. Ointments for burns, salves for abrasions, tinctures and teas, sutures, and even a leaching to a swollen, pooling of blood under an eye; the poor man took a branch to the face, while felling trees outside the city. Although I walk through a daze as I work, I'm on top of the world. My thoughts are astray to a certain soldier who keeps curiously winding up at the surgery door; ten days in a row now, never an injury to be had, thank goodness. Aaron is clever to time his arrivals to coincide with the end of my work day and we have been sneaking out of the city and spending time together, walking the surrounding woods every night.

I've given up my denial since the night at the tower, accepted my strong attraction for this man and I couldn't be happier. Every day has been better and every day another little piece of my worry slips away.

As the afternoon drags along, I find myself spending less time with my work and more time peering out the window wishing for the end of the day so I can see Aaron again.

Draping my apron over a stool in my little side room workspace, I hear the main door open. A smile breaks over my face and I bound in the other room, expecting it to be him. Stopping short, my shoulders slump at the sight of Doctor Greaves.

"Expecting someone else were you?" He says as he closes the door behind himself.

The man's eyes are too inquisitive and I do my best to hide my disappointment as he places a large book on the table and pulls up a stool.

"Nope, just…Keeping busy." I say shifting my gaze around the room.

Having already tidied up ages ago, in anticipation of sneaking out early, I bounce on my feet, trying to find something to make myself look busy. I was hoping to find Aaron even earlier tonight and have more time with him. The arrival of Doctor Greaves makes my need for departure even more dire. I would hate for Aaron to show up again, faking injuries, Doctor Greaves can't be stupid enough to fall for it, he's going to catch on sooner or later.

"I was thinking of heading out early if that okay, Richard. I have things going on tonight and I was hoping to get an early start." I say.

"Not a problem, son. You go on, have a good night."

I give him a quick smile and slip out the door before he can make any remarks on my plans. I'd rather not lie to the man. Checking down the street, in the direction Aaron should arrive, I don't see him yet. I wander slowly around back of the building to my room, keeping my eye on the road ahead, watching out for him.

"Looks like you're waiting for somebody."

The deep thrum of a voice behind me brings a smile to my face. I turn to find Aaron grinning back at me with his dark hair masking his rich brown eyes and I wonder how I missed him when I came out of the surgery.

"Hey, handsome." Aaron says as he shakes the hair from his face with the toss of his head.

"You're sneaky."

"I am." He steps in closer and stares at me through downcast eyes. "Want to be sneaky with me and head down to the pond? Scare a few toads, terrorize the fish, and throw stones at the birds?"

I scrunch my nose up at the thought.

"What are we, eight?" I ask and laugh.

"Come on, it's my favorite pastime. Just have to be home by dark or my mom will tan my ass and I won't be able to play tomorrow." He says egging me on with a grin and a wink.

"You stick a toad anywhere near my face and I'll tan your ass."

Aaron's halts his departure and turns back to me. His eyes grow a shade darker and he steps a little closer, lowering his voice. "Is that a threat or a promise, Doctor?"

"A promise. Now lead the way, Mr. Pryor, or are we going to stand here until night?"

Once we are a good distance from the city, I allow Aaron to grab my hand. He likes holding hands and makes sure we do it every chance we get. Every little touch brings us that much closer together and it feels completely natural now to have my fingers laced with his.

At the pond we find a soft piece of grass to sit, pull off our boots and roll up our breeches to sit with our feet dangling into the warm waters. The minnows swim up and inspect our toes, nipping them, tickling and making me yank my feet out in fits of giggles.

"Buggers are biting me." I say at Aaron's inquisitive look and he laughs as I extract my feet for the third time.

"You don't like to be bit." He leans in and takes a nibble at my neck eliciting another round of giggles as I try to shove him off. He clamps down and wraps his arms around me, not letting me go.

I squirm around, laughing uncontrollably at this point. "I'm ticklish. Stop."

I try to shove him off, but without success as he continues his attack on my neck. Nibbles eventually turn to kisses and a wet tongue and

I no longer feel the urge for him to move. I lean my head to the side giving him more access and enjoy the feeling of his lips caressing up to my ear.

"I definitely prefer you biting me over them." I say closing my eyes and reveling in the warmth coming off his mouth and breathing over my skin.

"Me too," he says between kisses, "but these aren't nibbles anymore, you didn't seem to like those from me either." He pulls back and waggles his eyebrows at me, making a chomping motion with his teeth and I jerk away laughing at the threat of being munched on again.

"You're a character, Aaron. Always the entertainer."

"That's what happens when you grow up in a huge family. You need to act out to get any attention you can, and I'm the master."

"How many brothers and sisters do you have?" I ask.

"I'm one of seven. The middle of seven to be precise. Three brother, three sisters."

"Wow, I can't even imagine."

"Yeah, so if you wanted attention at my house, you had to fight for it."

"Not me, when you're an only child, you get more than you need. In fact, you wish they would stop and turn their back for a bit and let you breathe on your own."

"I envy you sometimes."

"Don't. Look at the parents I have to deal with, remember my nightmare."

I risk putting my toes back in the water, but this time keep my feet kicking to scare away the nasty little toe nibblers. Aaron slides closer to me and pulls me to his chest. I rest my head there and listen intently for his heart beating under my ear. It has already become my most favorite place to rest and Aaron habitually draws me there every time we are sitting around talking. He plays with the stubborn strand of hair that is too short to tie back and I notice he likes to twirl it around his fingers over and over. It's amazing how comfortable we've become around each other and how quickly we've developed our own little rituals and routines.

Just as we have every day before today, we spend our time in intimate conversation, closely connected, always touching as we get to know one another better. However, once that contact begins, at some point, it always escalates. I can hear Aaron's heart race a little faster when I place my hand on his thigh and rub methodically up and down with a soft, tender touch, brushing my fingers increasingly closer to places we have yet to explore.

We've never spent time anywhere that is truly private. We are alone in the woods, but there is always the slim chance someone may walk by, so the intimacy between us has never gone further than exploring hands and lots of kissing. Aaron has never pushed these boundaries and I wonder if it's nerves or him being respectful of my initial hesitation at this relationship.

"Do your parents know about you?" I ask.

"That I'm not into women?"

A gentle laugh escapes my lips. "Yeah."

"Well, I don't know. I'd say they would have to be blind not to have picked up on it through the years, but my parents have a knack for turning their heads and looking the other way when there is a problem they don't want to face."

"Huh. Do you think they would accept you if they did know?"

"I think so. They're not too judgmental, just purposefully oblivious when it suits them.

"How long has Caleb known?"

"For as long as I have. There isn't a single thing that little shit doesn't know about me."

"Did you and he ever…"

Aaron bursts out laughing at that remark.

"Hell no. Caleb's straight as an arrow. I tried to kiss him once when we were fifteen and got punched in the face. I learned where he stood. We've been best friends forever and he's the only one I trust with all my dirty little secrets."

"Is that so?" I say. I glance up to meet Aaron's eyes as they peer down at me. "You have dirty little secrets do you?"

Aaron shuffles under me as a look of hesitation passes briefly in his eyes. He brings a hand to trace over my cheek. "You have the most gorgeous eyes." He says, directing away from my question. "I've wanted to tell you that for a long time. I could just stare into them all night."

Lost in his gaze, and memorized by his words, I'm acutely aware of my labored breathing and how the rhythm of my heart matches his own accelerating pace. Aaron seems to have this way of turning my insides to mush and leaving me without words all too frequently. Before I can respond, he lowers his face to mine and takes what breath I have left into a crushing kiss.

As is our habit, the kiss deepens with more and more intimacy and I find myself on top of Aaron in the grass, devouring his mouth, snaking my hands up his shirt, tracing the hard contours of his muscles with my fingers. Every day is a little more intense and a lot harder to keep in control. Aaron commands my senses and I feel myself giving way to him. Every tingle across my skin when he touches me, every flutter of my heart from his words, tells me I'm getting dangerously close to falling in love with this man. Which seems ridiculous since it's only been a short time since we got together, but tell that to my heart. This should scare me, but it doesn't any longer. I'm at peace for the first time in a long time and welcome all he has to give.

Aaron runs his hands over my ass, squeezes through my breeches, and thrusts his hard cock to rub against mine. I could forget myself in the next moment and tear into him, let him have me right here in the fading daylight under the open sky by the pond, but it wouldn't be right; no matter how badly we both seem to want it. I don't want to worry over someone strolling by and fear would niggle at my brain the entire time if we crossed that line right here and now. I want the first time we are together to be only us and the moment we are sharing. I want no worries to be present in the room whatsoever.

Trying to tear my lips free, I want to ask him to come back to my rooms, to stay with me tonight and make love to me, but a sudden loud splash, like a large rock being tossed in the water, has us both scrambling to our feet. Aaron has ahold of my arm and is yanking me back from the water's edge before I can turn my head to see the cause of the splash. Danger and panic fill my head as I run – more like dragged - stumbling after him.

About ten paces away, Aaron turns and squats down, pulling me to him and wrapping his arms around me in a protective manner. We both stare back down to the pond we so hurriedly vacated. A momma bear and her two cubs have decided to take to the pond for a swim. Once I realize the bears have taken no notice of us, and our rapid flight to get away from them, my heart begins to calm in my chest. The bears continue about their day, swimming and diving in the waters, splashing and playing as though they didn't just scare the crap out of two innocent bystanders. I should be disappointed at the intrusion but they are quite the fascinating sight to see.

Ducked down by the base of a large oak, we watch the three bears in silence as they continue to paddle along in the waters, eventually dipping their heads underneath in search of a meal. Mamma bear manages to snag a large fish and her cubs knock each other over in their frenzy to get the most food.

Aaron takes my hand and stands, helping me up. He kisses our interlocking fingers and motions for us to take off through the woods away from our unexpected company. We continue to stroll, hand in hand as the sun sets. The heat between us simmers warm, although, it doesn't ignite again like it did before, but I know it's on both our minds. As we approach the city, I toy with the idea of having Aaron come home with me. I want him there. I want to ask him. But as the words race around my mind, they never pass my lips. We are at the city wall, and in a few moments we will be back behind the surgery at the door to my rooms and Aaron will be saying goodbye again. I don't want this night to end. Every day together gets better and every night I lay in bed lonelier, wishing Aaron was there; wrapping me up like a blanket in his arms. As we approach the surgery and are about to head around back, I prepare my words carefully, feeling the jitter of excited nerves inside my body; rolling the words on my tongue, finding the courage to voice the request, and take this relationship in the direction we are both anticipating.

Lost in my muddled planning, I startle as the surgery door swings open in our wake and Doctor Greaves pokes his head out. He makes a brief glance at Aaron, unaffected by finding us together, then rests his eyes on me.

"Chase, thank goodness. I came looking for you, but couldn't find you. I need a hand if you could."

He disappears behind the door before I can object.

Damn.

I swing around to Aaron and can see the disappointment in his face as well. He too had been anticipating a longer night together.

"I'm sorry." I say. "He wouldn't ask for me if it wasn't important."

Aaron hides his disappointment behind a warm smile.

"No worries, Doc. You are in high demand. I'm glad you could make time for me tonight."

I can tell he wants to kiss me goodbye, but his respect for my boundaries is always first on his mind. He gives me a wink and a lingering smile before he heads down the street.

I watch him go, feeling instantly empty without him.

Chapter Six

Aaron

"Seriously, interrupted by bloody bears? Damn that sucks." Caleb says.

"Yup. Scarred the shit out of us too."

"And then what happened?"

"We wandered through the woods a while and then I walked him home." I say.

"That's it? You didn't invite yourself in and finish what you started?"

"I'm a respectable gentleman, Caleb. I won't force the issue."

"Horseshit. You're practically a horny teenager whose been chasing this guy since we got here and you're telling me it's been almost a fortnight and all you've done is kiss him?"

"A lot of kisses…In between a lot of talk. We've spent a lot to time getting to know each other. Our hands wandered a little…well…a lot sometimes."

My eyes drift across the field to where a group of men are being taken through a variety of specific drills. Something is going on today. Captain Leeson has been joined with Captain Harris, Commander Corban, and the King himself. They have been huddled together all morning and are slowly taking small groups of men through different maneuvers while they watch them intently, talking and discussing amongst themselves. The rest of us have been made to stand around and wait our turn. I get the feeling this has something to do with the march north to hold the border.

Things have been slowly falling into place and the talk is that the armies should be on the move come winter.

"So, when are you going to step it up?" Caleb waggles his eyebrows at me.

We've been waiting patiently for most of the morning and Caleb has been on an unending quest for more details about my nights with Chase.

"I don't know. I don't want to scare him off. He seemed tentative with this whole thing at first and I want it to be his decision. I get the feeling if Doctor Greaves hadn't needed to pull him in to work last night he was going to invite me to stay."

The recent group of men who have been taken through drills are released and my attention shifts as they walk off the field.

"What do you think they are doing?" I ask Caleb, changing the subject.

"Probably deciding who stays and who goes."

The higher-ups all gather together and are talking again. I notice Captain Leeson pointing to a few of us. When he turns to where Caleb and I are standing, I grow rigid. I'm not nervous, or at least I don't think I am. I want to go north with the armies, it's why I came here to Ludairium with Caleb. We want to be amongst the fighting men to save our land from the Outsiders. If that is what this is all about, then I'll need to make sure I perform at my absolute best. Leeson's finger points to Caleb and I and I know we will be called forward next. The huddling and whispering continue for longer than I expect and I'm becoming increasingly antsy as I wait.

Finally, the higher-ups break apart and spread out and I see them walking in different directions toward groups of soldiers around the field. The King himself makes his way toward Caleb and I. The man is the sheer definition of intimidating. He carries himself with confidence, broad shoulders squared in his approach, each step measured and unrushed; yet somehow giving the impression that if you tried to run from him, you would never get away. His blond hair is cut short. His jaw is set firm and the few days' worth of stubble across his chin only adds to his daunting appearance.

"Moment of truth, Aaron. Hope you're ready for this." Caleb says.

I nod at him and turn to face the fast approaching King. He is a slightly shorter man then myself, but regardless, if I'm being honest, he kind of scares the crap out of me. The few times I have had the privilege of seeing him, he is always stern and serious. Today is no different.

Nearly at us, the King waves his hands for us to come forward to meet him. Caleb and I rush forward and stand at attention giving our King an appropriate bow before waiting for instruction.

"Mathers and Pryor, correct?" He asks.

"Yes, Sir." Caleb and I say in unison.

His gaze scans up and down Caleb before turning to me to do the same. I notice his eyes are a shocking blue as they study my forehead before landing on my face, meeting my gaze. Indicating to my injury with a nod of his head, his brow knits.

"What happened?"

My heart sinks. What am I supposed to say? According to the report, I was technically "injured during training" because Caleb and I disregarded and did not "comply with the rules".

"Intense, long hours of training take a toll on the mind and body, Sir. It was an accident. One that will not be repeated, I assure you."

He lets a humph pass through his lips as he looks between us again. I'm not sure if he's satisfied with my answer or not but he seems to have moved on.

"I'd like you two to come run a few specific maneuvers. I'm not going to dance around the matter. We're looking to assemble an army to march north. I need you to show me what you've got. Understand?"

"Yes, Sir." Caleb and I say.

The King indicates for us to follow and we are joined with a few other men.

For the next little while we run through a number of different drills, nothing new, but the intensity and expectation makes everything all the more exhausting. Finally, allowing for a small break, the higher-ups gather in a tight circle and talk in low voices. We haven't been dismissed, so we hang back and wait to be told what to do. Caleb wanders up beside me and nudges my arm.

"What?" I say, keeping my voice low.

"Field gates. Look."

I turn my head to glance over my shoulder and am shocked to find Chase walking out onto the field. He is carrying a stack of papers and is headed directly for the higher-ups. He hasn't seen me. A smile curls the edges of my mouth as I watch him cross the field. He is the sheer embodiment of gorgeous.

"Rawr! Sexy." Caleb teases.

I jab him in the gut with an elbow and lower my head not to look directly at Chase, but I follow his movements with downcast eyes. I promised we could be subtle and I will not break that promise.

Chase joins the group of higher ups and hands the stack of papers he is carrying over to the King. I don't miss the glare that is passed. The tension between them could be cut with a knife. The King leafs through the pile of papers, skimming over whatever is written on them and nods to Chase. Chase turns to leave and Caleb is in my ear.

"Go ask him if you can see him tonight."

"I can't," I hiss, "discreet remember?"

"Come on, Aaron. You can think around this. Go." Caleb shoves me forward and I stumble a few steps.

I glance to the higher-ups to see if they are watching, but they are deeply engrossed in whatever Chase handed them. I follow after Chase, picking up my pace as he makes ground ahead of me.

"Doctor." I call out.

Chase slows his pace and turns to me, a look of unease crosses his face.

"How can I help you, Mr. Pryor?" He asks as his eyes do a scan of the men around us.

"These sutures, they are irritating me and pulling at the skin. Any chance you could take a look at them?"

Chase steps forward, giving me a warning look before brushing my hair back and running a finger over my forehead. His touch is light and professional, but it still manages to get my blood flowing a little faster. Chase meets my eyes and I see he's not angry. He is struggling to hide a smile that wants to flood his face, but it pulls at his eyes and I see it clearly.

"They can probably come out. How about you stop in later today and I'll remove them for you."

"I'll be there. Thank you." I let my gaze linger a while longer as we share a moment, thick with unspoken desire before I back away and let him go.

I watch as Chase makes his way off the field before I turn and head back over to Caleb.

"So?" Caleb asks.

"Going to head to the surgery later, get these damn sutures out." I say with a grin.

"And get yourself a piece of ass?"

"It's more than that with him you know?"

"Sure it is." Caleb says rolling his eyes. "He's all I hear about now."

I don't expect Caleb to understand the connection Chase and I seem to have developed. It may not have been all that long, but we have connected on such a deep level I feel like I've known him my whole life. Conversations between us run freely and we make each other laugh. It doesn't bother me in the slightest that he wants to keep us a secret. All that matters is how incredibly good I feel when I'm with him.

With a sharp whistle, the higher-ups pull us together and ask a few random questions before dismissing the group. I head off to the gates with Caleb, when I'm halted by a hand on my shoulder.

"Pryor, if you'd hang back a moment please." Captain Leeson says.

My heartrate picks up again and I share a glance with Caleb as he turns to go.

"Come find me after." He says, as he heads off the field with the other men.

Standing at attention, I wait while whispers are passed between Captain Leeson and the King. Harris and Corban have moved off and are no longer involved in whatever is going on. They have pulled more men in a group and are working with them across the field.

The King raises a hand to motion me forward. "Come." He says.

I stand before him at attention. My nerves are frayed. Being singled out is never good. Why do they want to see me? I try to calm my jitters with a few deep breaths while I wait. The King is looking at me again with his penetrating blue eyed stare. I feel split open like he can see into my very soul with that gaze of his and I steel myself not to react. Leeson is standing close to him and is still scanning the papers in his hand.

There is no indication of their personal relationship in their behavior on the field. Unless you know about it, like everyone does, you would never be able to tell by watching them right now that they are lovers. As terrified as I am right now in the Kings presence, I'm equally fascinated by these two men and what they have achieved.

"Pryor, I'm concerned," the King says.

I remain silent, not sure if I'm supposed to respond to this or not. Concerned? Concerned about what? What did I do?

"When were you recruited?" He asks, no indication in his voice telling me where this conversation might be going.

"Late spring, Sir."

"So you haven't been here all that long."

"No, Sir."

The King turns to Leeson. "How many?"

"Five." Leeson answers.

Five what?

Turning his attention back to me, the King narrows his eyes. "Records indicate you have been treated by Doctor Schuyler for injuries on five separate occasions."

I swallow a hard lump that has instantly formed in my throat. So that's what this is about. I'm being evaluated as being a potential klutz all because of my stupid methods at trying to get Chase's attention.

"Yes, Sir. That's correct."

"Were these all field related injuries?" He asks.

I lower my eyes to the ground as shame washes over me.

No, they are the calling of a desperate man injuries.

"Umm...Sort of, Sir...Yes and no."

"It's a simple question, Pryor. Answer it. Are they field injuries, yes or no?"

I let out a sigh. "Yes, Sir," I raise my head to meet his intense stare, "but I can explain. I'm not a bad soldier, I assure you."

"Don't put words in my mouth, Pryor. I never said you were a bad soldier. Explain yourself."

"Sorry, Sir...Umm...Well..." How am I supposed to explain this without breaking Chase's confidence? Lost for words, I gape at the King with a blank stare.

"Never mind." He says. "Leeson tells me you hold your own on the field. You've proven that today. Everything I saw was impressive, but these injuries are what concern me. To me, they are evidence of goofing around. Of one of my soldiers not taking his training seriously. Every incident recorded has gone unobserved during training. You seem to manage to hurt yourself every time your Captain's back is turned. I require a certain element of self-discipline with my soldiers. I can't have men who need constant supervision-"

"I have self-discipline, Sir-"

"Don't. Ever. Interrupt me." The man steps in close to me, invading my personal space and drilling his eyes into mine. "You want to be here? You want to march north with *my* army? Then you need to prove you are mature enough and reliable enough to do so. Do I make myself clear?"

"Yes, Sir. I'm sorry, Sir." I say as I struggle not to break eye contact with the man again.

"You are a better swordsman then you are showing on the field. Leeson is observant and tells me what he sees and I don't question his judgement. Now, pull your shit together, Pryor, or you will be staying behind."

"I will, Sir."

The King turns from me and goes back to Leeson, taking the papers from his hand. Leeson leans in close and says something to him I don't hear and I see the King's demeanor soften and a smile crawl onto his face. It's amazing anyone can crack through that man's rough exterior. He scares the shit out of me, and he know it.

Turning back to me, he sees I haven't left.

"Go, you're dismissed."

I give a short bow and spin on my heels, trying hard not to run off the field.

Ouch. I haven't gained a good reputation at all. It's a good thing I have finally been able to snag Chase's attention and I shouldn't need to do anything more to get myself in trouble. It was a stupid move to begin with and I knew it. I should be grateful he's even giving me a second chance.

Leaving the field, I nearly run into Caleb as I turn the corner.

"What happened? Why did you need to stay?" He asks, following me as we continue toward the city.

"I've been warned to behave or I won't be going north."

"What? Seriously? How have you not behaved?"

"Every time Leeson turns his back, I wind up needing sutures to fix a field wound, it looks like I need constant supervision. I got told."

"Ouch."

"Yeah."

"What are you going to do?" Caleb asks.

"Turn it around. If not, I don't march with the rest."

We walk in silence for a while as we head back toward the city and to the east end where Caleb and I split rent on a small room above the local tailor's shop.

"You want to grab some food and a drink and Statin's once we clean up?" Caleb asks.

"You seem to forget, I have a nasty head wound that needs a certain sexy ass doctor's attention right now."

"Right." Caleb laughs. "How could I forget? I won't fret if you don't come home tonight then."

Caleb turns off down a different road while I continue my trek toward the surgery. The closer I get, the faster my heart pumps. The warm rush of blood washing over my body quickens my pace with the anticipation of seeing him again. I love being around Chase. The time we go between seeing each other feels like it stretches on for days when in actuality I've seen Chase almost every day for a fortnight. It's never enough.

Responding to my knock, the door swings open and Doctor Greaves peers out at me.

"Good afternoon, son. Here to get those blasted sutures out are you? The young doctor said you'd be by. Come on in."

I hesitate on the threshold, not moving. "Is he not in?"

"Nah, sent him home. He was up half the night preparing some lists for His Grace. Come on in."

I can feel my good mood draining from my body as my shoulders slump and I reluctantly follow the man through the door. Guiding me to a stool, Doctor Greaves proceeds to poke and prod at my forehead. My confusion at not finding Chase at the surgery must be etched on my face. I'm relieved when the doctor mistakes it for concern over my head wound.

"Cheer up, son. Looks well enough to be removed I'd say. Shouldn't take more than a moment, so find that smile of yours while I get to work and you can be on your way in no time."

"Thank you, Sir." I say trying to muster a smile to my face.

Disappointment doesn't quite describe how I'm feeling at not finding Chase here. Did he not want to see me? No, Doctor Greaves said he sent him home. As the doctor proceeds to cut and pull sutures from my head, I think about how I might proceed, wincing and grunting every now and then when a small tug causes the sensitive skin to pinch. Should I go around to his place? Will he want to see me? Is he upset that I approached him on the field? I was careful, like he wanted. Too many questions and not enough answers.

Another tug makes me flinch back and grit my teeth. The doctor puts his cutting tool in his mouth while he squints at my forehead, yanking the last few, pesky bits out from where they have imbedded themselves under my skin. Smoothing a hand over the area, he nods his head.

"That's all of them. You're good to go, son." The doctor steps away and begins tidying up.

"Thanks, Doc."

Leaving the surgery, I stand undecided for a while, looking down the street. Watching people wandering by, going to and from the market in the city square.

Spinning on my heels, I make my way around the back of the surgery to the alley and Chase's rooms. Not allowing myself to think on it any more, I knock on the door. A fleeting thought crosses my mind. What if he's sleeping? The doctor had said he was up half the night last night. What if he-

The door swings open and there he is. By the look of him, he might have been laying down. He's no longer in his standard "doctor attire" of white blouse, apron, and breeches. He is dressed in a simple cotton shirt, laces undone halfway down his chest, and a simple pair of dark breeches. His hair is not tied back, as I normally see it, and it hangs in long waves around his face and in his eyes. The urge to run my fingers through it is strong but I resist. His eyes are slightly red and tired looking, something I didn't notice when I saw him earlier.

"Hey, handsome." I say giving him a warm smile. "Did I wake you?"

Swiping a hand over his face and through his hair, holding it back, he returns my smile. I take it as a good sign.

"Yeah, I had a long night." He peers down the street in both directions. "Want to come in?" He asks.

Accepting the invitation, I follow behind him into his small room. I take note of the obsessive tidiness around me. There are two tables, one organized with a variety of jars, clearly labeled and ordered so they stand biggest to smallest along the tables back edge. A basin of water sits to the side. The other table has a stack of books on one side and a small pile of papers with an ink bottle and quill at the ready. There are a few shelves with pots, jugs, and an assortment of foods. A pallet by the hearth with blankets that look recently slept in and a trunk against the wall at the end; which no doubt contains Chase's personal belongings and clothes.

Turning to Chase, I see him squinting tired eyes at me. "Your sutures are out."

"Yeah, Doctor Greaves took care of them. Although I admit, you have a gentler hand then the old man."

Chase laughs. "Yeah, he's less patient in his old age."

He turns to the book laden table and picks up a ribbon. Combing through his hair with his fingers, he works to pull it back off his face. I place a hand on his arm and give it a gentle tug to encourage him to release his hold on his hair. He lets it fall back down, sending it to brush over his shoulders as he studies me quizzically. I tuck the few strands that fall in his eyes behind his ear and linger my finger against their softness.

"Keep it down, I like it."

His head dips down and I can see his cheeks flush as he hides his face from me, placing the tie back on the table. Not being in our common territory of the wooded forest, I'm feeling quite nervous and sense Chase feels the same. He invited me in reflexively, something we have been edging toward and wanting, I have no doubt, but I'm not sure if he thought it through that far and meant it as an invitation for anything else.

"Can I get you a drink?" He asks.

"Nah, it's okay. You look tired, I'm not going to stay."

"No." He says abruptly. "I'm all right...stay...for a bit."

We both stand awkwardly just watching each other. It's the first time we have had true privacy and my body seems to know it and is responding to the invisible pull between us much more forcefully than it ever has before. I ache to touch him and hold him. Hell, the animalistic side of me - the one I've suppressed and not let out - wants to throw him down and give him a night he'll never forget, wants to take him violently until he's screaming my name and writhing under me. I hold my breath and still my feet.

My eyes drift from his face to roam his body. His exposed chest shows the gentle contours of fine muscles on fair skin and I can't help but linger there, staring hungrily, while my brain peels away his layers as it tries to imagine the rest of what remains covered by his shirt. Have I mentioned I have quite an active imagination? I like what I see. I'm so mesmerized by his beauty and what my mind is creating, I don't realize when he closes the gap between us. When his hand reaches up and his thumb traces along my jawline, my eyes climb back up to meet his.

Deep emerald pools beckon me, inviting me in; I so want in. He is giving me that distinct "kiss me" face again that I'm coming to know well.

There is no way I'm going to deny him. Leaning in to capture his mouth, Chase's face comes up to meet mine halfway and I melt against his lips. My heightened senses remind me of our complete seclusion. We are alone and this can go anywhere we want it to go. The heat between us mounts higher and my cock stirs as Chase deepens the kiss. I delve in to the far reaches of his mouth with my tongue, to lick and taste all he has to give. Everything about Chase is intoxicating. Despite the dozens of times I have kissed him recently, I'm still surprised at how deliciously good he tastes. I can never get enough of him.

Chase's hands wrap around the back of my neck and he holds me in place, sucking my tongue in his mouth, and kissing at me with more appetite than he has ever shown. My body's response is immediate, waves of heat run from my head to my toes, making my skin super sensitive to his touch. He presses against me and I feel his stiffness grind against my leg. His arousal makes me groan into his mouth. I need to touch him and look at him, explore his incredible body, and get to know what I have been deprived of for too long. I let my fingers trail down his back, feeling every curve and muscle of him easily through his thin shirt. Slowly down until they are at his waist where I climb them back up again under his shirt.

I've been so nervous of scaring him off, have been nothing but a gentleman around him, allowing him to take the lead at every turn, never pressing the issue but not now, not today. If I'm crossing a line he'll need to stop me because I've wanted this for too long to hold back.

Nothing alerts me to slow down, so I trace my fingers up his warm, soft skin. I'm afraid my rough, callused hands will feel awful against him, so I keep my touches light as I run my hands around his body and up over his chest. Chase's hands begin doing the same to me and just the feel of his delicate fingers running across my lower bare back sends goosebumps to prickle down my arms.

Chase begins working at the buckles securing my armor and expertly relieves me of its heavy weight, letting it fall to the ground. Next thing I know, my shirt is being pulled from my body and discarded as well. Our lips crash back together in a desperation of tongues and teeth, the frenzy of need elevating us even higher. Hell if a fortnight of waiting and wanting hasn't made this moment almost frantic between us. I slide my hands around Chase's hips, bringing them down to take a firm grip on his perfectly round ass before lifting him up against me. Chase wraps his legs around my waist and I can feel his cock straining against the confines of his breeches as it rests against my belly. I take him to his pallet and lower him carefully to the tousled blankets. Chase's lips lock back onto mine as he rolls me bodily and straddles himself on top of me, staring deep into my eyes. Chase, no longer the meek and mild man I have come to know, rids himself of his own shirt and is back on my lips again, licking and sucking at them with a furious need.

All clear thoughts vanish and the only focus I have is for Chase, this moment, and the need pulsing through my veins. I'd be lying if I said I didn't want this, or haven't been thinking about it since our first kiss, but the actual event is proving to be far more intense than I ever imagined.

Chase's mouth moves from mine to kiss down my neck. He nibbles and bites at the soft skin sending my body to arch up and another moan to escape my lips. Tracing his tongue up the curve of my neck to my ear, he takes the lobe in his mouth suckling gently before popping it out again. His breath is burning hot against me and I'm trembling when he whispers.

"No more messing around, Aaron. I want you to make love to me. I want you inside me."

Holy hell, pants on and everything, the man nearly undoes me right there. I had no expectations coming over here today, but I surely am not disappointed with where it's going. Chase has become more than a want, he's a need. Someone I can see myself getting lost in time and time again.

His mouth moves back to mine and takes command, hungrily eating at my lips and tongue. It's suffocating, but I have no desire to breathe anything but Chase. The next thing I know, his hand is between us, removing whatever clothes are still left intact, until we are completely naked. For someone who started off tentative and unsure he wanted this relationship, Chase sure does know what he wants now.

Pulling his nakedness to mine, I revel in the feel of him against my skin. I want him to slow down, not because I don't want this - I do, desperately - but I want it to last and it feels like we are in a frantic race to the finish line. I want to take in and remember every touch and feel with clarity so I can cherish and relive it again and again.

"Slow down. I need to feel you. Don't rush it." I pant against his mouth.

Chase follows my lead and our kisses become less desperate and more intimate which only increases our need for each other tenfold. Finding a slower, smoother rhythm, we take our time exploring each other's bodies. His is heavenly. Every curve, every muscle and contour under my touch makes him respond as I only hoped he would. Every move made sends our desire for each other to grow exponentially until we are aching to be joined and can't hold off any longer.

In a moment that can only be described as euphoric, we allow our urgency full rein as we succumb to one another. I never could have imagined just how deliriously intoxicating being inside Chase would be. As desperately as I need him, when we come together it isn't violent or aggressive at all but raw and open. The look in Chase's eyes and the ache pulling at my heart is almost frightening. I feel split open in that moment. Exposed and vulnerable with more awareness of our connection than ever before.

* * *

Exhausted from a night up writing lists for the King and a captivating afternoon filled with an exuberant amount of love making, Chase falls asleep wrapped in my arms. It's just short of dusk, but there is no other place I would rather be than right here. The heaviness of sleep takes its hold, pulling me under. I secure his warm body tight up against me and bury my face in his neck, breathing in the sweetness that is him as I feel myself being drawn down to join him in the pits of sleep.

Chapter Seven

Chase

Opening my eyes, I'm surrounded by darkness. Slivers of moonlight illuminate the shape of the window where its light leaks in around the drawn drapes in almost a perfect square. Night has fallen and Aaron's warm body is wrapped so completely around me, I struggle to turn around in his arms and face him. He's fast asleep; soft snores passing through his parted lips making them flutter with each exhale. Even at our close distance, the soft contours of his face are the only forms I can make out in the darkness and I reach up a hand to run my fingers over his scruffy, slack cheek. A smile curls his mouth at my touch and his eyes try to open but give up, still heavy with sleep. Memories from earlier are still fresh in my mind and I wiggle in even closer, brushing soft kisses along Aaron's jaw up to his mouth. Moving his face to mine, he kisses me with little energy before his body loses its battle with sleep again and his deep, even breathing rhythm continues.

This man has completely broken down my defenses, leaving nothing but a mess of rubble where my protective wall once stood and now I'm scared to death of hurting him. That tiny little voice inside me, who I suppressed that night at the tower, has been screaming at me that this is a mistake, but I haven't listened. Whenever I'm in Aaron's presence, I'm stripped of all reason and am left with an all-consuming need. It feels so good, so right, and I have deprived myself of this feeling for so long. Aaron makes my heart smile, and it has been a long five years since it knew that sensation; it hasn't forgotten how freeing and liberating it can be. Being with him feels right in so many ways and I'm not altogether sure I can remember why this is a bad thing anymore.

Aaron's eyelids flutter and his breathing hiccups once before he readjusts himself, squeezing his arms tighter around me. Sighing into the comfort of his embrace, I bury my face in his neck and smooth a hand down his back to rest on his thigh. The small action stirs Aaron from his slumber and his eyes manage to open. His smile glows in the dark and he draws me in closer and takes my lips in his. Becoming lost in each other again, the last of my fading doubts – and that nagging little voice deep inside - disappear into nothingness. Aaron's touch is tender and sweet, never rushed. It's almost as though he is making sure his every move is accepted before going forward and I accept. I accept him wholeheartedly, no longer afraid. Without being told, Aaron knows what I need. He is gentle, but confident, and makes love to me with a passion I could have never guessed this exuberant man could possess and I know I'm in deep.

* * *

Waking again to find an emptiness beside me where there was once a warm body, I lift my head in confusion, feeling instantly lonely. There is movement in the darkness and I look around to see Aaron fishing for his clothes.

"Are you leaving?" I ask, sleep making my voice raspy and broken.

Aaron makes his way back over and bends down to plant a soft lingering kiss on my lips.

"Dawn is on the horizon. I have to be on the field at sun-up."

"It's morning?" I turn a sleepy glance to the window, but see no evidence of daybreak around the drapes. The world still appears to be blanketed in darkness beyond.

"It is, handsome. You were tired." Aaron tucks my loose hair behind my ear as he sits on the pallet edge before pulling on his boots.

Stealing the attention, I wrap my arms around his neck and draw him down on top of me, kissing at him with a renewed appetite. Last night was amazing and I'm not ready for it to end. I pull Aaron's hands away from his boot, and encourage them back on my body.

"Stay a little longer, be late one time." I beg between kisses.

Aaron doesn't struggle or resist me and he returns the kiss feverishly for a while longer. Pulling back after a moment, a look of reluctance mares his gorgeous face. He says, "I want to, believe me, but I can't. I'm already in all kinds of shit and I can't be late. Not today."

"What do you mean?"

Aaron snags his shirt from the end of the bed and sits to pull it over his head. "You know those injury reports you had to draw up?"

"Yeah."

"Well, the King confronted me about how many times I've been treated by you. He's unhappy with the fact that I seem to have poor discipline on his field and is concerned that if I require such constant supervision that maybe I'm not ready to march north with the men."

"Aaron, those weren't true field injuries."

"He doesn't know that. Now he has Leeson watching my every move and if I don't prove myself, then I'm staying back. Leeson's a dick and I know he'll use any excuse he can to go running back to lover boy and tell him I have no business going."

I pull myself to sit and grab at Aaron's arm, stilling his dressing, turning him to face me.

"Brandon's not like that, Aaron. If he thinks you're a good soldier, he'll make sure Alistair knows it and you'll go with the rest of them."

I see confusion crease Aaron's forehead before realization raises his eyebrows.

"Oh right, you and Leeson were…" he trails off.

"That has no bearing on what I'm telling you, but I do know the man a little bit and I'm saying, if you are a good soldier, he will recognize it. If you're under scrutiny right now, it's Alistair initiating it. Brandon will do whatever is asked of him, but in the end, Brandon will be the decider of whether or not you go. Trust me."

Aaron seems unsettled. He has stopped dressing altogether and is watching me with uncertainty. There is a distance between us, if not physically, emotionally for sure. I reach a hand out and take his to still his unconscious fidgeting and move closer to him.

"I know these men, Aaron. Trust me. I spent a long time on the road with them. Alistair may call the shots, but Brandon holds a huge influence over him." I pull myself up and swing a leg around him to straddle his lap. "You are right though; you shouldn't be late."

Aaron's eyes search mine and I can see him hesitate before he finally speaks. "What happened between you two?"

"It doesn't matter. It was a long time ago." And the pain I have for what I did to Brandon is something I can't share with Aaron. It's a weight a carry and I own it, it belongs to me alone.

"Do you still love him?" His voice is faint and uncertain.

I cup Aaron's face in my hands and look deep into his brown eyes, smoothing his creased brow with my thumb. "I do, and I probably always will, but I'm not in love with him anymore. Brandon has the kindest soul I've ever seen and he would never hesitate to help someone in need. Anyone who is lucky enough to know him for who he is, can't help but love him. It's just who he is. And I assure you, he will not wrong you. He doesn't have a vindictive or cruel bone in his body."

When Aaron's eyes drop from mine, I dip my head to meet them again. "You have no competition and nothing to worry yourself over, Aaron. Brandon and I went our separate ways five years ago. It's history."

With that, I push Aaron down onto the bed again and collapse on top of him, holding his hands to the bed above his head with all the force I can muster. It's a sad amount I admit, but I need to lighten the mood and if I know one thing about Aaron it's that he's playful.

"Listen to me, Pryor. I'm all yours so quit looking so damn worried or I'll hold you to this bed and kiss you raw until you submit and believe me."

Aaron's laugher makes me bounce on his chest. The worry is instantly gone from his face and has been replaced with a look of warmth and happiness, followed by a raised eyebrow of humorous doubt.

"You really think you can hold me down?" He asks, easily wrenching free of my grasp with a grin so he can wrap his arms around my naked body. "You're half my size, Chase."

I squirm in his grasp, laughing until I am able to get my arms free again and bring them to hold his face to mine.

"If you have to go, can I at least give you something to think about before you leave?" I ask, drawing his lips to mine and sucking him into a hungry passionate kiss, delving deep into his mouth and making him groan.

Coming up for air, Aaron breathes a heavy sigh and grinds his already hard cock into me. "Like last night didn't already give me something to think about."

"I want to be sure you are coming back later." I say.

"If you want me here, I'll be back."

"Come back, and bring this," I grind against his erection with a smirk, "with you."

After a few more lingering kisses and evidently rising passion between us, Aaron is in jeopardy of missing his training session completely. I pull back, gasping for air from Aaron's hold on my lips and roll off him.

"Go, Pryor." I shove him away with mirth, "or I won't be able to let you leave."

Resigning with a low growl in the back of his throat, Aaron gets up to finish dressing, but his eyes never leave my own. They are filled with not only desire, but a reflective pool of emotion I know I'm feeling as well. I fish my own shirt off the floor where it was tossed last night and meet him at the door as I pull it over my head.

"Go prove you're worth taking north."

"I will." He turns to the door, but dives at me for one last kiss before heading out into the morning.

* * *

After Aaron leaves, I decide to clean up and head around to the surgery to start my day. Doctor Greaves is rarely in the building this early and unless he knows I'm not available to come in, he stays away until long after midday. I promised the man I would try to replenish our supplies before winter set in and this morning is looking like a good time to finish the lists of what I will need to acquire.

The sun has just broke the horizon and the day is warming up fast, leaving a soft misty fog in its wake. Summer seems insistent on holding on this year, which is fine by me. I hate the cold, especially after having spent so much of last winter on the road, never knowing what it was like to truly be warm. I'm not sure the memory of that bone deep chill I carried with me every day we were gone will ever leave me. Although, the idea of having Aaron warming the bed beside me every night this year lends a certain desire for winter to get here faster. I grin to myself, remembering last night and the sheen of sweat that covered both our bodies as we rode each other to climax. Definitely no chill in the air last night.

Once inside the surgery, I start pulling the drapes away from the windows to let in the morning light. The two rooms used for our practice are small, but adequate. The main area consists of a few tables for working and organizing supplies. They are old and the thick wooden surfaces are cracked and pitted from decades of use. A number of stools sit against one wall by the door, none of them are the same; having been gathered at random over the years. They sit as extras because sometimes families like to hover around while we work on patients, better they have a place to rest their butts than have them shadowing our work and getting in the way. The opposite wall consists of shelves that run all the way up its length to the ceiling, filled with vials and jars of every thinkable ingredient that may be used to treat anything from a headache to a broken toe. The joining room is smaller, and where I do most of my treating of patients. I insisted that patients should be respected and given as much privacy as we can offer them, a product of my teachings, therefore, I treat them in this separate room. Within the four walls is a small work table where I prepare the instruments I require and a larger table for patients to lie down, should the need arise. Apart from a couple stools that sit around this table, the room is relatively bare and uncluttered; just the way I like it.

I make my way to the back room, and the smaller table, to gather a stack of papers, ink, and quill to begin my task of taking inventory of our supplies. As I'm about to turn around, a slightly yellowed, folded parchment, sitting on the table's edge, catches my eye. My name is etched on the front in a familiar hand and I stiffen at its sight. I shuffle my supplies to one arm and grab the letter, turning it over. My face drops when I see the seal on the back, confirming what I knew in my mind. Six stars surrounding a crescent moon, all embodied in an upside down triangle. My family seal. The letter is from my parents. Hesitating with it in my hand for a moment, I race through all the possibilities of what it could mean. Written correspondence from my parents is never good news, maybe in their eyes, but not mine. I have no desire to open it right now. Whatever news they send can wait. My day has started off on a high and I'm in no mood to have it ruined. Leaving the letter where I found it, I head back into the main room to begin my task and try to distract myself from the feeling of dread lying heavy in the pit of my stomach.

Midway through my morning, I have already been pulled away a number of times to handle minor patient needs. Ludairium, being a large city, and this being the only surgery with me being the only full time doctor, makes for busy days. Surprising me, Doctor Greaves makes his appearance before noon as he clamors through the door with a cheerful hello.

"Mornin', son. How's the day going?"

"Steady. I've been working on the inventory. We are going to need a fair number of things by the looks of it. I may need a day away just to ensure we are stocked up. I'll have to talk to the trader and see if he can get some of these harder to acquire items while on his travels."

"Let me know, I'll make sure I'm available so you can get out of here." He pulls up a stool beside me and scans the list I have been busy making. "Your friend was by yesterday. The young soldier who's always hurting himself. Did he come find you? Handsome lad he is. Seemed disappointed you weren't around."

I peer up from my work at the table to look at the older man. The sideways smile plastered to his face and the nonchalant way he continues to skim my work without looking over to me says everything. I'm not fooling him. Was I ever?

Bloody hell, does everyone know about me?

A knock comes to the door and I'm relived at the interruption. Maybe the old man knows, or thinks he does, but I'm not too sure I'm ready to admit it to him just yet. Doctor Greaves rises to get the door and my momentary relief at a distraction evaporates when I look up to see Aaron standing there holding his arm to his chest. Doctor Greaves steps aside to allow Aaron to enter and turns to me with a grin.

"It's for you."

Between the Doctor's smug, knowing grin, and Aaron's "apparent" discomfort in what appears to be yet another injury, I'm unsure how to react and find myself shuffling my gaze between them.

Breaking the uncomfortable silence, Doctor Greaves indicates for Aaron to head into the joining room. Settled back to his work at the table beside me, he leans in and whispers. "I don't think he's hurt this time. Call it a hunch."

My head shoots up to meet his eyes, and the doctor gives me a wink and nods to the door.

"He's waiting." He says.

Damn, blasted, bloody hell. I'm an open book to you aren't I, Doc?

Closing the door behind me, I stand staring at yet another smug smile. This one coming from the man who shared my bed last night. My anger evaporates and I can't fight the smile creeping its way to my face. Aaron is rocking his braced arm carelessly with a smile on his face that could light up the room on a dark night. He is terribly adorable, but I would never tell him so. It would only encourage him.

"Are you really hurt?" I ask.

Aaron releases his arm from its hold and swings it around. "Nah, just wanted to see you."

"You're not fooling anyone. He knows." I say, indicating over my shoulder to the next room. "Apparently we are blatantly obvious to him."

Aaron's face drops and I realize he probably thinks I'll be mad at him.

"It's okay. I'm not sure I've ever fooled him. The man has some kind of parental type wisdom to him. He sees through all the horseshit I attempt to send his way."

I walk toward Aaron who has taken a seat on his stool. I wedge myself to stand between his legs and wrap my arms around his neck.

"So. How can I help you today, Mr. Pryor?"

"Well," he says, pulling me closer, dark, warm brown eyes staring up at me, "I've had this terrible aching, almost tugging sensation in my heart since I left your house this morning. I thought maybe something was wrong, so I rushed right over after training. Turns out it must have been nothing, because the minute I laid eyes on you, it seems to have settled."

"Heartache. Hmm. Careful, that could be serious."

"Oh, it's very serious. Surprisingly serious." Aaron pulls me down and claims my lips.

My knees grow weak as his kiss intensifies and he urges me up to straddle him on the stool. His hands deftly untie my apron and he pulls it over my head before untucking my shirt and kneading up my bare back within moments. Managing to pull my lips free, I stay his hands.

"At ease, soldier. As much as I want you right now, it's not a good time. I have a lot of work to do today." I say.

Aaron buries his face in my neck, nibbling little kisses along my collar bone, but slowly brings himself back down with a sigh.

"Last night was incredible," he says, "but what of my aching chest?"

"I have a cure for that. When you come back to my place tonight, I'll take care of it."

"I look forward to it."

Aaron lifts me to stand and chases a strand of loose hair back behind my ear.

"Thanks for kissing me better, Doc. You have the magic touch." Aaron says, as he gives my hand a squeeze and heads for the door.

Once I'm sure he's gone, I spend a minute trying to wipe the grin off my face. His little visit was exactly perfect. The warmth he left behind in my chest radiates through my body and has left me aglow. Just as work was beginning to feel monotonous too, and my day was dragging on, Aaron comes and rises me up as only he knows how. My stress evaporates along with the worry of Doctor Greaves knowing about us. Aaron manages to leave me with a bounce to my step. Yup. I'm in deep. Deep. Deep. Deep. Not for the first time, I send a quick prayer up to the Maker that things stay this way and I don't end up leaving Aaron a broken mess around the next corner.

Fully composed again, I head back out to the main room. Doctor Greaves knows better than to haggle me and keeps his head down as he works through more of my inventory, but the smile across his damn face does not go unnoticed and I can't help but to smile inwardly at the elation I'm feeling.

Settling back into my work, I do my best to focus on the task at hand and not on my upcoming evening. Betraying me, my mind wanders continuously back to Aaron, our shared nights wandering outside the city as we learned more and more about each other, the kiss in the other room just now, our night together last evening, and our anticipated night together tonight. In the short time we've known each other, so much has grown between us. The unexpected surrender of my heart has me forgetting to be nervous and rather enjoying the excitement I am feeling instead.

My happy energy makes me work faster and I'm finished long before evening meal. Doctor Greaves looks up from where he is folding strips of cloth, still apparently enjoying the new bubbly me, and smiles.

"How about you head out for the day. I'm going to be here a bit. Still have a few things I'd like to take care of. I anticipate you have things to do."

I nod while hiding my reaction as I turn to go to the other room and put away my quill and ink.

Things have their designated place in my chaotic life and as I return my tools to where they belong, I catch sight of the letter from my parents still precariously on the edge of the table where I left it and frown. The weight in my stomach returns with full force. What can they possibly want? Why are they writing me? No amount of racking my brain can conjure up a plausible reason why my parents should need to contact me. Ordinary parents might write strictly because correspondence with their only child is the right thing to do, but not with my parents. They only ever write when they want something or need something of me. It's always news and it's never good.

With a resigned sigh, I snag up the letter and shove it in my apron. I hate that even though they are far away in another city, they still manage to somehow wreck my perfectly good day. Why can't they just forget about me? Maker, but life would be so much easier if they did.

Once home, I shed myself of my dirty clothes and wash up before making some porridge to feed my hungry belly. It's the first food I have eaten all day and my stomach thanks me for it. I pull the letter from my discarded apron and settle in at my small work table. Setting it down, I simply stare at it. Too bad my name is written in my father's hand; that in itself dispels all hope that it is news of his passing. Maker help me, I'm a terrible person wishing for such things.

Would it be wrong to throw it in the fire and pretend I never got it? They would see right through that, I have no doubt, I pick it up and turn it over in my hands running my finger under the wax seal on the back. My heartbeat quickens as I hold the still folded letter in my hands.

I came to Ludairium to doctor because it was as far from Saldrium as I could get. Being the King's city, it was busy and in dire need of a new doctor. I was able to convince my parents to let me go, telling them I would be doing the King's soldiers a justice by offering my talents in mending wounds and having a knowledge of field training. I had fudged the truth a little saying the King had been thrilled at my offer, when in truth it was Doctor Greaves who was the one eager to have me. I also gave them assurance that my father did not need assistance in running the lands. I learned all I needed to know to eventually follow in his footsteps someday and placated him by telling him he was strong and capable and didn't need me hovering around.

On that note, my parents wasted no time in getting me here. In their minds, if I got in good with the King, it could only move more land and power to our family name; because that's what's important. I was finally free of them. If only they knew how much the King came to hate me once he discovered who I was.

An uneasy feeling grips my insides as I toy with the lip of the paper. Closing my eyes, I inhale a deep breath, letting it out slowly. Opening them again, I unfold the paper in my hands to find my father's carefully scrolled hand filling the inside. My eyes follow the words as I read.

My heart races faster with every finished sentence and my breath catches in my throat when their meaning becomes clear. I can hear the blood pounding in my ears with sickening, hard thumps as the letter falls through my fingers, missing the table and lands on the floor. My mouth is dry and my throat sticks to itself as I try to swallow. I stare blankly at my empty hand, trying to decide what to do. Thoughts race around so fast in my brain my head spins in nauseating circles. I feel as though I have just plunged deep into a horrific nightmare where everywhere I turn there is no escape and the walls are pressing in on me, closer and closer.

A loud knock at my door startles me back from my thoughts and I stare at the wooden frame with confusion, before the pieces start coming back together in my mind.

Shit! Aaron.

It has to be him. He was coming over tonight. Dammit! I scramble to the ground in search of the letter and scoop it up shoving it haphazardly inside the pages of a book on my table before tucking a few loose strands of hair behind my ear. My movements feel choppy and erratic, like they are happening in super slow motion, yet I can't seem to get them under control.

Shit! This can't be happening. Not now. No.

Chapter Eight

Aaron

"Hey, handsome." I say as the door swings open. I step inside quickly after checking that the coast is clear and close the door behind me before wrapping myself around Chase. It feels like forever since I felt him against me, when in reality it has only been a little more than half a day. I missed him, everything about him. His lips, his touch, his smell…Gah…Everything. Wasting no time, I cup his face in my hands descending on him, smothering him in an array of kisses I've been saving up all afternoon. I intend on showing him just how much I've missed him in our short time apart.

Something isn't right. It registers that his lips aren't moving against mine, his body is rigid and his hands are stiff at his sides. Pulling back to look him in the eye, I notice he is ghostly white and his eyes are unfocused, staring into nothingness.

"Chase? Are you okay?" I ask, keeping his face cradled in my hands. "You're really pale. What's the matter?"

Chase remains silent as he peels my hands from his face and backs away. I snag his arm and hold him in place. "Hey, are you okay?" I ask again. I get the sinking feeling like something terrible must have happened. He looks like someone died, and being a doctor it's not out of the question. Chase pulls free from my grasp again and walks across the room turning his back to me.

"You should go, Aaron. This isn't a good time."

"Why? Is something the matter? You really don't look good." I approach him again, but he flinches away from my touch.

"Just go."

I'm not sure what to do. Something is clearly not right. He's distraught and I'm not prepared to just walk away and leave him like this. The idea that something is troubling him or that someone might have upset him makes me defensive and I want to protect him from whatever could be causing him pain.

"I just need to know you're okay before I leave. I'm worried about you."

He spins on me, his green eyes void of emotion, "I'm fine. Go. I just need to be alone. I need to think."

"Chase. Did something happen?"

"Go!" His words are harsher and full of venom causing me to startle back a pace and hold my hands up.

"Whoa, whoa, what's going on?"

Chase scrubs a hand over his face and turns his back to me again walking away. Why can't he look at me? Why is he so edgy right now? What the hell happened?

"I can't do this."

"This? This, what?"

"This." He throws his hands up in exasperation. "You and me. You should have listened, Aaron. I told you I couldn't. I need you to leave."

What the hell!

I close the few steps between us and pull on his resistant shoulder, forcing him to turn and look at me against his will.

"What are you talking about?"

He wrenches free from my grasp and place two hands on my chest to keep me back. "Go, Aaron. Please."

Taking his hands in mine, refusing to allow him to pull them away, I try to get him to look me in the eye. He is purposefully avoiding my gaze, shifting his eyes away at my every effort. My heart is hammering in my chest and I feel like I'm going to be sick.

"This afternoon you wanted me here. You asked me to come. Last night was incredible, you said so yourself. What changed? What's going on, Chase? Talk to me. Don't push me away."

Chase's face goes stone cold as he gives in and meets my eyes. His glare is chilling.

"I told you it wouldn't work. You should have listened, Aaron. I didn't want to hurt you. I didn't want to hurt anyone again. Go. Please. Don't come back."

Despite his strong resolve, I can feel him trembling. My insides twist together as his words stab into my heart one by one. His eyes have lost their usual sparkle and I barely recognize the look I'm being given. *What's happened to you?*

Is this really happening? I try to find my voice and work even harder to keep it steady.

"Are you serious?" I fail. My voice is shaky and barely audible, cracking against my will.

Chase's eyes seem to be looking through me now. He has put up a wall and is pushing me out of his life after just having let me in and I have no idea why. He doesn't answer me. Dropping my hands, I back away reluctantly. My legs are shaky and my body feels almost too heavy for them to bear my weight. At his door, I try to encourage him look at me again, but he is hiding behind a newly erected barrier and as far as he is concerned, I no longer exist.

Walking aimlessly down the streets of Ludairium, I try to piece together what just happened. To say I'm confused is a vast understatement. This afternoon, Chase had been right there with me, eager to revisit our previous evening and blatantly invited me to come over tonight. Something happened between then and now and I'll be damned if I have any idea what it is. His tone and demeanor changed completely and the more I pushed him to talk to me, the angrier he seemed to get.

After circling the same city block twice and not feeling any more clear-headed, I decide to find myself a drink at Statin's local tavern. Being the city's most frequented tavern, I find it bustling and crowded. Many people have come for an evening meal, socialization, and games; so it takes me a moment to find a free spot to sit. The available table sits against the wall near the door away from most of the rowdier patrons and suits me fine. The bar maid comes right over and brings me a full mug of ale without asking. I've been here enough times as a regular, it's just time saving to assume I'll take a mug at least. I toss her a few coins as payment and stare at the tankard before me.

This whole thing with Chase started off confusing on day one, but I was sure we had ironed out those kinks a fortnight ago. Apparently, I was wrong. Why is he so adamant he can't do this? What scared him off? His earlier uncertainties clearly weren't resolved. He had been okay with this, with us, but something…Happened. What? Did I overstep my bounds? Did I read him wrong? There's no way. He asked me to make love to him last night. It was his idea, his words. I would have been perfectly content to wait even longer if he wanted to. He's said before he didn't want to hurt me, like somehow he knew he would eventually, like he apparently had before. *Again*. What does that mean? He said he didn't want to hurt anyone *again*.

Bah…Too many questions. My mind is spinning and it can't keep up.

I pick up my drink and drain over half of it before setting it down again. So lost in my own thoughts, I don't notice when a familiar face approaches until he plops down heavily on the bench across from me.

"Hey, I thought you were getting busy with a certain doctor tonight."

Caleb looks as though he has been here a while. The drink he sets down next to mine is nearly empty and his eyes are glassy and unfocused. I manage a half smile that I know doesn't reach my eyes and pick up my mug, draining it. Waving over the bar maid, I let the warmth of the first drink wash over me. Setting my new drink down, I toss her more coin. Once I have drained more than half of the new mug, I meet Caleb's inquisitive glare.

"We're through. I screwed up and he told me to leave and not to come back." I blink back the sting in my eyes and lift the drink to my mouth again, savoring another long gulp, trying to drown out the sorrow, numb the hurt and not let it surface. I can't let the pain of Chase's dismissal get to me. Knowing what that would entail, I try to submerse myself in the alcohol buzzing around my head instead.

"What?!? What did you do, Aaron?"

I have Caleb's full attention now and he shoves his drink aside putting both palms on the table in front of us staring at me dumbstruck.

"Why is this my fault? I have no idea. One minute we're all over each other, the next he's throwing me out of his place and telling me it never should have happened."

"Something must have happened. Last night you guys-"

"I know. It doesn't make sense. He just kept saying I should have listened to him and that he knew it would never work. Caleb, seriously, I'm lost here. I have no idea what happened."

"Bloody hell, I'm sorry."

We drink in silence for a while, Caleb fidgets and eyes me like he should say something but doesn't. Caleb and I have always been pretty open with one another, but he's not exactly the heart to heart talk kind of guy. Spilling about emotions and feelings brings out the awkward, "I know I should try to help but don't know what to say" side of him. Right now, I'm not so much looking for Caleb's sympathies as I am just plain confused over Chase's sudden change of heart and wishing I had answers. Part of me wants to go back over to his house and just confront him again. Pull an explanation out of him. Maybe I can fix this. Maybe it's just a misunderstanding of something I said or did. If it's something else, maybe I can help him work it out. Everything was moving toward such a good place and our connection is so strong, almost palpable. There is no way of denying the look we shared last night when we were joined together.

Rolling all of Chase's words around in my head, I keep getting hung up on something he has said to me on more than one occasion. *I didn't want to hurt anyone again.* What does that mean? It's like he premeditatedly knew this was going to happen and didn't know how to stop it. *Does that even make sense?*

"Caleb, can I run something by you?"

Caleb sits up straight and looks almost relieved to not have to come up with a way of helping me on his own.

"Hell yes. Anything. What's up?"

"The night when I took Chase to the tower, he said something to me that kind of stood out. I didn't really think much about it then, but he said it again to me just a little while ago. He said we couldn't be together because he'd only end up hurting me and he didn't want to do that to anyone again. What do you think he means by that? Again?"

"No idea. Wait. He said he didn't want to get involved before?"

"Yeah, but I figured it was nerves, Caleb. He was just afraid people would find out and the thing with his parents and whatnot. Once I proved I was willing to keep this quiet, he very quickly came around to it. It's not like it took a whole lot of convincing. There is a huge connection between us, Caleb. I've never felt this way about anyone before. I can't describe it, but I know Chase feels it too. It's deep and it's intense. When I was there earlier and Chase told me we were over, I could see it wasn't what he wanted. It was killing him to do it. I just don't get it."

"Maybe he's just freaking out. Maybe getting serious so fast scares him and makes him run. Maybe that's what 'Again' means."

It was sinking into serious between us really fast. Faster than I expected and if Chase felt what I did last night - and I'm certain he did - it could have caused him to get nervous and back off. Maybe Caleb is right, but I just get the feeling there is more to it than that. I slump over the table and let out a heavy sigh. I'm so tired of thinking. I can't let him walk away. I just can't. Not when I can see the hurt in his eyes as he pushes me away. The idea of not being with him anymore is causing the most excruciating ache in my chest and the sense of panic ripping through my body at the thought is enough to make me want to sit in a pile on the floor and weep. Maker, I need to control myself, I'm slipping.

I spent the better part of spring and summer lusting after this man. I finally snagged him, and had a taste of what could be between us, and it's even better than anything I imagined. My heart is tripping over itself not knowing how to take this rejection. Is it possible that I have fallen for him so soon? My head says no way, but the pain in my chest begs to differ.

Shoving my empty mug away from me, I stand to go.

"I have to sort this out. I'm going bloody crazy. Something isn't right, Caleb. I'll see you on the field tomorrow."

"Wait." Caleb barrels out of his seat to stand I front of me. "Aaron, where are you going?"

"I don't know. All I know is it really hurts right now. Right here," I pat my chest over my heart. "I have to shake this off. I'm going for a walk."

"Holy hell, Aaron. You love him, don't you?"

I shuffle on my feet and look up at my friend.

"I don't know. Maybe. Yes, I think. All I know is I can't let him walk away. Not like this."

"Are you going to see him?" Caleb asks.

"I have no idea. I just need air. My head is swimming. I gotta go."

I shove my way through the crowded tavern and burst out the doors into the cooler evening air. Standing in the street, I try to decide what to do. I need to see Chase, but he made it clear I shouldn't come back. What do I do? The turmoil ripping through my gut is crippling and making it harder and harder to come to a rash decision. I palm my forehead, smacking it a few times, trying to still the mounting flood of thoughts racing in my brain. My first reaction is to do what I always do. He's a doctor. Doctors treat patients. I just need to…*You can't do it*. I rip my fingers through my hair. I made a promise to myself. I've been good. I have a handle on things…but…

"Don't do it, Aaron." Caleb's voice pierces into my clouded mind. He is on my heels, following me down the road. I didn't even know I was on the move.

I turn around and we nearly collide. He is teetering on his feet, his alcohol buzz evident even more outside the tavern than it was inside.

"Do what?" I'm instantly on the defensive. "You don't know what I'm doing." But Caleb knows me better than anyone and I know he can see the thoughts in my head right now, no matter how hard I try to mask them.

My body is shaking and my lip quivers as I speak. I don't know when I became so upset, but the sinking feeling in my gut and strain in my heart is suddenly overwhelming and I want to run from it, escape it. I need to get away.

"I'm not an idiot and I do so know where your thoughts are going right now, and it's not the answer." Caleb's hand latches onto my wrist and holds me in place. I make an attempt to pull free, but he holds tight and yanks me closer so his face is in mine. I'm hot, I'm angry, and his restraint is only augmenting the panic.

"Listen to me, Aaron. When things go wrong you can't resort to sinking a knife into yourself just to see him again. I should never have condoned it in the first place. I know better and I'm not going to let you do it now. You know where you'll end up if you do it. You know where it will lead you and I know you don't want to go down that road again. This needs to stop. Control it. Don't let it control you."

"Let go of me, Caleb." I jerk my arm again, trying to free myself from his hold. He fights back and I shove my weight into him. "I just need to talk to him."

Caleb stands firm. "I know you do. Let him cool off. Give him a day or two, then go see if he'll talk to you. Worry about you right now. You need to refocus. You can't talk to him when you're like this anyhow. You're spiraling. Stop it. Breathe. Control it, don't let it control you."

I quit tugging against Caleb's hold and he eases off my arm. I wobble on my own feet, but I know I haven't had enough ale to make me unsteady. Caleb has me pegged. He knows and he's right. The world feels as though it is pressing in on me and the crushing, suffocating feeling is all around me. This is the feeling Caleb is referring to. I need to control it. He's right. I need to stop it.

"I feel sick. I need to make it stop. Let me stop it."

"Not like this. You know it's not the answer. Come inside, have a few drinks with me, play some games. Refocus. Get your ground beneath you again."

Nodding, I follow Caleb back inside and let him pull me over to a table where men are drinking and gambling away their hard earned coin. No matter how many mugs of ale I manage to have, the sinking feeling in my stomach doesn't seem to want to go away. I hope Caleb is right. I fight against all my ingrained urges and try to trust in my friend. I need control.

Chapter Nine

Chase

Aaron should have listened. Maybe I should have better stood my ground. I let his free spirit and charm break down my defenses and now the look on his face when I asked him to leave is burned in my memory. It tore into my heart like a knife and left a gaping hole behind to bleed out shame and self-hatred without mercy. I couldn't watch him go. I know he was confused and I know I didn't give him any feasible answers but I couldn't, it hurt so much. I warned him, dammit, I wish he'd listened. At least I hadn't had to see the broken look on Brandon's face the day I left him years ago. I was never plagued with that nightmare. But Aaron, I almost crumbled apart at seeing the devastation in his parting glance. It broke my heart.

How did I become so deeply involved with him? And so fast. He snuck his way in, saying all the right things and before I knew it, I let down my defenses and welcomed him into my heart. Now, I've hurt him. *Dammit to hell!* My stomach hasn't stopped turning since he left. Where did all these feelings come from? Aaron made me feel so safe and happy. I opened up to him and gave him all of me without pause, without a second thought to the consequences I knew were coming.

Dammit, dammit, dammit!

I strip out of my clothes, dropping them in a heap on the floor and bury myself under the mountain of covers on my pallet. It's a warm evening, almost hot, and I'm sweltering underneath them, but I don't care. I have no concern for my own discomfort.

The last thing I wanted to do was to hurt Aaron. I already have more than enough guilt at causing another's pain to last me a lifetime and yet I drew in this innocent man selfishly when I knew I could never have a life with him.

Five years ago, I allowed this very thing to happen to my relationship with Brandon, and I spent years unable to forgive myself for the hurt I knew I had caused him. Brandon and I had been young. Neither of us had been in a relationship before and we were exploring what we knew made us different from other men. It was young love, and maybe it would have naturally ended on its own in time, but I destroyed it and left a world of pain on his frail shoulders, without explanation. The last thing Brandon needed was more hurt in his life, the man had suffered enough. I have never wanted to repeat that mistake, yet here I am, doing it again.

There is something undeniably special between Aaron and I, and I was falling for him fast. He made me feel like I have never felt before in my life and yet, I had no choice but to destroy all of it. Just like before, and I can't even find it in myself to tell him why. He would never understand. He hasn't known me long enough to. Brandon might have understood, but I never had the chance to try to explain it to him either, and any attempts I've made by way of explanation since finding him in Ludairium, have been in vain. He no longer wants to hear my excuses.

I'm a terrible man. I should never have allowed this to happen.

Long into the night, I eventually fall asleep. It is a restless sleep, full of dreams, nightmares, mocking the life I'll never have, the one I'm forbidden to live.

* * *

The next morning goes from bad to worse. Arriving at the surgery, ready to dive into a day's work, ready to forget Aaron, the letter from my parents, my aching heart, and my pounding headache, I'm met with Doctor Greaves.

"Don't get too comfortable, son. We have been summoned to make audience with the King this morning. Decisions are being made for the march north. He's organizing the troops and I reckon he'll be asking you to come along again."

Letting out a defeated sigh, I follow the older man out the door. My body aches from a restless sleep and the last thing I need is to fake my way through a meeting with Alistair of all people.

The Great Hall is crowded when we arrive. Weekly court is in session and a cluster of people have gathered to bring forth their problems and concerns to be reconciled by the King. The man himself sits reclined in his throne at the far end of the room. His look is passive, indifferent, maybe even a little bored. His eyes are glazed over and I doubt he is even listening to the two men arguing their points before him; a squabble over a bit of destroyed crops. Alistair chews his thumb and stifles a yawn before leaning forward to interrupt the argument and make his ruling.

Why did we have to come now? Alistair will be busy most of the morning, and I'm in no mood to stand around here waiting on a man I don't particularly even like.

Alistair Ellesmere - yes I call him by his first name, as most people do if they know what's good for them - is not your conventional King. Brought to Ludairium at nineteen upon the death of the late King, Chrystiaan Ellesmere, Alistair is his only son; his bastard son. Not having been raised in nobility, Alistair lacks a certain…ennoblement for ruling a Kingdom. Regardless, he has made a name for himself and the people love him. His methods fall short of what would be construed as typical, and most people need to have dealt with him once or twice before they truly understand just how he expects to be treated.

As we wait for the court session to run its course, my mind inevitably wanders to Aaron. I wish he would have listened to me. Dammit, it's not his fault. It's my own bloody fault. My own cowardice. I knew this would happen. I just didn't anticipate it would happen so soon. If I had been strong enough to hold him at bay this would not have happened.

"You alright, son? You don't look so well today." Doctor Greaves is peering over at me from the piece of wall he found to lean his tired body against.

I give the man a phonier than all hell smile and just nod, turning my attention to what is taking place at the front of the room. I have no interest in these events. Other people's business is not mine. Some people come to every court session just to keep up on the goings on around the city. They thrive on gossip. I get enough of it day to day in the surgery from the mouths of these very people squeezed into the hall right now.

As the crowd dwindles and court draws to an end, Doctor Greaves and I are the only ones left behind. Making our way forward, Alistair stands from his seat up front to great us.

"Gentlemen, if you don't mind, let's move this meeting to the council chambers. I need a bloody drink after all this crap."

Following the man down the long, winding castle halls we eventually settle in comfortably in the council chambers. A long mahogany table stands center in the room with six chairs flanking each side and single seats at either end. A large map of Edovia takes up much of the one end of the table and is riddled with markings and small figures, evidence of a war in the making. The wall down one side of the room consists of large portraits of past Kings, going back centuries. I find myself studying them, trying to pick out the Ellesmere family resemblance. Alistair has yet to have a portrait hung.

Alistair pours himself a glass of whiskey and offers us one as well. The doctor and I both decline.

Choosing to stand, Alistair paces the end of the table whereas the older doctor and I have chosen to sit. I'm restless and choose to perch on the end of my seat, jiggling my knees and twiddling my fingers together.

"I'm going to get straight to the point, because I have too much other bloody shit to deal with today." See. A true example of our King at his finest. "I'm in the process of organizing troops to march north as you no doubt already figured out. Blah, blah, blah, not really a secret. However, I'm hoping that won't become necessary."

Not necessary?

"What I'm about to share with you needs to remain confidential, at least for now. It's still a work in progress. Is that understood?"

Alistair stops his pacing and looks between both of us.

"Of course." I say. Doctor Greaves nods his agreement.

"I have a small group of men working quietly to organize a party to go north and cross the border to meet with the leader of the Outsiders. We are hoping to negotiate a peace. We've been in correspondence with them over the summer and it's all coming to a head quickly. It's an extremely dangerous mission and every man who steps foot outside of Edovia risks not coming back. Should negotiations go south, if this whole damn thing is a trap, then the armies will need to be prepared to march. We will secure our border once and for all, or die trying."

Alistair's leans his hands on the table and his eyes fall to me. I know what is coming. He wants me prepared to go north with the troops should it be required. I've anticipated this so it's hardly shocking. I warned Doctor Greaves it was coming.

I raise my head to meet Alistair's penetrating stare without fear or intimidation, I will never give this man that satisfaction no matter how hard he tries, but what I see hiding in his eyes is worry and uncertainty and I'm taken aback. Alistair lowers his voice and proceeds tentatively.

"Chase, I know it's a lot to ask, but I want you with the negotiating party when they cross the border."

My jaw falls open and all my attempts at hiding my emotions fail the instant the words leave his lips.

"I wouldn't ordinarily ask a civilian to put themselves in a position like this. I won't lie, it's dangerous and I cannot confirm your safety or your survival. But you are more than just a civilian, you are a trained soldier and more so, a trained doctor and we need a healer along."

"I'm not a soldier." I bark at him.

"You were. You have the training and you will need those skills along with your abilities to heal if it should come to it."

"I was a terrible soldier, you know that. That's why I stopped training five years ago."

Alistair draws a deep breath through his nose and pulls out a chair in front of me to sit. Resting his hands on the table he meets my eyes. The creases in his forehead are deep and I can see the strain this war has taken on him written all over his face.

"We will keep you as far away from dangerous situations as we can."

The anger running through me right now is making my skin burn. Turning to Doctor Greaves, I do my best to keep it from showing in my voice.

"Can you give us a moment please, Doctor?" I say through clenched teeth.

Without pause, the older man dips his head and leaves us.

Turning back to Alistair, I glare at him.

"This is personal and I know it. I'm not an idiot. Why in the Maker's name you still feel threatened by me, Alistair, I have no idea. If you send me out there, you are sending me to my death."

Alistair holds his hands up for peace.

"I assumed you would respond like this. I know how it looks. Chase, listen to me, please. Hear what I'm saying before you attack me. I'm sending twenty men across that border. Twenty. That's all. Every one of them hand selected by me, but not one of them is being ordered to do this. It will be their own choice. I will not send anyone to their deaths. My hope is for us to negotiate a peace. Every precautionary step is being taken so we can be ready for anything that may arise. I have the best minds at work on this."

Alistair pauses and studies my face.

"Chase, I'm not ordering you to go. I'm asking you. My intention is not to send you to your death, but to hopefully save our world from spinning into an ugly war. Please think about it. It's your choice. You don't have to let me know today or tomorrow, but soon. Please."

My heart hammering against my rib cage is so loud I'm certain Alistair can hear it too. I didn't anticipate any of this. I figured I'd be part of the march north, but this? This is so beyond dangerous, I don't even know what to think.

"Think about it? Please?" He asks.

All I can do is nod.

"Can I ask Doctor Greaves to join us again?"

Again, just a nod and Alistair is on his feet ushering the doctor back in the room.

Settling back in his seat, Alistair turns to the older man. He doesn't mess around, he's straight to the point.

"Chase is going to consider joining the men across the border. Should this happen, how will it affect you and the amount of care you can give our city's people?"

"It will be a rough move, Your Grace, if I'm being honest."

The older man, still stuck in his generational difference, insists on titling Alistair, despite his pleas that we don't. It's a respect thing for the doctor and Alistair doesn't seem to fight him on it as much as he does with others.

"I don't do a whole lot of the care any longer. My eyes aren't good anymore and I can't keep up with the long demanding hours in my old age. If Chase here decides to travel with your men, I must request assistance. We need to bring in another doctor."

Alistair nods and brings his thumb to his mouth to rip at the nail. His forehead remains creased as his eyes shift out of focus and he thinks.

"Hmm…Okay. I'll see what I can do." Alistair rises from the table. "Chase, let me know your answer as soon as you can."

* * *

Sitting at my small reading table later that night, I shove the book I have been trying to read away from me. It's impossible. I have read the same sentence at least two dozen times and I still have no idea what it says. From another book, I fish out the letter from my parents and turn it around in my hands, over and over. I've read it through five times to ensure I haven't misread it or interpreted it the wrong way. Every time I read it, the fire in my gut burns hotter. I thread my fingers through my hair, pulling my tie out. Feeling it fall free from its binds, my scalp almost sighs with relief. My head hasn't stopped pounding since this morning and the ever increasing throb is only making my mood more sour. Shoving the letter aside, I put a pot of water on the hearth and go in search of some dried featherfew. After shuffling through a few vials, I find a small amount left in the bottom of a bottle. Good enough. I pour what's left in a mug and wait for my water to boil. Hopefully some featherfew tea will ease the pain in my head.

Laying down on top of the blankets covering my pallet, I cover my face with my hands. This day needs to end. Now, on top of everything else, Alistair wants me to join in on what I can only see as a suicide mission across the border. The only good thing I can make from this mission is that dying in the field would instantly solve my other two problems. The thought alone is almost enough for me to agree to going.

I miss Aaron. I don't want to, but I do. The situation with him is not the problem, it is the unfortunate result of my only real issue. I need to find a way of getting him out of my head. I'm only torturing myself with thoughts of him and we can never have anything between us again. My heart and stomach both twinge in defiance of my decision, and I hate my head right now for the choices it had to make.

Chapter Ten

Aaron

"Okay men, break apart and work through some of these techniques. I want to see you changing it up more frequently. Mix it up. Challenge yourselves. Keep moving through the exercises and I'm going to make my way around and work with each group separately." Leeson barks out the orders as he lets his eyes fall to each man in front of him. They linger a little longer on me and I'm not surprised, I've barely made much effort at lifting my sword today and my distractedness must be starting to show.

I've been working with about twenty other men on the western edge of the field. The sun is almost at high noon and blazing its hot rays down on us, making me hot and exceptionally more miserable. I'm just begging for it to be time to quit. I have no energy left for this day at all and it's starting to feel like it's never going to end. Leeson keeps coming up with more and more drills and the end seems nowhere in sight.

"Aaron, get your ass over here. Take the left side." A fellow soldier, James Barkley, says.

Dragging my body over to where I'm expected to participate, I stand with the other men, trying to look engaged. Their voices drift into the distance and my eyes fade out of focus again. The weight of yesterday is still pressing in on me. I still can't believe Chase threw me out without even so much as an explanation. Nothing, just a "go and don't come back". How do you share a bed with someone at the crack of dawn and throw them out of your life come evening?

I drank far too much at the tavern last night with Caleb, trying to keep myself in check and stay clear away from old habits. I rarely drink to the point of intoxication, but last night was different and when Caleb and I had left, I was hardly able to put one foot in front of the other to walk home. In fact, I feel asleep on the floor six feet away from my bed because those six feet felt like a mountain's climb away at the time. Training came early and Caleb nearly had to drag me to the field this morning. I can't decide what hurts more, my body from having spent all night on a hard floor, my head from the awful headache pounding my brain to a pulp, or my heart from where Chase had torn it from my body and stomped all over it. My heart I decide.

"Aaron!"

My name is yelled yet again, breaking through my thoughts. I look around and see the men I'm supposed to be working with have shifted and I'm, once again, out of formation. Caleb shoos a hand at the men to keep them going and comes up beside me.

"You need to pull your shit together. You've been out of it all morning and don't think Leeson hasn't been watching you. You're already under evaluation, Aaron. Get your head together." Caleb says as he flicks a finger against my forehead.

"Pryor."

Caleb gives me a distinct "I told you so" look before heading back to join the men.

Dammit!

I squeeze my eyes shut tight and take a deep breath before turning to Captain Leeson who is headed toward me, brow furrowed. I fix a neural look on my face and stand at attention.

"Walk with me." Leeson says as he grabs my upper arm and turns me away from the other men.

The last bit of stamina I was holding onto drains from my body as I follow after Leeson, my feet dragging behind. I just keep burying myself deeper and deeper. Leeson stops after a few hundred paces and turns to me, arms crossed over his chest.

"What's going on with you today, Aaron?"

Trying to hide all telltale signs of emotion from my face, I force my body up straight and stand as tall as I can before him.

"I'm sorry, Sir. It's just not a good day. I'll do better."

Leeson's eyes narrow at me and he says nothing for a long time. I fidget under his scrutiny and avert my eyes to the ground. When he speaks, his voice is softer and he relaxes his posture, making himself appear less intimidating.

"You are a good soldier, Aaron. I've seen you perform well out there. You have no problem keeping up with daily drills and have proven yourself on more than one occasion. Here's the thing, I now have strict instructions to make daily reports on your progress. You are being monitored on a higher level and you know that. How am I supposed to make a positive report about you today when you've done nothing but be lost in your head every time I turn around? You've barely raised your sword effectively once. Now I'll ask you again. What's going on?"

"Umm…I'm just dealing with some personal issues, Sir. I'll do better. I'm sorry. I understand if you have to write a poor report. It's my own fault. I shouldn't let outside problems affect my performance. It won't happen again. If I could return to the drills, I will turn it around I promise you."

I continue to fidget anxiously in front of him, hoping for a dismissal. Leeson's eyes search my own and eventually he nods sympathetically and indicated for me to return to the men.

I need to focus. We can't have much longer to go before training is over. The sun is almost at the top of the sky. I can pull off the short time we have left. I have to.

* * *

After practice, I decide enough is enough, I need to confront Chase. No more messing around. No more guessing. I know I told Caleb I'd give him a couple days, but I can't wait any longer. It already feels like it's been an eternity. If I don't get answers soon, I'm going to fall apart.

Hell, I'm starting to think I've already started. Chase doesn't know this screwed up side of me, so I need to pull my shit together if I'm going to talk to him.

Figuring he'll be at the surgery this time of day, I head over there. When the older doctor answers the door and informs me Chase went home with a headache, I begin to worry. When I saw Chase the other day, he was so pale his skin was nearly white. Now he's home with a headache. Whatever he isn't telling me is having a huge effect on him. I need answers and I'm going to get them. I hate seeing him in such distress. There has to be a way I can help him get through this, whatever it is. At this point I'm convincing myself Chase is just panicking over the intense direction our relationship has headed and telling me to leave was just a knee jerk reaction in a moment of panic.

When Chase doesn't answer the door on the third knock, I start to hesitate and second guess everything. Doubt sets in and I wonder if confronting him is the right thing to do. As I'm reconsidering my options, the door swings open and a disheveled Chase stands before me. Clad only in wrinkled breeches that hang low on his hips with bed messed hair, loose and falling in his face, red eyes, swollen with sleep; he looks worse today than yesterday.

When his eyes meet mine, they close and he lets out a heavy sigh.

"Please don't do this, Aaron. Go home."

"No. What happened? Why are you doing this? I need to know, Chase."

"Aaron. Go."

He begins to close the door, but I throw my hand up and catch it, pushing it open again. When I go to step in Chase presses his hands to my chest and looks up at me, worry etched in his face. I stop at his touch, not intending to force myself into his home when clearly I'm not wanted.

"No, Aaron. I told you this would happen. I didn't want to hurt you, but I knew it was inevitable. I warned you. You refused to listen."

"Why is it inevitable?" I bring my hands up to hold his and bring his knuckles to my mouth to kiss them. "Why do you feel you have to hurt me? I don't understand."

"I knew this would happen again. I tried to keep you at bay. I tried to tell you."

Chase watches our linked hands, but doesn't pull away. I rejoice in the small victory.

"Again?" I ask tentatively. "What do you mean again? You said that before."

Chase looks up into my eyes and pulls his hands free. *And victory lost.* "Please go, Aaron. Don't make his harder than it has to be."

"No. Don't shut me out dammit. Explain it to me. Why were you so adamant you didn't want this when I can see clearly that you do? And what the hell does 'again' mean? You said that before. You didn't want to do this again? Again what? Come on, Chase, speak English. Give me some answers so I can understand this. I don't do well when people are cryptic with me."

Defeated at not being able to get me out the door, Chase slams his fist into the wooden framework startling me and raises his voice until he is practically yelling.

"Dammit, Aaron! Again. Again, as in Brandon again. Again, as in all I do is hurt people I care about. I let Brandon get close to me, and then I tore his heart to pieces. I hurt him so badly I can never forgive myself. I just have to live with the memory of what I did every day for the rest of my life. I knew, if I let you get close to me, it would just end up the same with you too. I didn't want to get close to you, Aaron, because I didn't want to break your heart too. I didn't want to like everything that we shared, but I got sucked in, and I did like it, and you. I like you more than I can even fathom in such a short time. It doesn't make sense and it's frightening. Now, you are just another person I have to hurt in this stupid bloody life of mine where I have to parade around and pretend to be happy. What makes me happy, I can't have. Anything I want, I can't have.

Like you. I want you more than anything, but I can't have you, Aaron. I can't. I need to start remembering that, and not let people suck me in where I don't belong. I was weak with you. I let you in and it felt so good, so right, and now I've hurt you even more. I'm an ass and I'm sorry you got stuck in the middle of my pathetic life. Now please, take your hand off my door and leave so I can go feel sorry for myself in peace."

Shocked at his harsh tone and pointed words, my jaw hangs slack and I remove my hand from his door. I'm pretty sure it was the only thing keeping me upright during his speech. Once I bring it down the door slams in my face, vibrating on its hinges. Staring at the marred wood before me, I squeeze my hands into fists to try and calm the trembling that is radiating through my body.

What just happened? What he said didn't clear anything up at all, except the "again". He hurt Brandon and now me. I'm the again. But why? Why does it *have* to be this way? He just said he likes me and everything we shared, he just admitted to wanting it, yet I'm standing, staring at a door instead of the gorgeous doctor I'm falling ridiculously in love with. That thought has me reaching a hand up to steady myself on the building. Am I falling in love with Chase? How can that be possible? I know I've been infatuated with him for a while, but anything we were developing has been so short lived I can't be. Can I?

For the second time in two days, I walk away from Chase's feeling defeated and lost. The spinning is stirring up in my head again and I know I need to quash it before it takes control. Letting my emotions escalate is a really bad thing for me and I know it. I've spend my adult life learning all kinds of coping mechanisms to keep myself in check, but I'm far from better and I know how easy it can be to slip back to the bad place. I need to clear my mind, so I wander the streets aimlessly until I find myself heading toward the watch tower where Chase and I shared one of our first beautiful kisses. I didn't tell Chase, but it is a place I frequent often when I need to destress and refocus my head, which is precisely what I need to do right now. The freedom I feel at the top of the tower helps me release the tension when it starts to build.

After removing the beam across the door, I scale the dark stairs with ease and find my favorite spot to sit; perched on the wall, high above the city.

I spend the afternoon mulling over the things he said to me. No matter how I look at it, none of it makes any sense. I still can't understand why he thinks he needs to walk away when he clearly doesn't want to. As the sun sets on the horizon, I realize the only thing I came away with after seeing him this afternoon is the knowledge that I'm not the first person he has pushed away. That, according to him, *had* to be pushed away. Captain Leeson has too. Maybe he is the key to understanding all this. I toy with the idea of bringing it up with him, but feel instantly awkward. The man is my superior, even though - I have no doubt - we are probably about the same age, we have never spent time together off the field. Can I talk to him about this? We certainly aren't friends. Would it be weird telling him Chase and I were together? Am I going to stir up angry feelings and will he be mad at me? I slump over with a sigh, resting my elbows on my knees. If I don't ask, I may never know what's going on in Chase's head. I guess I have no other option. Chase surely won't speak with me again. I have to see the Captain.

Engulfed in darkness, I run blindly down the tower stairs to the door I left propped open at the bottom. I've done this decent enough times, I know exactly how many steps there are and don't worry about stumbling. Heading through the city, I make my way toward the castle.

The Captain has taken up residence with the King since their trial, and I've been led to understand, it was quite the talk around town when it was made common knowledge to the people. At the time, there was even talk about whether or not, with the removal of the law, the two of them could be wed. With that question came more questions. What of an heir? How would the King secure the throne if he married a man? Can the King marry a commoner? Will more laws be looked at and rewritten? It was big news at the time. When I arrived to the city in the spring, talk had died down to whispers and eventually were forgotten when the King and Captain Leeson had not given the people answers one way or another about nuptials. For the most part, they have been left alone. Personally, I think it would be an amazingly bold step if he and the King did decide to be married. It would be a victory I wouldn't miss celebrating for the world.

As I approach the main entrance to the castle, I'm met with two senior soldiers on guard duty, fully dressed in leather armor and swinging swords off their belts. I never really put any forethought into whether or not I would need to request audience to see the Captain.

"Can we help you?" One of the men ask.

"Umm...I was looking to have a word with Captain Leeson. Is that possible?"

"Should be, take a walk with me and we'll find out."

I follow the one guard inside and down a long hallway. It's my first time within the castle walls and it is quite stunning. My eyes are drawn to the various paintings that are hung down the walls. I've never seen work like this before, ever in my life. The pictures are so real I feel I could step through them, right into another land. Rounding a corner, we are met by a maid servant scurrying down the hall in the opposite direction, a tray of picked over food in one hand balanced on her hip.

"Where are they hiding out tonight?" The guard asks the woman.

"Library." She says without stopping.

"This way." The guard steers us down another hall and after another two turns I'm officially lost. The plush burgundy carpet, squishes under my boots and I imagine this is what it would be like to walk on a cloud; bouncing and floating along. I want to take my boots off and feel the softness under my toes.

As we move along, I find myself absorbed in my surroundings of ornate furniture and decorations. Losing ground to the guard ahead of me, I pick up my pace for fear of being left behind. This place is huge and I may never find my way out on my own.

The guard comes to a halt at a set of closed double doors, expertly engraved with a forest of trees and elegant bird's swarming overhead. The door is a piece of art in itself and I lift my fingers to trails over the groves in the wood. The guard smiles, apparently amused with my curiosity.

"Who should I say is asking to see him?" He asks.

"Aaron, Sir. Aaron Pryor"

"Are you one of his soldiers?"

"Yes, Sir."

"Wait here." He disappears behind the beautiful doors and I continue my tactile exploration.

When he doesn't return immediately doubt sets in and I question my intentions. It never occurred to me that Leeson would probably be with the King right now and I'd be making audience with him in the room. *Shit! I don't want to see the King.* My palms begin to sweat and I wipe them down my breeches to expel some nervous energy. Maybe this is a bad idea. Just as I'm contemplating leaving and whether or not I know my way back to the front entrance, the door before me opens again and I'm being ushered inside.

"Go on in, he's waiting."

I give the guard a nod and proceed through the door, feeling ever the fool for being here. Like everything I do in life, this was not thought out. I didn't plan what to say or anything.

Upon entering the room, my eyes widen at the vast size of it. It is two stories high, with books lining nearly every wall. A balcony runs around the upper section where the array of bookshelves continue out of sight in neat rows. Wall length windows adorn the entire north side and I can imagine they must look spectacular in the daytime when the sun beams through them. Right now, this front end of the library where I stand is in shadows. All the way at the back of the room, a few lanterns are burning low and I see Captain Leeson and of course the damn King lounging around a low table. As I approach the men, the King's eyes come up to meet mine with a scrutinizing blue glare. The Captain's back is to me and he makes no move to turn and acknowledge my presence. He is flipping through a stack of papers, mumbling to himself. When I'm closer, I see the men are hovering over what looks to be a large map of Edovia.

Stopping a few paces short of them, I shuffle awkwardly and wait. Leeson continues to flip through the papers and eventually sighs and tosses them down.

"I'll find it later." He says to the King.

Leeson eventually turns and faces me, cocks his head to the side, and gives me a warm smile.

"Good evening, Aaron."

"Captain." I nod my head and turn to bow properly to the King. "Your Grace, pleasure to see you this evening. I hope I'm not interrupting anything."

I see the King's eyes narrow and he is about to say something when Leeson clamps a hand on his arm. "Be nice." He tells him.

The King shares a look with the Captain and relaxes back to whatever it was he was doing before, ignoring me. Leeson pulls himself up off the floor and motions for me to take a seat in one of the chairs nearby.

"You wanted to see me?"

Leeson moves to another chair and waits for me to join him. My eyes move to the King and then to the Captain. I realize a bigger mistake in my lack of planning. I'm about to ask Leeson about his past lover in front of his current lover. This can only lead to no good. Moving tentatively to the offered seat, I sit hovering on the edge. My knees begin to bounce as I try to figure out how I'm supposed to ask what I came here to ask.

"What's on your mind, Aaron?" Lesson tries again.

"Umm...Well, Captain, Sir. It might be better if we discuss this in private. I'm not sure you'll want what I have to say to be...Umm. Well... It's personal, Sir."

The King is glaring at me again, his gaze burning into me, as I slink back in my seat trying to avoid looking at him.

"Aaron." I peel my eyes off the ground and force them onto my Captain. "First of all, call me Brandon, we're not on the field. Second, whatever you have to say can be said in front of Alistair. Personal or not, I keep nothing from him."

Daring to look at the King, my eyes shift between the two men. Alistair's full attention is on us now, his maps and papers cast aside. I take a deep breath and try to swallow, but my mouth is so dry I can barely do it.

"Okay." I take a shaky breath. "Umm...Well, here's the thing. You know Doctor Schuyler?" Idiot, of course he knows Doctor Schuyler, that's why you're here. He probably knows him better than you, which is the other reason you're here. "I mean, of course you know Doctor Schuyler, you guys were, I mean..." My eyes dart over to the King. He is watching me with a scowl. Way to go, now you've done it.

This is going terribly. Leeson's face has lost the warm inviting expression it held a moment ago and the King proceeds to press his lips together so tightly they have gone white. I have already hit a nerve with both of them and I haven't so much as even explained myself.

Blowing out a breath I start again. "Chase and I are kind of together, or were together. Things were going really well between us and then out of nowhere, the other day, he tells me we're through. He won't talk to me now and he won't explain why. The only thing I can get out of him is his adamancy that we never should have started anything together. He says he knew he would only end up having to hurt me, just as he hurt you. He makes it sound like it wasn't a choice. He claims it was inevitable."

Hearing the words in my head, it is as close to what I wanted to say as I'm probably going to get. Leeson's eyes are narrowed and are looking past me. He has drawn his bottom lip in his teeth and is worrying at it. The King isn't watching me anymore, but has his eyes trained on Leeson instead, the harsh edge to him is gone and is replaced with what looks to be concern. Neither man says anything. The silence is unbearable.

Leeson pulls his lips from his teeth, but his eyes stay trained in the distance. "And the reason you came here tonight?"

"Answers." I shrug. "I get the feeling whatever reason he gave you for leaving is why he's running from me. I don't know why he's doing this. He said he knew it would happen again, and he hates himself for it. Why is he running? It was getting pretty serious between us. Fast. I know that and I worry that may be why. I know I may not get him back, but not understanding where I went wrong is killing me."

The faraway look in Leeson's eyes and unreadable expression on his face makes me shuffle in my seat. The King still watches him and concern is growing on his face too. When the silence continues long past what should be a normal time to respond, the King shuffles up beside the Captain and rests his hand on his knee.

"B?"

Shaken from wherever the man had gone, Leeson meets my eyes, there is fire burning inside them and I can see him set his jaw. I get the sense he is fighting off anger when I see his fists clench in his lap and the way he appears to be fighting to maintain his composure in front of me.

"I don't know why he does this, Aaron, but its horseshit, and I'm going to find out."

Brandon flies out of his seat and is halfway down the long room before I can make heads or tails of what is going on. The King is on his heels.

"B." The King calls after him, grabbing his arm to stop him. "You're not doing this."

"I am doing this. Let go of me."

The King drops Leeson's arm, but squares himself in front of the man, aiming for dominance and preventing him from walking away. "You said you didn't care. You said you didn't want to hear his excuses." The King says.

"It's not for me this time. You don't know the half of what I went through when he left me. I'm not going to let him do this to someone else, at least not without giving one of us the courtesy of an answer."

"B, it's in the past. Let it stay there. You tell me that all the time."

"I know, but every time I look at him, that past has a nice way of slapping me across the face and calling me a fool. It's infuriating, Alistair. I have to do this, not just for me but for him." He swings his arm in my direction.

"Then I'm going with you. If you can't get an answer out of him, I will."

What have I started? I feel as though I have just poked the hornet's nest and I'm stuck in the middle of a seriously personal argument.

Leeson has a hand on the King now, stopping him from following. "Alistair, stay here. It's not your business."

"It is my business. You've never told me how much he hurt you, you've never said a damn thing or shared any of that pain with me." The King says.

I want to melt into the floor and disappear. I never should have come here.

"You're right, I haven't, but to be fair you get fired up every time his name comes up. You make it really hard to talk about."

Deciding maybe they have forgotten about me, I slink out of my seat and shuffle toward a far wall, hoping maybe I can sneak out unnoticed.

The King's hand flies up at my movement, indicating for me to stop. I stop. I freeze and think that maybe if I don't move a muscle, I will disappear. I pray for invisibility so I can disappear. *Maker, please make me invisible. Please.*

"You're right. I do. I'm sorry. Let me come with you, B. You want answers, I'll make sure you get them." The King says to Leeson.

"No. I need to do this on my own. Trust me." Leeson leans in and kisses his cheek. "Stay with him, I'll come back here and let you know what I learn."

No! Maker help me. *No! No! Oh bloody hell, don't leave me here alone with the King.* This was a stupid, stupid idea. A stupid, stupid, stupid idea. I really need to learn forward thinking. *I said invisible not please paint a target on my chest. Dammit!*

The King begrudgingly nods and gives Leeson's hand a squeeze.

The Captain walks out the doors at the far end of the room and we are alone; me and the King. He returns to a chair and motions for me to sit down as well. I reluctantly obey and sit stiffly on the edge of the seat, fighting the frantic need to flee.

"I-I'm sorry I came here tonight, Your Grace. M-my intention was not to cause problems. I was only hoping the Captain could give me answers-"

"Aaron, is it?" He interrupts.

"Yes, Sir."

"If you don't bloody relax and start calling me Alistair, I won't share my whiskey with you. Understood?"

With wide eyes, I nod my head and slide my butt back in my seat. *I can do this…I think.*

Chapter Eleven

Chase

Having slept most of the day, I lay on my pallet, wide awake now, but having no desire to get up and do anything. It's late in the evening, the sun has set and my stomach growls, begging to be fed. I ignore it. My head still pounds along in time with my heart, none of my usual remedies having helped at all. I pull myself to sit and try to muster the strength to at least find a book to read. It hasn't worked to distract my thoughts so far, but I insist on trying again. As I rummage through stacks of books on my table and a sharp knock resonates from my door.

Squeezing my eyes closed, I press my fingers into them. Aaron needs to let this go. I refuse to answer the door and snag the first book I see off the top of the pile, not bothering to read the title, and head back to my pallet.

The door pounds again under a hard fist. He's determined this time, and I'm afraid if he knocks any harder he might succeed in breaking the door down completely. I continue to ignore him. Opening the book to a random page, I try to focus my eyes on reading the words in front of me, not caring what it says.

The pounding comes again, harder, longer, and increasingly intent on its mission to get me to answer it.

"Open the bloody door, Chase. I know you're in there."

That voice, I know that voice, but it isn't Aaron. My eyes shoot over to the closed door and I stare at it. Why is Brandon here? Confusion makes me rise from bed and shuffle to the door. I unbar it and swing it open, breathing a sigh of relief at finding him alone. I half feared Aaron brought reinforcements in the form of Brandon and the last thing I need is to be confronted by the only two men I have succeeded in hurting in my life.

"What do you want?" I squint at him. My head hurts too much to open my eyes all the way and his incessant pounding has only made the throbbing inside worse.

"We need to talk." He says, pushing his way past me and entering uninvited.

"It's not a good time, Brandon."

"That's too bad, because it's happening right now, like it or not. What the hell are you doing?"

Seeing he isn't going anywhere, I move to the small table, grab a shirt draped over my stool, and throw it over my head.

"You'll need to be more specific, because I'm pretty sure you're not looking for the sarcastic 'I have a headache and I'm trying to sleep' answer. Are you?"

Brandon crosses his arms over his chest and glares at me.

"Don't be a smart ass."

"See, I didn't think so. Elaborate."

"Aaron came and paid me a visit tonight."

Bloody hell…He would team up with Brandon on this.

"It's not your business, Brandon."

"He's made it my business. Now talk. What are you doing?"

"I'm busy not feeling very well. My head is pounding and I need to sleep. Once again, this isn't your problem, it's mine."

"Damn your stubbornness, Chase. Fine." He storms over to me boxing me in between him and the wall and glares at me. "You don't want to talk about Aaron, then let's talk about us then shall we? Me and you. Remember those days? Do me a favor and take a stroll with me down memory lane and enlighten me once and for all. Why did you turn your back and walk away from me five years ago?"

He would bring this up now. I gape at him trying to compose myself. Brandon hovers, staring down at me in anticipation, waiting for an answer. How many times was I willing to explain this to him and he never wanted to hear it? Now. Now he wants to know and the bloody man knows damn well it's the same reason I've walked away from Aaron.

I shuffle around him - clearly he has no intention of leaving without answers - and pace to the other side of the room to stand near my bed. I match his posture, crossing my arms across my chest, and glare back to him.

"Brandon, I've tried to tell you a hundred times and you've never wanted to know. You shut me down every time I want to talk. Why now?"

"Because you're doing it again. That man barely knows me. I'm his commanding officer on the field and nothing more, yet tonight he comes pleading for answers because you've hurt him and he's frustrated and doesn't know where else to turn. Gee…Sound familiar?"

"Aaron will get past it. We hardly started anything between us. He'll move on."

"By the sounds of it, things were getting pretty serious between you."

"Again, not your business, Brandon."

Brandon stalks forward and, being several inches taller, looms over me trying for intimidation. It's never worked. I know him too well and his soul is too soft for threats.

"Why did you leave me?" He asks.

I've always wanted to give this man the truth of it, so I relent and flop down on my pallet with a sigh.

"My parents showed up in Prag. Jefferson sent them reports of my progress and I was an embarrassment to my family name. I was no soldier, you know that. They showed up late one afternoon and informed Jefferson I was through. They had me pack my things and told me I was to begin my training to become a physician the moment we arrived back in Saldrium. They already had it lined up. I tried to make them wait to leave until morning so I could talk to you, but they wouldn't hear me. I was practically dragged from the city that night, Brandon. I couldn't even come find you to tell you what was going on. You know how overbearing they are. I told you."

"You couldn't say you had to make goodbyes to your fellow soldiers?"

"I tried, believe me. They were appalled with me. They went on and on about the taint I had brought to their name with my ridiculous notion of wanting to fight. They told me Jefferson would inform the other men that I left to seek other opportunities. It was for the best. It broke my heart to leave you like that. I told you that before. I wanted to say goodbye. I wanted to explain. I didn't want to just disappear into the night without telling you why."

I stand watching Brandon's face, his stone cold stare watching me. I'm not sure if he believes me, but it's the truth. I never wanted to leave him, but obeying my parents is what I was raised to do. After a moment, Brandon's face clears, but his forehead remains creased.

"Fine. I believe you, but what of Aaron? You haven't been pulled from the city by the scruff of your neck. You didn't disappear into the night. You're here. Your parents are miles away in Saldrium. This can't be about me... Is it?"

"It's not. We've long ago moved on, you know that. I like Aaron. I more than like him, but..."

"But what?"

Sighing, I rise and head to the small table. I flip through the book where I keep the letter from my parents and hand it to him.

"This came for me the other day." I say.

He takes the letter from my hand and studies my face before opening it. He bends his head and reads. I know every word he is reading. I've committed it to memory now, the words having burned into my brain so they can haunt me wherever I go, even in my sleep.

My parents are on their way to Ludairium and, if my calculations are correct, they should arrive in the next few days. Accompanying them will be Lady Maribelle Seymour, daughter to Lord and Lady Arthur Seymour of Gromishran and apparently, my future wife. According to the letter, arrangements have been made for us to be wed. The arrangement being in the best interest of both our families. Combining our families fortune and lands will bring both names more power.

Watching Brandon's face, I can see he has reached that point in the letter. Finished reading, he brings it down from his face and meets my eyes. The harsh, rigid demeanor is gone, his face softens with sadness and worry.

"You're not doing this, Chase." His voice is nothing more than a whisper. "You can't."

I take the letter back from him, tossing it back on the table, not bothering to put it in its hiding place. The pit of my stomach feels hallow again and the numbness is back.

"I have no choice."

"Like hell you don't. Times have changed."

"Barely, Brandon, and not in my world. There is no way my parents can know about me. No way." I emphasize. "I would not only be an embarrassment to them, but a disgrace to my family name. It would destroy their reputation."

"You can't marry a woman, Chase. Do you have any idea how unhappy you will be?"

"Oh, I have an idea, trust me. You think I haven't thought about this? It's all I think about, aside from the anguish of losing Aaron, but I don't have a choice. Besides, many men like us marry woman and live perfectly normal lives. It's what's been done for hundreds of years. It's what I'm supposed to do. It's what my parents expect of me."

"What about, Aaron?"

"I told him from the beginning it wouldn't work. I warned him he'd only get hurt."

Brandon studies my face and all I can do is look back at him. He's thinking. I can always tell when Brandon is trying to work out a problem, he gets this look in his eyes like he's referencing his "big book of Brandon knowledge" inside his head.

"No. Wait." He says, abruptly pulled from his thoughts. "More than like? You said 'more than like.' Do you love him?"

I sigh and turn, walking away, pacing in the opposite direction.

"Brandon, it doesn't matter. I can't pursue anything. I have to do as my parents bid. It's over."

"Do. You. Love him?" He asks pointedly.

"Brandon…" when I go to turn, his arms are on me and he jerks me back around to face him.

"Answer the damn question."

"Yes! Okay. Yes, I love him. But it can't happen. I shouldn't have led him on. I shouldn't have allowed it to come to this. I knew better."

Brandon laughs a humorless laugh. "Yeah. You're right. You shouldn't have let it come to this. But if you truly love him, then you owe him the courtesy of a proper explanation. Don't do to him what you did to me."

I rub a hand over my face. My eyes sting and all this talk has made my head hurt so badly I'm nauseous. I have to swallow the bile building in the back of my throat.

"I'll talk to him."

"Good."

Silence grows between us but Brandon doesn't turn to go, so I slump back on my bed and lay down. My body is so tired and I can hardly be upright anymore.

"You are wrong, Chase." Brandon has calmed some and his words are full of anguish and pity. "You can be true to yourself. You can tell your parents. Don't ruin your life like this. You'll never forgive yourself."

"None of this will matter soon anyway. The love of your life has asked me to join the negotiating party and cross the border. He's still itching to get rid of me so I figured I'd make his day and agree to go. It will save me a heap load of problems. It's a suicide mission and I know it. I'll be dead before my parents can marry me off and I will no longer be able to hurt anyone else. It'd be better if my parents believe I died honorably serving the King's wishes than tarnish my family name and be disowned. Aaron… He'll find someone else."

"You're agreeing to cross the border?"

"Yup, I just made my decision. I'll tell Alistair tomorrow."

"Chase…"

"Please go, Brandon. I feel sick. I'll talk to Aaron. I promise. Go."

He doesn't leave right away, but hovers nearby. Resigned, he moves silently to the door and rests his hand on the knob.

"Just think about what you're doing, Chase. I know you've always wanted to do right by your parents. I get that, but times are changing. Things aren't like they once were." He pauses as he seems to consider something. "You won't die crossing that border. Not many people know this yet, but I've become Alistair's tactical advisor, sworn in by the council, and I'm telling you, it's not a suicide mission. I'm directly involved in all the correspondence. You *will* come back. And then, when you do, you will need to follow through with this marriage unless you come clean with your parents. I hate to see you miss out on something really great with Aaron just because you're afraid."

His "happily ever after" outlook on everything is starting to get under my skin.

"How are you so damn hopeful all the time? You've seen the shit this world has to offer first hand, Brandon, yet you're so damn positive it's sickening. You have hope for these negotiations and this war. You have hope that my parents would be understanding in this controversial life I want to live. You have hope that things would work out with me and Aaron. Things aren't always so damn flowery and happy, Brandon. Things don't always work out, even when you *hope* they will."

I hit a nerve and Brandon's face reddens in anger. "Damn you, Chase! You say that to *me* of all people? My whole life is built on hope for a better tomorrow, because yesterday nearly killed me and you of all people know that. Sometimes we have to believe in a better future. Hope is what keeps people going and helps us rise to the day. Every day."

"Yeah, well, my hope for a future ran out a long time ago. Now, I just go through the motions. Turns out, I can't make everyone happy."

"That's a sad realization, Chase. You need to wake up and find yourself a little bit of that hope again or life will eat you up, believe me. The only person you need to make happy…Is yourself."

Without another word he slips silently out the door into the night and I'm alone again, with a raging headache and an unbelievable pain in my heart.

Barely nineteen when we got together, Brandon and I were so young. Hiding our sexuality from a realm that forbade it, we were held together more from a desire of not being alone in a scary world than from love. We were the best of friends and shared all our secrets and all our fears. Brandon's were dark and frightening, his past more than I could bear most days, but I always listened when he needed to talk.

I hit a cord tonight saying what I did, and I feel like a heel for doing so. The shit he went through as a child made him wise beyond his years and I have always respected the way he sees the world. The man standing here, lecturing me, giving me shit for my actions was like a flash to the past. He always called me out on my horseshit and today is no different. His words ring in my head and I know them to be right and true.

I didn't even realize until I said it out loud that I love Aaron. How can I love him? I know it's the truth. Aaron awoke something in me I didn't know was there and letting him go has left me so empty and afraid, I'm not sure I will ever fully recover. Empty has become my new normal. Unlike Brandon, I'm not brave enough to have hope. Despite believing in everything he said, I can't help feeling stuck following this road I have set myself on. I have come to believe that everything that is good, can't be had. I'm a conformer, a parent pleaser by nature, and I don't know how to break free of the chains and claim my life back.

Chapter Twelve

Aaron

Leeson was gone for a long time last night and I was left behind to make awkward conversation with the King. The whiskey he served was good, and after not too long, the mood relaxed allowing conversation to flow easier. I inquired about the reason for the maps, and asked how the plans were coming for our march north, but he seemed tight lipped about it and would change the subject every time I asked. Eventually, I took the hint and we moved on to other things. My initial impression of the man was quite cast aside once we got more comfortable with each other and surprisingly, I ended up enjoying his company. By the time Leeson returned it was nearing on midnight and his mood was somber. He explained that Chase had agreed to talk to me and would seek me out tomorrow. I was disappointed at leaving with no answers, but am hopeful I will know more soon.

* * *

This morning's field training is going by painfully slow. I swear we have been here longer than our usual sessions normally run, but seeing the sun just reaching high noon, I know it is just my nerves making everything seem like it is moving extra slow.

Once we are dismissed, I make my way home to change. Leeson promised Chase would speak to me today, but he didn't say when or where. The not knowing is draining on my nerves and part of me wants to run over to the surgery and force the confrontation. I know it's the wrong decision and try to distract myself with a stroll in the market instead.

The market is the same clamor of bodies it always is, people pushing past one another, bartering deals with merchants and having general disregard for one another in their effort to get what they need, at the best price, first. After being bumped one too many times, my toleration of people meets its peak and I steer my way to Statin's instead for a bite to eat and a few mugs of ale. The food curdles in my upset stomach making me nauseous and the ale does little to help my feelings of anxiousness. After pushing food around on my plate and watching the patrons for a while, I decide to venture back home.

Walking with my head down, I nearly run into a man who blatantly steps out in front of me, blocking my path. I'm about to curse who I think is a rushing, market goer, when I raise my head and am met with all too familiar, gorgeous green eyes, only the sparkle that usually shines behind them is gone and they look sad and tired. Pain tugs at my heart and I'm unsure what to say. The last two times I was around Chase, he made it clear he didn't want anything to do with me. Alas, my promised explanation has arrived, and I'm not sure anymore that I'm ready to hear it. Breaking the awkward silence, Chase looks to the ground and lowers his voice.

"Can we go somewhere and talk?"

I nod my head, not trusting myself to speak. The wave of emotion flooding through me is in danger of making me fall to my knees to beg and grovel for him to take me back, and I need to be a man right now and hear him out.

Chase walks down a few roads before turning off and heading out of the city walls. Once into the woods a few hundred yards, he finally comes to a halt under a huge oak tree. I come up to stand a few feet away from him and shuffle awkwardly on my feet. My body is vibrating uncontrollably and I squeeze my hands to fists to try and control it. My eyes are fixed on his and the turmoil I see racing around behind his beautiful emerald eyes ties my stomach in knots. It is so obvious ending this relationship is not what he wants. I wish I could just take him in my arms and hold him until all this ridiculous confusion subsides and he comes to his senses.

"Aaron, please hear me out. I'll do my best to explain. I don't think you'll understand, but I know I owe you the truth at least."

All I can do is nod as he paces small circles in front of me. The air feels thick and I have to fight to pull air into my lungs. The tension in nearly palpable and I can't help but watch his lips as he speaks. They've always lured me in, full and soft. I could hardly ever resist kissing them, it's no different right now, only I know I can't. I just stare at them, needing a focus, afraid to look at the pain behind his eyes.

"I told you before I can't live open and free with my sexuality like you, even though the laws are gone. My parents are long believers in the old ways and would scorn me. I would be disgraced, disowned, and would bring utter shame to my family. You understand that, don't you?"

I lift my eyes to his. "No. But I respect it. I told you I'd hide for you." My voice is strained and I can hear my attempts at sounding strong and brave have failed miserably.

Chase sighs. "My parents have always dictated my life. They are the deciders of everything I do, and I'm their only son. It is my duty to take over the family estate and lands when my father passes. My parents have told me how to live my life since the day I was born. The only time I tried to do things my own way was when I wanted so badly to be a soldier. Begrudgingly, they tried to go along with it. No matter the private tutoring they provided me, I was the worst soldier ever to carry a sword. I became a mockery in their eyes. They went along with my blasted dream until it brought them shame and was tainting the family name. I was the joke amongst their friends and it embarrassed them. One day my father decided enough was enough. I was pulled from the ranks in Prag and was ushered into schooling to become a doctor before I even knew what was happening. My father reprimanded me for years about never going against his word again. He knows best and it is my duty as their son to do as I'm bid."

As the story flows from Chase's lips, all I can do is feel sorry for him. He has lived his whole life under his parents' thumb and now, he's afraid to be his own man. He doesn't even know how to be himself.

"Chase, I told you, we can keep this a secret. I have no problem with that. Your parents aren't even in the city. They will never find out."

Chases shoulders drop and his hands go to his face and through his hair. I see him inhaling and exhaling deep breaths and I struggle to understand what it is that makes him so afraid to even try.

"That's not it, Aaron. I wish it was that simple, I do. I just wanted you to understand how it is with my family first before I tell you the next part."

"Okay..."

"I got a letter from my father a couple of days ago." Chases comes to stand in front of me, taking my hands in his. It's the first time he has touched me since I was kicked out of his home. My heartrate picks up at the warmth and I can feel him trembling where we are joined. I want to kiss him and take him into my arms, make all his words stop right here because I know whatever is coming next is bad, but I keep listening.

"My parents are on their way here right now. I expect them to arrive any day." Chase swallows hard and I can see the emotions flooding into his eyes. "They are bringing Lady Marielle Seymour, daughter of Lord and Lady Arthur Seymour of Gromishran, to meet me. They have arranged a marriage between us."

Chase keeps talking, but the blood pounding in my ears drowns out his words. Marriage? Did I hear him right? A marriage has been arranged? I don't understand. My thoughts are muddled and I roll the word around in my head trying to make sense of it. My head starts its too familiar spin.

"Aaron." Chase's hand goes to my face and pulls my attention back. His other hand is squeezing me tight and is holding me up more than he knows.

"Married?" My voice sounds hallow. "They want you to be married?"

"Yes."

"And you are going to?"

"I have no choice, Aaron. That's what I'm trying to tell you."

No choice? He's going to marry a woman and be miserable instead of perusing happiness in a relationship with me. Yes, he has a choice. The spinning panic stirs inside me sending my heart to race and goosebumps to snake up my arms. Pain stabs me to my core. I grab Chase around the waist and back him into a tree. Closing him in with my body.

"Like hell, Chase. You have a choice. You can throw caution to the wind, stand up to those bloody, overbearing parents, and tell them no. Tell them who you are. You have a right to be happy. I know you don't want to walk away from us."

"I can't, Aaron."

"That's horseshit. What about you, Chase? What about what you want?"

"Aaron…"

"No. Marrying her isn't going to make you happy. You know that."

"Neither is being cast aside by my family in shame."

Chase's other hand moves to my face and holds me gently as he looks deep into my eyes. His touch feels so good, so right. How can he do this? How?

"Aaron…I told you this wouldn't work. I told you we shouldn't get involved."

"But we did." I pull him tighter against my body, pressing up against him, leaning my forehead on his. His red rimmed eyes stare back at me, pleading me to stop, "Are you saying this means nothing to you, Chase?" I crash my lips to his and kiss him with everything I have. I make love to his mouth and he doesn't fight me off like I expect. When I taste the salty tears running down his face, I pull away. His hands have moved to the back of my head and he is caressing them through my hair.

"How can you say you don't want this?" I whisper. "It's so obvious you do."

"I do, Aaron, but I can't, you need to understand. What I want to do and what I have to do are two separate things."

Swiping the tears from his face, I kiss him again, more gentle this time, never wanting to part, feeling need flowing from him as well. Need he won't allow himself to have, need he is going to bury and walk away from if I let him go. My body shakes more violently at the thought. The burning in my core intensifies. I can't let him go.

"Don't push me away, Chase. You can right this with your parents. You have the law on your side now. You have the King on your side. They can't punish you when you share the same beliefs as him."

"Aaron…Please don't make this harder than it has to be."

He is trying to squirm out from under me now, but I keep my body close, holding him there, fearing what happens if I let him walk away. I fight against him and hold his face to mine. I know he doesn't want to see what's right in front of him. I know he doesn't want to believe it can happen, but I'm grasping onto anything I can.

"Chase…Listen to me, please."

Chase's hands cover my own and he stares deep into my eyes. I have his attention, but his look is far away and I'm afraid he's already given up on me, already shut out my pleas.

"I know this sounds crazy, and I know we haven't known each other that long, but listen to me. Everything we have and everything we've shared is so perfect. We are so in sync with one another. I am falling in love with you. You can't walk away from that."

The tears fall even harder from his eyes and I hope that means I'm breaking him down. He needs to see reason. He can't live a lie his entire life, not when he doesn't have to.

His lips meet mine and the passion and emotion conveyed in that short moment leaves me breathless.

Pulling back, Chase lowers my hands and edges me to back up. Defeat weighs my body down. I have lost this battle. I retreat a step and give him the space he wants. He stares long and hard into my eyes and the silence is unbearable. Letting out a heavy sigh, Chase squeezes my hand.

"Goodbye, Aaron. I'm sorry."

My heart shatters into a million pieces as Chase turns and walks away without even so much as a glance back.

Chapter Thirteen

Aaron

Chase is gone. He has disappeared back into the woods toward the city. Gone, and not coming back. But damn it all to hell, it's not what he wanted to do. My body feels drained; empty and heavy. It's being pulled down to the ground. My brain fogs over as I take a few wavering steps before slumping down to land on my bottom. My eyes trail after him, praying he will re-emerge from where he has disappeared, but he's out of sight now. Gone. My vision blurs and I can feel the hot tears roll down my face. I taste their salty sadness as they trace my lips and fall to the ground. I swipe them away and bury my face to hide them as they continue to fall unbidden in waves. The griping pain in my chest squeezes tighter and won't let go. Won't let me take a full breath as I sob for the loss of a man I barely know, but whom I have fallen hopelessly in love with.

He chose not to fight for us. He chose a life of obedience over love. He's gone and not coming back. I was so careful too. I tried to give him everything he needed, but it wasn't enough. He wouldn't hear my pleas, wouldn't stay and fight for this, for us. He wanted it too, he said as much and I saw it in the tears he shed, yet he walked away.

I clutch at my chest, trying to calm the hurt. Maker it hurts. The spinning is back. My mind races and I can feel myself slipping into that dark place of my childhood, the place I have tried so hard to avoid for years. The place where danger lurks within my reach and I fear I am not strong enough to control right now. I cover my ears and try to make it stop. I know I can't go there. I can't…I know…

"Aaron, your sister is trying to tell me something important. Whatever you need, it can wait."

"But, Mama, I'm next. I was already waiting while you talked to Kyle and then Marjorie too, it's my turn."

"Aaron that's nonsense. I'll talk to you when Erica's done. Help Mommy out and go check on the baby would you."

"But, Mama, I did check the baby last time. Mama, listen to me. You never listen to me. Why do you always ignore me?"

Pressing fingers into my eyes, I try to force it to stop. I stand and spin circles trying to decide where to go. I shake my head, clearing the memory. I have to focus. I need control. I need to stop the pain crippling me right now because it's going to break me down. I can't let it win. I stumble over a branch and nearly fall before I catch my balance again.

Oh, Chase. Why won't you listen to me? Why can't you see what we have?

Back in the city, I head home. I barrel around market goers, ignoring their quips and comments at my disregard for their space. Climbing the stairs around back of the tailor's shop, I keep one hand on the wall for balance. I let myself in and nearly collide with Caleb who is on his way out. My wavering vision makes his face fade in and out of focus in front of me. I'm pretty sure there must still be tears in my eyes. I duck my head and move past him, hoping he doesn't notice. I need to lie down. I need the pain to stop. I need to gain control.

"Aaron? Geez, you look like shit." Caleb says, placing a hand on my arm and spinning me back to look at him.

Pulling my arm from his grasp I continue across the room and collapse onto my pallet, burying my face. I don't want to see anyone right now and I certainly don't need Caleb's concern over my wellbeing. I can do this myself. It's been years since I had an episode. I don't need help. I've got this.

Only everything hurts. Most of all my chest; my heart. The feeling of having it ripped in two is almost too much to bear. It's more painful than a sword breaking skin, a pain like none I have ever felt, and I can't make it stop. I can't get away from it. I need it to stop.

"Aaron?"

I didn't notice Caleb was still here until he places a hand on my arm and says my name.

"Aaron. Talk to me. What happened?" The pallet shifts under his weight as he sits down beside me.

"He's getting married." I say into the blankets.

"Married? Who, Chase?"

"Yes."

The words said out loud send another stab through my chest, deeper this time and I pull my legs up to curl into a ball.

"I don't understand…To a woman?" He asks.

"Yes."

Caleb goes quiet beside me. I don't have the energy to explain more and besides, I can't explain something I will never understand.

"Go." I say. "You were leaving. Just go. Leave me alone."

"And what are you going to do?" He asks almost accusingly.

Worry has worked its way into my best friend's voice and I know where his thoughts are right now; exactly the place I'm trying to avoid.

Caleb and I have known each other since we were both five years old and his family moved down the road from mine. Caleb has two significantly older sisters who couldn't be bothered with a pesky younger brother following them around all the time. Me, I have more than enough siblings, being the middle child of seven, but no one paid any attention to me and I was a lonely child. Always the one cast aside, always the one forgotten about. I somehow slipped between the cracks and got lost in the shuffle. I sought out a friendship with the new boy down the road and we hit it off right away. From the day we met, we have been inseparable. The problem is, Caleb knows all my secrets and the ongoing struggles I suffer. I know he isn't going to leave right now, because he doesn't trust me, and he shouldn't. I don't trust me either right now. I have a bad reputation.

"Aaron, why don't you come out with me? I was going to meet up with Bill and Morgan and go have drinks at Statin's. Maybe gamble a bit. You like that, come with us."

"I just want to sleep. I'll be fine. Go."

It's not a lie. It is in fact my plan. If I can sleep, I can't hurt. If I don't hurt, then I'm safe from myself.

"I don't think I should leave you."

"I'm fine."

"You don't seem fine."

"It's not that bad. I'd tell you if it was." I lie. It is that bad but I'm too afraid to admit it. I hate to admit when I'm losing control.

Caleb hesitates a long time before the bed shifts and he stands up.

"Promise me you won't do anything stupid. Promise me you'll come find me if you need me."

Nothing stupid…

"Daddy, I was just trying to help cut the wood with Andrew, I didn't mean to."

"Get back in the house, I can't turn my back on you without you doing something stupid, Aaron. What were you thinking?"

"But, Daddy, listen…I didn't mean to. I was trying to help Andrew and it slipped out of my hands…It was really heavy, Daddy. Daddy…you aren't listening."

I pinch the bridge of my nose hard enough to hurt and shove the memories down again.

"Go, Caleb. I'll be fine."

"Promise me, Aaron. Promise you'll come find me if you can't control it."

"I promise."

After a moment, I hear the door close after Caleb leaves and I lay still on my bed. My mind swims with the voices of another time. Words and memories from long ago, brought to the surface, unwanted. The pain brings them on. I'm familiar with the cycle. I need to stop the pain.

"Mommy, I picked you some flowers."

"That's nice, Aaron honey. Marjorie, I need you to come help me prepare this meal or we won't be eating tonight."

"Where do you want your pretty flowers, Mommy?"

"Aaron honey, you're right in the way. Mommy is busy. Get moving."

"Can I help?"

"Aaron, not now."

"Mommy, I put your flowers on the table...okay, Mommy?"

"Marjorie, knead this dough while I peel potatoes would you? What would I do without someone to help me around here?"

"Mommy, I said I could help...Mommy?"

I roll over on my bed, pressing my hands to my ears as though I can block out the sounds and stare at the ceiling, trying to find focus in a concrete object, trying to center my thoughts. I need to stop the hurt. My heart feels literally broke in half and I'm losing control. I can't lose control. I can't let myself. I'm stronger than this. I need to dull the pain somehow. I don't want to feel anymore. I need it all to stop.

I peel my heavy body from my bed and stagger to the door. I don't know where I'm going, all I know is I need to be gone.

I know what will help the pain. I know how to make it stop, but I can't. It's the place I can't go. The place Caleb fears I'll venture and the one thing I can't do. I haven't gone there in so long. Years and I can't give in now. I need to find another way. A drink maybe? That may dull it some, it may help. I know I should go find Caleb at Statin's, but I'm not one who can easily admit defeat so I wander past the tavern and weave through the dark streets instead.

Down a dark, quiet alley, I trade a man way too many coins for his full jug of whiskey and head out of town. Swallowing a few long pulls, I wait for the sting, sliding down my throat, to start to kick in. I walk deeper into the woods. It's dark tonight, the stars and moon are mostly hidden behind scattered clouds. Fall is slowly sneaking into Edovia and with it generally comes an abundance of rain. Maybe we will have rain. I wouldn't mind tonight. Maybe a little rain will wash away the emptiness. I lean hard against a tree and drain another quarter of the jug down my throat, begging for numbness. Please work. Please.

If Chase could have given me a chance, I would have shown him just how special a person he is to me. I would love him and cherish him and show him the life he deserves. He doesn't think he deserves love or happiness. I would have given him both. That man became a part of me in the short time we spent together and now I feel like he has stripped me of half my soul. Maker, but Chase never knew this part of me. This messed up person who has fought for balance my whole life. Nobody know this part of me, except Caleb. I thought it was under control. I thought I'd outgrown it somehow, but the void left behind from Chase's rejection continues to pull and ache. Despite the whiskey seeping into my blood, I'm sinking fast out of control. I'm not fixed like I want to believe. My vision swims. *No. Stop.* I bang my head against a tree, trying to refocus…Trying to stay my ground…

"Aaron honey, oh my goodness, you're bleeding, what happened?"

"I cut myself with Daddy's knife."

"Oh, baby, you had an accident. You need to be more careful, knives are sharp, let me clean you up you poor thing. Mommy will make it better and then we can have snuggles. Okay, baby."

Bringing the jug to my lips, I empty the last few mouthfuls down my gullet and toss it to the ground. My body is feeling its effects, only not the way I hoped and I stumble deeper into the woods. The hurt is still there, under the haze of whiskey, it's still there raking across my heart. Why isn't it helping? Maker, please, make it stop. I don't want to feel anymore. I can't do it. I clutch at my head as the voices yell inside my brain.

"Simon, you need to bring a tutor in to train him with a sword. He's into your weapons constantly and walks away a bloody, bleeding mess every time. He's obviously interested in learning but he's klutzy and needs to be properly taught."

"I'll see what I can do, Belle, but it will cost us, tutors aren't cheap."

"Figure it out, please. He's going to really hurt himself one of these times. I've already bandaged him up three times this week. Look at him!"

My fingers fumble blindly for the hidden dagger I keep strapped to my leg under my breeches. I pull it loose and turn it about in my hands. My vision wavers and shifts, the whiskey's effects are hitting me hard. I'm unable to focus. I run a finger along the blade, testing its edge. It is sharp and so it should be, I spend a part of every day making sure all my weapons have the sharpest blades. I stare at it as the moon glints off the hammered steel, before hiding once again behind a cloud.

I don't want to do this. I know I should just tuck it away again and go home. I'm beyond intoxicated and will no doubt pass out before long and the pain will subside on its own in time.

I know every one of these things to be true, but habit and an underlying need to make it all go away right now keeps the blade in my hand. It's just so much easier. It always was easier this way.

I rip my shirt over my head and cast it aside, staring down at my body. I'm littered with tiny scars all over my chest and across my upper arms. It's a habit I have fought so hard to break. I hate every one of them. They each tell their own story of a time I couldn't break free. Each one is a sign of my failure to cope. They serve as a reminder of my weakness. Shame fills me up and my vision blurs with more tears. A lifetime of trying to get my parents attention is written all over me. Something else I discovered as a child, was just how effective cutting into my own flesh is at relieving my turmoil and emotional pain. Two birds with one stone as the saying goes. Sinking a blade into my flesh not only made my mother bend over backward to make her baby better, but it alleviated the sadness and heartache I felt at being constantly cast aside for more important things. This discovery sent me down a path of self-harm that I have struggled to break my whole life. One that I know is wrong, but I can't get away from.

Examining the blade, I wander deeper into the woods, one faltering step after another. The moon has made its appearance again and I'm easily able to make out the ground before me. I stop at the edge of a drop off. About twenty feet below, I can hear the creek flowing rapidly past. Chase and I came here once to wade our feet in the water as we shared stories of our past. I didn't share this one. I couldn't. Wavering on the edge, I looking down into the dark waters below. An old elm tree blocks the moon as it tries to shine through again. I bring the blade up, turning it in my hands. I forgot my shirt back somewhere on the path. I don't care. Turning the blade so it points in at my body, I let the tip trace along my chest as I decide where to make the cut. Knowing relief is coming quickens my heart. Lower...Lower...I stop at my abdomen. I can see it better here. Seeing it is as therapeutic as the sting itself. I trace the blade to my left side, letting the cold steel prickle my bare skin. I close my eyes and press into the knife, sucking in my breath as the blade pierces the skin. I trail it across the flesh for about an inch before pulling it back. I feel the warm flow of my emotional turmoil pour out of me and my body relaxes at the release and I can almost feel a physical realignment of my thoughts as I regain control. The relief is consuming and I welcome it.

    I open my eyes to see my handy work, to watch the blood trail from the cut, but the ground beneath me waivers as my eyes don't instantly adjust to my surroundings. Teetering off balance, I sense I'm about to fall and grab feebly for the tree beside me. It's farther away than I thought, and the ground rushes up. I'm precariously close to the cliff edge and in a panic, I try to move away, but lose my footing. I feel myself pass over the edge and my last coherent thought is of Chase as I plunge to the creek twenty feet below.

Chapter Fourteen

Chase

Pounding at my door jars me from a heavy, dream laden sleep. I can still feel Aaron's lips on my own and I don't want to wake up. I want more. I refuse to accept the act of waking up and keep my eyes closed, remaining in their dark veil in an attempt to force myself to stay in my dream world. My efforts fail, the banging at my door persists, and Aaron's face is soon gone. Remembering how things were left last night sends the heavy sadness to weigh my body down again, making rising even harder.

Last night I made myself an exceptionally strong mixture of valerian root, lemon balm, and chamomile tea to ensure I would not lay awake thinking about the upside down mess my life is becoming. This morning I'm groggy and having trouble responding to the incessant banging at my door, mostly because I don't care. Aaron tore my heart to shreds last night with his declaration of love and I wasn't sure if I was whole yet this morning. He said he loved me and I couldn't tell him back because it wouldn't have been fair. How do you tell a person you return their feelings and in the same breath reject them, turn around, and walk out of their life? The look in his eyes when I went to walk away will be forever burned into my mind. Every part of me just wanted to run back into his arms and keep kissing him, but I couldn't and I didn't.

Damn my life, damn my parents, and damn this stupid marriage!

The door pounds again, reminding me why I have awoken and for an instant I wonder if it's Aaron. My spirits rise slightly at the thought, even though in my heart I know it won't be him.

I drag myself out of bed, pull on a pair of breeches, and comb my stubborn hair back out of my half open eyes with my fingers.

Yanking the door open, I find a young man silhouetted in the morning light, dressed in riding clothes.

"Good Morning, Sir. Are you Doctor Chase Schuyler?"

"I am." I say squinting into the bright day.

"Message for you, Sir."

He extends an arm and hands me a letter with a courteous nod of his head.

Accepting the letter, I indicate for him to give me a moment while I rummage about at my small table to find him a few coins in payment. Once the man is merrily on his way - bouncing down the road looking far too happy with life - I close the door and turn the letter over in my hand. Six stars, a crescent moon all inside an upside down triangle. I let out a sigh.

"What now."

Wasting no time, I tear into it and unfold the parchment. My eyes skim over the words. It's short this time and to the point. My parents and future wife will be arriving this afternoon. As my body shakes off the remnants of sleep and the news of my parents pending arrival sinks in, I realize my waning headache is threatening to come back. Perfect.

Washing up in the cool water of my basin, not having time or energy to warm it, I scrub at the crawling sensation worming its way over my skin. I'm not ready for this. Although, all the time in the world will never make me ready. With the intention of changing into more appropriately fitting attire later on, I find a simple shirt to pair up with my wrinkled breeches. Once I have shrugged it on, I snag a tie off the table to pull my hair back. I curse the damn strands that aren't quite long enough and inevitably fall into my face before tucking them behind my ear.

Rushing out the door, I head to the surgery. If Doctor Greaves isn't in, I'll need to find him. My parents will insist on taking up most of my time while they are in the city and I won't be able to help out as much as I usually do with patients.

Grateful - and somewhat surprised - to find the doctor already at the surgery, slumped over the table working, I pull up a stool and breathe in the first real breath I have taken all day. The doctor lifts his eyes from his work giving me a soft smile and settles back to his task.

"Morning, Chase."

"Morning, Richard. You're here early."

"Mm hmm. Sometimes the birds get me up at the crack of dawn. Thought I'd wander over and see what was going on here."

"I'm glad you're here. I'm going to need some time away over the next couple days. My parents are arriving to the city this afternoon and I'm pretty sure they are going to expect me to be available to their every beck and call, as much as I'd prefer to hide in that room over there and hope they never find me."

"Fredrick Schuyler, Lord of Saldrium, is planning to be in Ludairium and this is the first you're telling me? Surely you knew before today."

I let out a sigh. "I did. I'm sorry I didn't bring it up, I've been trying to absorb the impact. Not exactly exciting news from my perspective."

Doctor Greaves knows I'm not a huge fan of my parents, but he also has the utmost respect for them seeing as his father, the old city's doctor, was good friends with my family.

"So why the sudden visit? Are they missing their only son?" He asks with a smirk.

That makes me burst out laughing. Miss me? Doubtful. The only thing I can see my parents missing would be having someone to lecture all the time and put down.

"No. I doubt that." I fill my lungs with air and let it out slowly. It will probably be best if I just tell Richard the truth rather than letting him find out when they get here. "My parents have arranged a marriage for me, they are bringing my future wife here for me to meet."

That makes Doctor Greaves stop everything he is doing and his eyes come up to meet mine. First he studies me to see if I'm being truthful. Why would I make this up? I mean really, why? Then I can see concern fill his eyes and crease his forehead. I put a hand up to stop him before he can say anything else.

"I know what you're thinking, Richard, but it is my duty as their son and I will not disrespect my parents by turning this down."

"Chase," his voice is warm and soft, "have you thought about what kind of a sacrifice you'll be making?"

"That's all I've done is think, and yes, I know. It doesn't matter, it's my duty."

He's quiet for a long time and his sympathetic look is almost too much to bare.

"What of the young lad who comes seeking your company all the time? I can see the way you look at him, Chase. You may not come out and admit anything to me, but I'm not a fool. You care about him."

Lowering my gaze, I can feel my cheeks flush. I didn't think I was fooling him. I never have, but the mention of Aaron brings renewed pain back into my heart.

"You're mistaken, Doctor."

"All right, my apologies." Again, not fooling him. "I can take care of things around here. Take all the time you need, son."

"Thank you, Sir." I say rising from my seat. I keep my head lowered as I make my way to the door.

Just as I'm about to walk out, Doctor Greaves' strong voice stops me in my tracks.

"I'm not trying to interfere, or make assumption when you clearly aren't ready to admit anything, but you only live one life, Chase. Make sure you are living the one *you* want to live not the one someone else dictates."

His words sting and I nod my head before dipping out the door, securing it behind me. I wish it were that simple. I wish I could be free to have that life everybody thinks is so easily achievable, but I can't.

I head back to my rooms. I need to prepare for later, more mentally than physically. Spending any time with my parents is exhausting, but after the last few days, I'm all but drained already and I'm not sure how much more I can take.

* * *

Straightening my blouse under my vest, I smooth it down before tucking it in the top of my black silk breeches. As I secure the clasps along the vest, my mind drifts to my future. What kind of future is it going to be now? Are my parents going to allow me to continue to stay in Ludairium after I'm wed? Will they insist I relocate? How am I going to keep a wife or even pretend to be happy with her? Can I find satisfaction in bedding a woman? Will I be expected to have children? Of course I will. It will be top of the list as far as my mother is concerned.

Letting out a sigh, I fish through my chest and find a black silk tie to match my attire and pull my hair back to secure it. My father will hate that I've let it grow so long and will no doubt have an opinion about it. I pull on tall, black leather boots and begin securing the buckles up the sides, when a knock comes to my door. Hopping over, one boot on one boot off, I come to a halt at the door and swing it open to find a young page looking quizzically at me.

"G'day, Master Schuyler. I've been sent to summon you to the castle, Sir. Lord and Lady Schuyler have arrived."

Squeezing my eyes shut, I try to keep my breathing steady. Here we go.

"Thank you. Let them know I'm on my way. No escort will be necessary."

The page bobs his head and is off down the road, skipping with the innocents of a child.

I pull on my other boot and sit on a stool to finish securing it. Taking a few deep breaths, I try to steel myself for what is about to happen to my life. It's bad enough I need to meet up with my parents, but with them staying in the castle, I will be no doubt be under the scrutinizing eyes of Brandon and the cocky, pigheaded ruler of the realm as well. Just what I need.

I'll never forget the day when Alistair pieced together who I was, or rather when Brandon finally told him of our past. Alistair had flown off the handle with jealousy, nearly destroying his and Brandon's entire relationship. Jealousy still flows through his veins whenever we are together, but he is much better at hiding it behind carefully constructed walls, keeping it at bay. I take too much delight in watching him flounder around me when Brandon is in the room and it is for this reason that Brandon and I have never been able to stay friends. The three of us are civil with one another, but never more than we have to be.

Approaching the castle, I'm greeted by two guards standing out front. I'm admitted right away and am escorted along the winding halls, and up a flight of stairs to the top level where I'm granted entry to the Lords apartments.

The young page I met earlier is scurrying around setting all the Lords belongs in their proper place. The room is large and exquisitely furnished, as expected. My father should be pleased. A few large embroidered, floral chairs sit on either side of a currently unlit fireplace. The lingering, warm summer air leaving its use unnecessary. A large, circular oak table sits on a round plush rug where I see my mother has pulled up a chair. She works to adjust her already perfect, sliver streaked hair in a looking glass, pinning back fallen hairs behind her silver, pearl lined pins. The curls that ringlet down her face are evidence of the youthful beauty she refuses to let go of. She is a small woman, whose tiny frame and green eyes I inherited, much to my father's disappointment. He would have preferred a much larger, stronger son I'm sure. Beside her is seated a young woman, who I can only assume is my future wife. Thick, striking blonde curls spill from a carefully fitted kerchief on her head. Her skin is the color of milk with a smattering of freckles dancing across the brim of her button nose. She is stunningly beautiful. Any ordinary man would fall to his knees to be chosen to marry her. Breaking my eyes from the ladies, I glance over the rest of the room; my father is nowhere to be seen.

At my entrance, my mother flies up from the table and rushes toward me in a ruffle of rose colored skirts to wrap her arms around me.

"Chase, my darling boy."

Her embrace is crushing and she plants a wet kiss on my cheek before pulling back to take in my appearance. I force a smile to my face that I know doesn't reach my eyes and hope she doesn't notice.

"It's nice to see you, Mother. How were your travels?"

Ignoring my questions - as she always does - she starts brushing the stubborn strands of fallen hair behind my ear, tsking and shaking her head. She takes my chin in a tight grip and steps back to look me up and down.

"Have you grown? I think you've grown."

"Not likely, I stopped growing years ago." I say while removing her hand from my face and drying her lingering kiss on my sleeve.

Kissing her cheek, I then encourage her to return to her seat. The young lady has risen from the table and is standing, poised beside it, awaiting introduction, sizing me up. I'm sure I must be a disappointment and quickly avert my eyes feeling increasingly uncomfortable.

"Chase, darling. I'd like you to meet, Lady Maribelle Seymour, daughter to Lord and Lady Arthur Seymour."

Keeping myself in check, but remembering my manners, I put a neutral look on my face and step forward. I take her hand and plant a chaste kiss on top.

"My Lady, it's a pleasure to make your acquaintance."

All I receive in greeting is a shy smile and a nod. I drop her hand and move away quickly, peering into the adjoining chambers, continuing my search for Father. This is going to be harder than I thought. I can't even look at the woman. How is this going to work?

After a quick scan of the other rooms, I notice my father isn't in the apartments at all and wonder at his absence when he knew I was on my way over.

"Where is Father?" I ask, returning to the main room.

"Making audience with the King and arranging a meal for tonight."

"He's more interested in seeing his King than his son? I see how it is."

"Chase Alexander," my mother darts her eyes to me, "you will not speak of your Father in such a way."

"I'm sorry, Mother." Setting my jaw, I reprimand myself for letting my tongue slip. I know better. "How were your travels?" I ask again.

"Dreadful. How is your apprenticeship going?"

"It's finished. Doctor Greaves has given me full title, Mother. I'm acting as the city's full time Physician now. Doctor Greaves is slowly stepping down."

"It's about time." My mother returns to fixing herself in the mirror and Lady Maribelle fiddles beside her, toying with a ribbon on her dress.

The awkward silence sets in. I have never been good at small talking my parents, mostly because it's all meat and potatoes with them, if it's not important business, it's not worth speaking of. And I certainly don't know what to say to this woman.

My father's boisterous return breaks into the quiet room making the Lady Maribelle jump in her seat. I hide a grin, realizing she is no doubt unaccustomed to my parents' bold, uninhibited behavior.

"We are set for a meal at sundown, although, how I'm to keep company with such a disgrace to the crown I have no idea. Can you believe the man insists on having his blasted lover at the table with us? Disgusting, filthy sodomite I tell you. The late King would be appalled at what is become of his crown."

Standing off to the side, my father has yet to notice me.

"Darling." My mother nods her head in my direction.

Catching sight of me for the first time, my father makes no more than a curt nod in my direction - oh the warmth of my family - before turning to the mantle above the fireplace. My father snatches up a bottle of whiskey and pours out two mugs. He makes his way to me in two strides and slams the mug into my hand before marching away to the adjoining room.

"Nice to see you too, Father," I mumble under my breath. Taking the hint that I'm to join him, I nod to the ladies and follow after him into the next room.

My father has plopped himself into another lavishly upholstered chair near the window and has raised his feet to rest on a trunk that has been brought up by a servant. Knowing what is expected of me, I follow suit, making myself comfortable in a similar seat across from him. I bring my mug to my lips, to delay our conversation, and let the amber liquid graze my lips, just dampening them. I despise whiskey and getting through this mug and the rest of the evening just may be the death of me. Thank the Maker.

"You've met your future wife I assume."

Just like my father, straight to the point, no mincing of words.

"I have, Sir. She seems a lovely woman."

"She is more than just a lovely woman. She is daughter to Lord and Lady Seymour of Gromishran. A fine specimen and of high birth, young man. You'd do well to remember that."

"Yes, Sir." I say. Taking a chance, I gulp my whiskey. Maybe I'll choke and die. That could work too. Save me the trouble of another moment of this day. I shudder at the taste as it singes my mouth and throat.

"The joining of our families will mean greater wealth in your future. More lands, and a firm position." He says.

Deciding to remain silent, I focus instead on keeping a neutral face. The idea of marrying this poor woman in the other room saddens me, for as much her sake as my own. She will have no idea that my path in life tears me in the opposite direction. That any advances I make on her are from necessity and not lust. That I can never even learn to be okay with this and ever love her the way she deserves.

"How is the apprenticeship going?" He asks.

It's all my parents care about, not "how are things with you?", but "how's your work?" and "Ta-da! Here's your life". You're welcome.

"It is finished, as I told Mother, I have been deemed a full physician."

"Excellent. Saldrium needs a good doctor."

"Saldrium? My position is here. I'm not leaving, Father. I run the surgery and Ludairium has higher needs."

"Nonsense. They will replace you easily enough. Once you are wed, we will have a manor erected on the lands and you and Lady

Maribelle will live comfortably there. Do not argue with me. I know what is best. You will come and be closer to your family and the lands. Run the surgery there and help me out in my old age."

I shrink down in my seat. "Yes, Sir."

Forcing down another mouthful of whiskey, I struggle to keep myself in check. I don't want to leave Ludairium. I've made a name for myself here and the last thing I want is to be anywhere near my parents. This whole thing just keeps getting worse.

"When do you plan for me to wed, Sir?" I'm afraid of the answer, but I need to know. I need to prepare for the inevitability ahead of me.

"We are hoping for this winter. We will send for you once the arrangements are made. You will pack your things and return to Saldrium at that time for good."

This winter. With any luck, I'll be across the border getting slaughtered by the Outsiders. In the event that everything there goes as planned, and I come back alive - as Brandon seems to believe will happen - I may have to just do myself in at this rate. I wish I could taint my father's plan and tell him of my intention to go north with the negotiation party, but I have been sworn to secrecy and Alistair would be one pissed off man if I were to tell my father of all people.

Shuffling in my chair, I attempt to change the subject.

"Did I hear we are meeting the King for a meal at sundown?"

"Indeed. Impertinent man he is. Lacks all necessary skills to run this realm. How in the world Chrystiaan felt he was capable of this position, I'll never understand."

"The people like him, Father. His methods may be slightly unconventional, but he's honest and fair." Despite my own opinions of Alistair, it is true.

"The people are dolts. The man is a disgrace to the crown. For the council and courts to find his sodomite behavior allowable is preposterous.

It's disgusting. He's not a man, he's a barbarian. Men do not act in such ways."

I straighten up in my seat and clench my jaw together achingly hard. I need to stop the words that want to flow right out of my mouth. If this man had any idea that his own son was no different than the King, it might just give him the apoplexy I've been waiting for. Maybe I should come clean. How fantastic would it be to watch the man choke and die on his own words? *Maker help me, I'm a terrible son.*

"The realm has accepted his ways, Father. You should watch who you express yourself to in this city. He has many close companions and he can be ill tempered at times. You don't want to be on his bad side, I assure you."

"Do not speak to me in such a manner. Clearly you've been subject to this city long enough. It will be best once we can bring you home."

Best for who exactly?

My father lets out a sigh and changes the subject.

"We will be in the city for a few days. Get to know Lady Maribelle while we are here. The next you see her again, she will be made your wife. Remember yourself, Chase. Do not disgrace this family. You treat her with the utmost respect."

"Yes, Sir."

Chapter Fifteen

Chase

I can hardly sit still in my seat. This has to be the most uncomfortable situation I could possibly find myself in. Not only am I stuck having dinner with my future bride to my right, who coincidentally seems just as uncomfortable about this arrangement as I do, but, to add insult to injury, Brandon has sat to my left, causing Alistair to be continuously glaring at me and flaring his nostrils. I won't be surprised if fire starts shooting out of his ears at any moment. Oh, and did I add that my parents haven't stopped rambling on since we sat down?

"Chase darling, eat your carrots." My mother reprimands as she reaches across the table with her spoon and pushes them together into a neat pile on my plate like I'm a child.

"Mother." I swat her hand away, feeling my cheeks flush.

"You're entirely too skinny. Maribelle needs a big, strong husband to take care of her. Now, eat up!"

Dear powers that be, is this conversation really happening?

"Mother, I'm certain eating six measly carrots swimming in butter isn't going to miraculously alter my build, but thank you."

"Humph…His Grace eats his carrots and look at him all strong and muscled." She mutters under her breath.

Seriously?!? Is this actually happening?

I turn my eyes to a snickering on my left and see that Alistair is clearly amused by my mother. In fact, he makes a dramatic display of plucking up a carrot from his plate and popping it in his mouth, chewing with exaggeration as he smiles at me.

Great.

Have I mentioned, I hate my family?

"Maribelle, darling, you'll need to stay on top of him about eating once you are wed. He can be justifiably stubborn as you can see."

"Mother." I say sharply. "Can we please change the subject?"

My raised voice earns me a glare from my father before he clears his throat and pulls himself to sit more upright, shifting his gaze to Alistair.

"How are the armies fairing, Your Grace? Should we expect them to be on the march before winter?"

"Curb the titles, Fredrick. I'm not going to ask you again. I prefer a more relaxed atmosphere at my dining table, if you will." Alistair says.

I smile inwardly hearing my father being put in his place.

"Preparations are in the works," Alistair continues, "but for the most part, I will not be discussing our plans openly at this time. I assure you though, I have the biggest brains at work on this and I have hope for a successful outcome."

Alistair claps Brandon on the shoulder and the two of them share a look between them. I pick at a carrot on my plate and watch my father closely for a reaction through downcast eyes.

Oh, yes indeed, the man looks right ready to burst watching Alistair and Brandon have their little moment. I chew my carrot slowly as I continue to watch for signs that the man might truly crack and start on a rant about "disgusting sodomite behaviors". And then, it gets even better. Adding to my father's discomfort, Alistair chooses this exact moment to get up and brush a soft kiss on Brandon's forehead.

"I think we need something a little stronger than wine to drink. If you'll excuse me, I have a particularly nice bottle of whiskey hidden away. I'd send a servant to fetch it, but I can't have them knowing where I keep my secret stash now can I?" Alistair gives a wink and heads out the door to the dining hall.

I'm pretty sure my father has developed a quite evident twitch above his right eye that got exponentially more noticeably after the small kiss was administered to Brandon's head. This is far too enjoyable to watch.

My father picks up his wine and drains it in two large gulps. He shifts his eyes to me and I swallow my well chewed carrot as I stare wide eyed back at him. And suddenly my enjoyment at the situation is gone.

"Chase," his voice booms in the silent room, "Would you speak to your future wife at least once before dinner is through? You are supposed to be making her acquaintance, but you've not said a single solitary word to each other all night."

I gape at my father and feel Lady Maribelle tense up beside me as well. I shift my eyes from my father to her and then drop them to the table to stare at the glossy surface. I stammer, trying to find words, but I have nothing to say.

"Good grief, Fredrick. The boy barely knows what to say when you put him on the spot."

Umm…Mother to the rescue? That's odd.

"Well how's he supposed to marry a woman he can't even look at, let alone talk to? He needs to be a man and learn to properly court a woman." Turning to me he says, "You only have six days, son, before we head back to Saldrium. Maker help me if you don't get over this uncomfortableness by then I should say it will make for an awkward bedding on your wedding night."

Somebody kill me now.

* * *

Last night was excruciating and this morning I'm lying in bed with a well-deserved hangover. When Alistair returned with the whiskey, I slammed back at least a half dozen glasses despite my fierce dislike for the stuff just so I could get through the rest of the evening. I ended up drifting into conversation with Brandon and Alistair just to avoid having to be the center of any more embarrassing situations. It's a sad day when I'd rather be in the company of Alistair and Brandon over my parents, but last night was exactly that. I clung to their end of the table, and come the end of the night, I think even Alistair felt sorry for me.

This morning, being the dutiful son, I have agreed to take Lady Maribelle about the city to show her around. Without my parents hovering and pressing conversation upon us. Hopefully, it won't feel as awkward being in her company as it did last night. Lady Maribelle had little to say outside the brief answers to the questions my parents put at her - all for my benefit of course. She preferred playing with her food rather than engage with anyone at dinner. She seems as happy about this marriage arrangement as I am. Maybe today we can simply find a comfortable silence between us and move forward.

My plans for her, after taking a tour of Ludairium, are to take her for a meal at Statin's, probably not a suitable display of nobility in my parents' eyes, but they don't need to know about it, and right now, I need a little more of my normal life back since the last few days have managed to make me forget how to feel human.

* * *

With Lady Maribelle on my arm, we stroll through the streets of Ludairium. We first head to the surgery, I show her where it is I spend most of my days. She is intrigued by the vials and jars of ingredients lining the walls and drills Doctor Greaves on their uses. The doctor respectfully explains what he can and I can feel his eyes studying me between her questions, but I refuse to make eye contact, knowing full well he disapproves of my decision to go along with this charade.

"So by combining any of these ingredients you can make teas or concoctions to aid in the healing of any number of ailments?" She asks.

"Not quite, My Lady. Not all of these herbs here can be ingested. Some are deadly poisonous."

"So what purpose do they serve?"

"They can be used to make a poultice and be applied to help with reducing inflammation or soreness of a wound."

"So you have the power here on this wee shelf to not only heal, but kill a man should you choose?"

The old doctor chuckles. "The doctor's job is that of healing, My Lady, not hurting. The hurting is generally what brings people here and the killing we leave to our soldiers."

Lady Maribelle's interest shifts from the vials on the walls to the number of different kinds of ailments we might treat in a given day. Doctor Greaves seems enchanted with the attention, whereas I'm finding myself nothing but board. Finally steering the conversation to an end, we leave Doctor Greaves to his work and head back out into the streets.

I suggest we take a stroll through the market and Lady Maribelle clings to my arm as we walk past the many booths admiring the wares set out by the merchants. The crowded square makes the market visit less enjoyable and as we move around to a more open section on the outside of the market, Lady Maribelle pulls me aside. Stopping abruptly, she turns and stands in front of me, hands on her hips.

"What are your views on this marriage we are about to undertake, Doctor?"

Having been nothing but silent with me most of the morning, her bold statement catches me off-guard. Looking everywhere but at her, I stare at my feet as I think about how to respond with as much honesty as she deserves.

"It seems a fitting union and benefits both our families. I'll abide my parent's wishes. If they feel it is for the best, they are no doubt correct. They have selected only the most perfect wife for me. I'm more than pleased."

I hope it was honest enough. This poor woman will never have the full truth from me, but she never can, and I will live with my secrets until my death if I must.

"You lie rather well, Doctor."

My eyes shoot up to meet hers for the first time since greeting her this morning. I never noticed their intriguing color until this moment. They are a deep blue, like the sky just before night fall and when the light hits them just right, you can see a fleck of violet swimming within. Her eyebrow raises at me in question and her face is stern.

"How have I lied, My Lady?"

"You have barely made eyes at me since we met, Doctor. Yet you call me a 'perfect choice for a wife'. Am I not to your liking?"

Damn, I'm not doing a good job at pretending it seems. I hadn't noticed I was being so inattentive.

Taking her hands in my own, I make a display of admiring her beauty. She is wearing a long ivory gown, weaved with a soft blue ribbon down the ruffles of her skirts. A finer lace of the same soft blue crisscrosses up the front of her bodice on either side ending in a ruffle around the low neck line. I let a soft smile form on my lips and tilt my head to the side.

"On the contrary, My Lady. I fine you most exquisite. You'll pardon my behavior, I did not want to seem too eager and frighten you off." Stepping in closer, I trace a finger over her cheek. "You are indeed very beautiful."

Appeased with my answer, her face softens and she presses her body to mine. I instantly stiffen and fight the urge to step back to get away from her.

"And you, Doctor, are indeed easy on the eyes." She leans in and plants a light kiss on the end of my nose.

Unease sets in as I realize I will eventually need to be intimate with this woman and I'm not sure I can be what she wants. Her close proximity already has me prepared to flee. Luckily, I still have enough time ahead of me to adjust to this situation. The wedding is not planned until winter. Breathing out an unsteady breath, I pull back from her close connection and relink her arm into mine.

"What else would you like to see, My Lady? I feel as though I have shown you everything already and it is too soon to eat yet."

"Where do Ludairium's soldiers train, Doctor? My father has a great interest in the building of the armies for the coming war. He spent a good deal of time with the King last winter when he visited Gromishran. I would like to be able to share with him that I saw the King's men as they trained for battle."

"Of course, My Lady. The Kings training field is in back of the castle, this way."

Steering her through the city, we make our way toward the castle and through the courtyard to the main gates leading out on the field. It is mid-morning and I know Brandon will be working with the newer recruits until midday.

Her interest in the training is evident the moment we pass through the gates. Her face lights up as her eyes try to look everywhere at once. Her knowledge of tactics and maneuvers tell me this woman has spent a lot of time watching men train before today. Her father has schooled her well and she knows what she is talking about. At one point she nudges me in the ribs.

"You're not a soldier." It is a statement more than a question, but the look she gives me seems to warrant an answer.

"I'm not."

"Sons of Lords are ordinarily trained to fight for their King. Yet you're a doctor."

Of course they are, only I failed miserably as a soldier. She would touch on a sore subject. I pat her hand and leave my eyes trained on the field ahead.

"It turns out, I'm better at saving lives than taking them. Does that disappoint you?"

"Not at all, Doctor."

Returning to her musing of the field, she says no more about it. As she continues to chatter about the goings on in front of us, I find my mind wandering with lack of interest until I'm sullen and lost in thoughts of Aaron. I haven't noticed him about with the men, but figure he's purposefully staying out of sight in anger of what I have done to him. I deserve nothing less. If the man was truthful when he said he loved me, then I know I broke his heart. If only he knew how much my own ached in sympathy.

I don't notice when Brandon wanders over us until Lady Maribelle squeezes on my arm and pulls me out of my trance.

"Is that Captain Leeson, from last night?" She asks.

A groan escapes my lips. The last thing I need is to deal with Brandon's scrutiny right now. Last night's dinner was bad enough. He whispered his disapproval of my decision in my ear all night, never letting the matter rest.

"It is." I say as he closes the distance between us.

Brandon's eyes inspect mine and Lady Maribelle's linked arms before landing on me.

"Chase." He says in greeting, nodding his head to me before turning to address the future Lady Schuyler. "Lady Maribelle, it's a pleasure to see you again." He takes her hand and kisses it in greeting.

"Good Morning, Captain," She says, with a grin. "The kind doctor has brought me to see your army at work. It's impressive. I can't wait to share what I've seen with my father. He talks all the time of the King and his plans."

"Not my army, My Lady, the King's, but thank you."

"Of course." She says, a flush reddening her cheeks.

Brandon's analytical gaze in back on me.

"If I could have a private word, Doctor." He spits the title off his lips in disgust. His unspoken thoughts searing into me.

"It's not a good time, Captain. I have promised the Lady Maribelle a bite to eat and I should fulfill that promise before she wastes away." I give him a warning look, trying to tell him not to push this matter.

"Nonsense, Doctor. I want to watch the men train some more. Go, I'm quite all right." She's oblivious to the silent conversation between Brandon and me.

Yanking me by the arm until we are about thirty paces away, Brandon then rounds on me.

"What are you doing, Chase?" He hisses.

"Showing my future wife around the city before taking her for a nice meal. It's my business, Brandon, not yours." I keep my voice low and find I'm speaking through clenched teeth.

"Are you mad? You know you can't go through with this."

"I can, and I will. It is not your concern, stay out of it."

"You should be ashamed. You're not only being unfair to yourself, you are being unfair to that poor woman. You can't give her what she needs. You can never love her the way she deserves to be loved and you will be lonely your whole life if you continue this way." He says.

"Why do you care so much? I'm sure Alistair would be spitting mad if he knew how much my life mattered to you, wouldn't he?" That quiets him, I see him bite back his next words and just stare at me. "I will make her a fine husband and I will learn to love her the best I can. Now quit interfering. I need to take my future bride to dinner now. If you'll excuse me." I spin around and make my way back to Lady Maribelle without another word.

Peering back over my shoulder, once my future bride is secure on my arm again, I see Brandon shake his head at me in pity. I'm so sick and tired of everyone's pity.

"Hey, Chase," he calls out. "Enjoy your meal and don't forget to eat your carrots."

I've officially decided, I hate Brandon.

If everyone would mind their own business, maybe, just maybe, I can ruin my life in peace.

* * *

After a decent meal at Statin's, I decide I've had enough pretending for one day and escort Lady Maribelle back to the castle. I hope I have shown enough interest in the woman for one day to make everyone happy.

On our way back, I'm slowed in my step by the sound of my name being yelled frantically behind me. Glancing over my shoulder, I see Caleb in a mad run, trying to catch up with me. My stomach twists at the thought that Caleb may not have been informed of my situation with Lady Maribelle and may inadvertently say something inappropriate. I know he and Aaron are good friends, but I have no idea just how much Aaron will have shared with him. My mind muddles as a slick sweat breaks out down my arms at his approach.

"Chase." He yells again, ensuring I have stopped to wait for him.

Caleb's eyes shift to the Lady Maribelle's arm linked with mine and he frowns before meeting my eyes with a knowing, disapproving glare.

"Have you seen Aaron?" He asks.

My heart beats a little faster at the mention of Aaron's name and I try to set my face to neutral as I answer Caleb. I want to show no indication of emotion.

"I haven't, I'm sorry. If you'll excuse me, I need to-"

"I think somethings wrong." He breaks in, not letting me finish or walk away. "I haven't seen him since yesterday. He was home when I left last night and said he was going to bed, when I got back, he was gone. I haven't seen him since. He didn't show up on the field today either. He was really upset, Chase. I'm worried about him. Did he come see you again?"

Stiffening under the implication that Aaron might seek me out, I try to keep a distance from what he is saying.

"I'm sorry, Caleb. I haven't seen him. I'm sure he's fine. If you'll excuse me."

"Chase." Caleb stops me again and shuffles uncomfortably before continuing. "You don't understand. Aaron doesn't handle stress very well. He's a danger to himself, I don't think you realize that. There are things he hasn't told you. Things you don't know about him."

My façade slips and I know Caleb sees the panic in my eyes. I try to hide it, try to fix my feature back to something appropriate and passive. It's not working. I need to get out of this situation and quickly before Lady Maribelle reads too deeply into what Caleb is saying.

"I haven't seen him." I say again.

I turn and pull Lady Maribelle along with me as I walk away. I pray Caleb knows enough not to follow me or push the issue.

"Chase." He calls out. "Please let me know if you hear from him?"

I give an absent nod and continue walking. My mind races with the implication of what Caleb has just said. What things? What don't I know?

If Caleb hasn't seen Aaron since yesterday, something is certainly wrong. They are good friends. They room together. I know Aaron was a mess when I saw him last, I was too. It was the hardest thing I have ever done; walking away from him. The man was destroyed and I knew it. Where is he? He didn't show up for training either? That explains why I didn't see him earlier on the field. Aaron knows he is being monitored, he wouldn't jeopardize the possibility of marching north with the armies. It's why he came here. It's what he wants to do. Something about this isn't sitting well.

"Doctor?"

I'm so lost in thought, I don't realize Lady Maribelle's tugging on my arm.

"I'm sorry, My Lady. What was that?"

"I asked if you knew this man who is missing."

"Umm…He's a patient. I've mended his wounds a few times." It's not a lie.

"That man seemed concerned about him."

"Do not worry yourself on the matter, My Lady."

I pat her arm and lower my head to stare at the ground.

I can't get the niggling feeling in my gut to go away. My stomach twists at the thought that something is really wrong about this whole thing. What did Caleb mean when he said Aaron is a danger to himself? I get the sinking feeling Aaron is in trouble.

Absently climbing the steps to the front doors of the castle, I don't notice the questioning looks the Lady Maribelle is giving me until she turns me to face her once more before we enter the doors.

"You're white as a ghost, Doctor. What that man said has upset you."

"You're mistaken, My Lady. I'm just tired. I have a lot of work to do this afternoon and the thoughts are overwhelming me just now. I apologize for my distraction."

This damn woman can see right through me and the look she gives me says she doesn't believe a damn word I just said. With an audible humph, she secures herself on my arm and allows me to take her back to the Lords apartments.

Greeted by both my parents, I'm asked to stay and visit for the afternoon and join them for a meal in the late evening. Declining, making similar excuses as before, I dodge the looks of scorn from my mother and Lady Maribelle before making my escape.

I've spent enough time fumbling through this day. Worry grips around my gut and I need to be alone before I give away too much.

Chapter Sixteen

Chase

The nightmare grips me and holds tight, long after I open my eyes. I'm soaked in a cold sweat and throw myself out of bed to stand in the middle of the dark room, if only to ensure I do not get thrown back into its hold. I move blindly to my table and throw cold water from my basin over my face, rinsing away the fear clinging to my skin. My heart slowly begins to settle in my chest and my breathing returns to normal. It was so real.

In my dream, Aaron had been teetering on the edge of the tower wall, like the night when he brought me to see the stars. He was laughing and kidding with me, ignoring my pleas for him to get down. Submitting, he was about to descend when he lost his balance. I could see him falling backward and I ran up to grab hold of him. Our hands locked and with all the strength I had in me, I held onto him, but he was slipping. Leaning back, gripping his hand with both of my own, I tried to pull him back over the wall, but I didn't have enough strength. Our grip loosened more and more and I could feel him slowly slipping from my fingers. I knew I was losing him, I couldn't hold on. Our eyes met as he slipped from my hold and I watched as he went over the edge with fear and panic in his wide brown eyes as he fell away into the night. Then, I was blasted awake in utter terror.

I know it was a dream, a nightmare, but the tightening in my gut is real and hasn't subsided since I spoke with Caleb yesterday. The uncertainty of Aaron's whereabouts, prickles my skin anew.

Pulling the drapes from my window, I see the sun illuminating the horizon. It is barely morning, but I know I will not be able to sleep anymore.

As I pull on clean clothes, I wonder if Caleb has found Aaron. I need to find out first thing, so I can put my mind at ease.

Checking in at the surgery first, I'm surprised to find Doctor Greaves already working through some logs at the table in the front room.

"You're up with the sun today." He says at seeing me. "How are things with the family, son?"

"Meh, pretty much how I expected." Pulling up a stool, I join him at the table. "My father wants me to relocate to Saldrium once I'm wed. Says they are in need of physicians and I would fit right in, so hopefully Alistair moves quickly on finding you new help. I'm afraid my days here are numbered."

I see his eyebrow raise, but he doesn't look up from his task.

"Saldrium? When is the wedding?"

Letting out a defeated breath, I scrub a hand over my face. "This winter I'm being told. You know I don't want to leave you. I explained to my father I'm needed here, but-"

"You don't have to explain anything to me, Chase. You will always do right by your parents. It's who you are. The King will find us a replacement. I'm not worried. He should already be looking into it. Have you given him an answer yet about going north?"

"No. I was going to the other day, but things got busy and it slipped my mind."

Going across the border may at least buy me a little more time, push the wedding plans at least until spring. *If* I come back. Ideally, I'd be better off if I didn't.

As daylight slowly wakes up the city and its people, I excuse myself and rush through town to Caleb and Aaron's rooms above the local tailor shop.

Having pounded on the door until my fist hurts, I figure no one is home. Someone should have answered by now.

Shit! It's sun-up. Caleb and Aaron should be on the field for training. Why didn't I think of that before now? Of course they aren't at home.

Walking as fast as my legs can carry me to the field, trying not to run, but tripping over my fast pace, I try to convince myself Caleb's panic yesterday is premature and that Aaron has turned up and is on the field training with him right now. Deep inside, lodged somewhere in my gut, refusing to let go, is that seed of doubt that says "what if" and it quickens my pace even more. Swinging around the stone wall to the courtyard, I nearly run smack into my mother and Lady Maribelle, as they head out into the city.

"Chase Alexander, you nearly knocked the two of us over. Why the rush? Slow down, you'll hurt someone." My mother says.

"Sorry, Mother. I didn't expect anyone to be there."

This is the last thing I need right now. Trying to slip around them, I'm snagged by the cuff of my shirt and yanked back to face my mother.

"Never mind. I'm glad we ran into you. Lady Maribelle and I were about to take a stroll, do join us."

My mother offers up Lady Maribelle's arm for me to take. I shift my eyes between the two women, one the look of steel determination the other of wavering uncertainty while I hesitate on my feet. I need to go. I don't have time for this.

"Mother, I need to take care of something first. I'd be happy to join you when I'm finished. I shouldn't be too long."

I tear my arm away and rush off in the direction of the field. The irritation in my mother's face is not missed, nor is it intended to be. Behind me, I hear her raised voice.

"You'll have to excuse my son's terrible manners. He forgets his priorities sometimes."

The little snip is fully intended for my ears, but I ignore it as I quicken my pace, my boots slapping on the dirt packed pathway as I continue my race to the field. I'll pay for this later; I have no doubt.

Entering by the north gates, I scan and see groups of men gathered together near midfield. Brandon is still giving out the days' instructions, barking order at the top of his voice to ensure he is heard. I tuck the stubborn strands of hair from my face behind my ears and study the huddled men surrounding him, trying to pick out the familiar face of either Aaron or Caleb. There are too many men bunched together, I don't see either of them and my heart beats a little faster in my chest. I stand on my toes and worry my hands as I wait for Brandon send them off to start their drills.

It feels like an eternity before the men disperse, and I take a few steps forward, rescanning the group. Caleb sees me first and starts running toward me, his sheathed sword bumping and bouncing off his leg at his side. I know by the anxiety on his face and his panicked approach that Aaron is nowhere to be found. My knees go weak and I take a few stumbling steps backward before I regain my balance.

"Have you seen him? Tell me you've seen him." Caleb is yelling the question at me long before he is by my side. The sickening tone in his voice gives indication that he knows the answer already.

All I can do is shake my head and Caleb's face drops even more. As he closes the last few steps between us, I try to find my voice.

"He's not here?"

Of course he's not here. It's a stupid question that needs no confirming, but I asked it anyway despite its redundancy.

"I have a bad feeling about this, Chase. I know Aaron too well. Something is wrong. I'm telling you."

I stare into the distress wrinkling the man's face. A twisting in my gut sends bile to rise up my gorge and I swallow it down as I struggle to find words.

"Caleb." My voice is gruff and I hardly recognize it as my own. "What did you mean yesterday when you said Aaron is a danger to himself? I have to know."

Caleb's shoulders slump and he looks at me with indecision like he is trying to decide if he trusts me enough to tell me. The worry in his face deepens and I know whatever he is about to say is bad.

"If I tell you this, you need to promise me it stays between us."

I nod my head, wanting him to get to the point, but it isn't good enough.

"Promise me, Chase. Say it or I'll tell you nothing. I'm defying Aaron's trust right now, but I think it's important you know."

"I promise."

Caleb glances behind him to ensure our privacy and lowers his voice.

"I don't know where to start." He lets out a sigh. "When things get too much for Aaron to handle. When stress grips him too tight or his emotions go on overload…he," Caleb looks to the ground and purses his lips, "he…hurts himself."

"Hurts himself. How? What do you mean?"

"He cuts himself. He told me once, it releases the pain, stops the spinning when it starts overloading inside him. It allows it to flow out of his body and helps him regain control. The worse the pain he feels, the more times he cuts and the deeper he goes. He's been doing it since we were kids."

Caleb raises his eyes to me and my stunned silence paired with my gapping mouth makes him continue.

"I'm worried because, he can't help himself sometimes. Even though he doesn't want to do it anymore, and he hasn't for years, he sometimes thinks it's the only way out. The only way it will stop what he's feeling. I've tried to help him find other ways. I thought he'd come to me if it got bad enough, but when I found him gone that night... I'm afraid he could do real damage to himself, or seriously hurt himself just to get his head to stop spinning. I don't think it would take much to make him go back down that road."

The fire igniting in my gut as Caleb speaks is one fueled from hurt, anger, worry, heartache, and a mountain of other emotions that all spill over at his words. The more Caleb explains the hotter the fire burns. It spreads through my belly and out along my every limb. I'm vibrating and my next move is a shear reaction to what I'm hearing. It's unplanned and even more unexpected. My hands fly up to grip the front of Caleb's armor and I shake him hard enough his teeth should rattle. The rage in my eyes must look violently dangerous, because Caleb flinches and tries to pull away from my restraint.

"All those scars on his chest and arms. He did that to himself?" I can't believe what I'm hearing.

"Yes." Caleb's eyes are wide.

"But... What of all those times he came to my surgery needing to be sutured? He did those too didn't he? I know he did. And here I thought it was you. It was the excuse he used to see me. You knew he was doing it! You supported it and you knew he had this problem? What the hell is the matter with you?"

Caleb flinches and I grip him harder, pulling his face to mine, seething mad. Caleb is a much bigger man than me, but my bristling anger makes him cower.

"Answer me." I yell in his face.

"No. No, he didn't do those. Aaron knows he has a problem. He's been trying to stop and he hasn't cut himself in a long time. He was afraid to do it himself, was afraid of stirring up old habits. He's been in control for years, but it always hovers at the surface when life throws tough shit at him. I wouldn't let him do it to get your attention. He... He convinced me to cut him. I know how that sounds. I didn't want to, Chase, I begged him to stop. I knew if I didn't do it for him he would just end up doing it himself and what he would do, would be worse, a lot worse. I thought it was the lesser evil. He was determined to get your attention and in case you haven't noticed, when Aaron sets his mind to something there is no stopping him. He was determined that that was how he was going to do it. It was either him or me cutting. I hate myself for even agreeing to it. I probably just made everything worse."

I let go of Caleb's armor and take a few steps away from him. I stumble and nearly fall. He's right, I know he's right. Aaron is in serious trouble right now, I know it. I can feel it. He's been missing for two nights. If he has cut himself badly enough…He could even be dead. My extensive knowledge of the human body and how it bleeds is a curse. Every possible scenario plays through my mind in the few moments we stand there and each vision is more gruesome then the last.

"What's going on?"

Brandon's voice breaks me from my thoughts and I meet his eyes. The worry etched in my face must be distinct, because Brandon's initial rough demeanor falls from his face and is replaced with a reflected worry.

"What happened?" He asks shifting his gaze from me to Caleb.

"Aaron is missing." Caleb says. "No one has seen him for two days and I think something bad may have happened to him, Sir."

Brandon eyes drift over to mine and it's all I can do not to fall apart.

"You haven't seen him?" He asks me.

"No." I say. "Brandon, Caleb needs to help me look for him. He knows Aaron better than me and is more apt to know where to look. Please dismiss him."

Brandon nods.

"I'll get things going here and I'll see if I can find Fergus to take over. I'll help you look."

The thing about Brandon is, no matter what his feelings are toward you, he will always help a person in need and he doesn't care who they are or what the circumstances.

With Caleb on my heels, we fly out the gates back toward the city.

"Where should we start?" Caleb asks.

My stomach flops and my steps falter as I flash back to my nightmare from last night. The shaking in my core rattles my teeth and I shiver, but not from cold. I need to check the tower. I need to know my dream wasn't trying to tell me something, but I'm terrified of what I might find.

"Follow me." I say, taking off in a dead run.

Winding through the city, I can't move fast enough. Caleb senses my urgency and keeps my pace easily. Weaving through the market, I'm slowed as I try to avoid running into people. Morning is the busiest time of day for market goers and the streets are packed with a crowd of bodies moving about slowly from stall to stall without a care in the world, oblivious to my panic and need to get by them quickly. I'm nearly through the crowd when someone grabs hold of my arm with enough force I'm surprised it remains in its socket and spins me to face them, almost knocking me off my feet in the process. Caleb collides into me at my abrupt halt, his head smacks my own with a deadening thunk, making me wince. Once I have been turned around fully, I find myself face to face with my mother…again.

Bloody hell, I don't have time for this right now.

"Young man. You have kept this poor woman waiting long enough, and look at you, flying through the city without a care in the world for anyone around you. You were raised to have more respect than that, Chase Alexander. I'm dissappo-"

Ripping my arm free from her hold, shocking her silent, I spin around and keep moving.

"I don't have time for this, Mother. I need to go."

With Caleb hot on my heels, I glance back over my shoulder as I run full long ahead. I see the recognition in Lady Maribelle's face at seeing Caleb and the look on my mother's face could kill a buck where he stood from twenty feet away. The amount of lecturing I'm certainly in for will probably leave me shoving daggers in my ears before she is through, that is, if my father doesn't tan my ass for this - like he would have when I was ten.

Shoving the pointless thoughts of my imminent chastening aside, I turn down the tower road and continue my run.

Approaching the tower, I slow my pace, suddenly in fear of what I might find. My eyes move along the ground in front of the tower and to the sides for as far as I can see. Nothing. No body. No Aaron. Climbing the mangled stairs in front, I notice the door is still barred and the nails are in place. A relieved breath escapes my lungs and I nearly collapse to the ground. He isn't here. Thank the Maker. Satisfying my own needs, I still make a point of circling the tower and checking every angle to ensure my dream holds no merit.

I look to Caleb, who has been standing by watching my meticulous checking and rechecking of the tower grounds, as I shake my head. "He could be anywhere. How do we know where to start?"

Caleb considers this for a moment before meeting my eyes. His expression is blank.

"If he did something to himself, he will have wanted seclusion. That's the only thing I can know for sure. When he was a kid, he used to go to this decrepit old wreckage on the coast where we lived. An old shipwreck. He wouldn't chance someone catching him in the act. He will have probably wanted to be alone."

That left us no further ahead. In a city like Ludairium, you could go down any alley in the night and find seclusion from prying eyes. Helplessness settles uninvited into my bones as I turn circles, looking at the great expanse of woods beyond the city. Aaron could be anywhere.

Chapter Seventeen

Aaron

Darkness.

Darkness...and pain.

Cold water splashes my face again and pulls me back to the surface of consciousness.

Pain. There is pain everywhere. And heaviness, such immense heaviness, weighing my body down. Pushing it into the ground...I can't lift myself...I can't move. It's so cold. Where am I? The world is too dark. I'm blind and lost somewhere in a blanket of terrible pain. My eyes...I need to open my eyes. I need to pull the veil and see. I need to find my way out. I try to force them open. I try, but they won't respond. They are stuck, like the skin of my lids has fused together leaving me stranded in this terrifying place of obscure agony and cold. I hear something. Faint. In the distance. It's the sounds of a faraway, familiar existence. I give up my fight against this tormenting world and follow the voices back to their pain free haven of warmth.

"Mommy, why does Marjorie always get to help? I want to help too."

"Aaron, honey, don't be silly, little boys don't help in the kitchen, they help the men in the fields and do manly things. Go ask your father if you can help."

"But, Mommy, Daddy says Andrew will do it. He doesn't want me to help."

"Then run along and play, baby. Go find your friends."

"I'm not a baby. I want to help, I'm big enough. Please, Mama."

"Aaron, for crying out loud, you need to get out from underfoot."

The water licks the insides of my ears. It muffles the sounds around me and tugs me back from the peaceful solace of this dream laden land. With it comes the misery of the darkened world of pain. So. Much. Pain. Please stop…I don't want to feel anymore. I want to go back…Back to the cushioning cloud of tranquility. Back to the place without all these uncertainties.

The water draws away and my ears pop with a sudden rush of sounds. There is a distinct buzzing that grows in intensity before fading into nothingness. The trickling noise of racing waters, a crinkle or rustling, and the buzzing is back again. What is buzzing? Before I can sort out the confusing mixture of sounds hitting my ears the water returns, squelching all noise until I'm deaf again.

I try to make sense of this strange world around me. Darkness. Water. Buzzing and pain. I don't like the pain. I don't like this world. The heaviness is back and I feel myself sinking as though the ground itself has opened up and is claiming my body, hugging around me as I sink down into its depths. A fog building in my mind makes my thoughts less clear and I can't remember what it was I was pondering a moment ago. They are calling again. The voices. The memories. The fog is thicker. I'm sinking…I…

"Daddy? Mommy says I need to help the men. I can't be allowed in the kitchen because I'm not a lady."

"Aaron, I told you, you're too little, you can't keep up. Winter is coming and I don't have time to teach you. When you're older, son. Andrew is going to help today."

"But, Daddy, I want a job to do."

"Your job is to stay out of the way right now, Aaron."

"That's not a job."

"Then go take care of Reilly and Jess so your mama and I can work."

"I don't want to watch the babies. I always have to watch the babies. I want a job like Marjorie and Andrew."

"Aaron, I don't have time for this right now. Off you go, you're in the way."

Cold wet hands tickle across my face and snake their way over my lips to dribble in my mouth. A fit of coughs rack my body and I'm pulled back up again to the surface of this strange world. The water hits the back of my throat, but my body doesn't remember what to do. Every weak sputter is a desperate attempt to protect my lungs from the invasion, but sends jolts of pain to stab at my head. Such a cruel place this is. Such utter torment and misery. I hate this place wherever I am. My lungs burn from hacking away the assault of the waters. Why do I keep coming back here? Why can't I leave this hellish life and keep the other one instead. I try to focus my thoughts. Try to discern this complex place I seem to have become a part of.

It has become an eerily quiet place since last I was here. The buzzing is gone. The water cushions my ears, no longer retreating, but the darkness remains. Why is this world so dark? Why are there no pleasantries here? Why can't I leave for good? Trying to make sense of it all is exhausting. I'm so tired. I want to sleep. I need to close my eyes and sleep. My eyes. I forgot about my eyes. Are my eyes still closed? Are they still stuck? I have little awareness outside the pain and the water that is threatening to dip in my mouth again. The effort it takes to focus on anything is so draining I want to give up, but something tells me it's important that I pay attention to this tiny detail of my eyes. Somehow, I know I must get them open so I can see. See what, I have no idea. So, I work on my eyes. I try to make them respond. Try to feel or sense them. I think they are already closed. I can't be sure.

Water hits the back of my throat again, and the choking coughs rattle my body. Stars burst across my vision and I'm certain someone stabs a knife into my skull, only it's just the sheer magnitude of the pain that is tricking my mind. I need to stop coughing. The pain is too much; I can't take it much longer. The water. I have to stop the water. Fighting with the thoughts cluttering up in my head, I try to understand. Again, I get the feeling I need to open my eyes, but that peaceful dream world is pulling me back down. I want to be there instead. There is no pain there. No physical pain at least. I give up the battle with my eyes and let my body float down again…down…down…

"What are you doing?"

"I have to make it stop hurting."

"Is that your dad's knife?"

"Yeah. I sneaked it out of his rooms."

"But doesn't that make you hurt more?"

"Only for a little bit. Then it all goes away. Then they will listen to me too."

Coughing. Lungs burning. Agonizing, stabbing pain in my head. No, I don't want to be in the pain world. I want to go back. I want to stop the pain. I can't do it anymore. My body jerks as my lungs expel more water that has snuck its way inside them. The coughing makes the pain worse all over now. I need to stop the coughing. I need to stop the water from going in my mouth. Fighting to find some element of understanding, I try to piece together the puzzle of this tormenting existence. I know I need to focus on my eyes. But why my eyes? The water is not in my eyes. I don't understand, but I try to concentrate on my eyes. To open them. I try to get my brain to send the message to open them, but they refuse to respond. Please open. Please.

Fine slivers of light sift into my vision, and give my body a new ache, a milder one, but another nonetheless. It's bright in this place and there are vague, dark forms all around me. They are fuzzy and shadowed. I squeeze my eyes closed again, blinking back the wet sting of this new sensation. Learning to control them, I reopen to more clarity. Tree branches. Leaves. A rocky, muddy, slopping edge climbing up above me.

Water splashes up over my face and into my mouth anew. The coughing pursues, only it is worse. My chest hurts and the water is not retreating like it was before. I can't get my mouth free and inadvertently suck more water into my seared lungs. I'm drowning. I can't get air. Panic races my heart just as the water draws away again. I gasp for breath. I shift my eyes around and take in my surroundings. My body is wet. I can see the cold water is covering me. My chest is bare. Am I naked? I can't be sure, but I'm so cold. Without moving, I let my eyes travel around my body and see I'm on the edge of a creek. The water is flowing past me, around me, and over me in a swift race downstream. How did I get here?

Water fills my mouth again and my brain finds enough comprehension now to not let it go down my throat. I spit out the mouthful and wait to take my next breath. I need to move. I know that now. I need to move or drown in these waters.

I try to make my mind focus on moving my body. First my arms. Start with my arms. I'm so tired, but I force myself to concentrate. I can't drift away now. There is danger present and I need to stay here. My arms, they won't move, I can't do it. The water is in my mouth again. I spit and cough. My head…I should move my head away from the flow.

I battle with myself and succeed at rolling my head ever so slightly to the side, but the movement makes the water dip in my eyes and shoot up my nose. I'm blinded. Fear clamps down on me and I turn it back to center again. I need to lift it. I need to bring it up, get it away from the water. Pain pulses through me. My body shivers violently, chattering my teeth. I work with all the strength I can muster and manage to lift my head enough to free my ears from the rushing creek and instantly, the buzzing is back. I breathe easier without having to fight against the rush of water flowing down my throat. With my head up, I look around again. One of my arms is laying over my chest in an awkward position. There is blood in places where my body is not submersed. I try to move the arm, but the effort sends more pain to throb over my body, so I stop. My other arm is beside me. I wiggle my fingers on that side. Nothing hurts over there. My legs are under the water. I try to move them. There is some pain, but it's not as bad. Using my one good arm, I reach out and grasp onto the ground near the shore and push with my legs. The strain is exhausting, but I inch forward with the effort. Excruciating agony dims my vision, but I don't stop, I can't. I know I need to move. I push again with my legs and pull with my arm, inching forward, closer to my goal. Dry ground, no more water. It's all I can manage. The darkness is seeping back in uninvited. I'm so tired. My teeth continue to clack together. I rest my head down. There is no more water. The buzzing is loud, but begins to fade as my eyes close again. The pain is subsiding. I welcome the dream world back. I let it wrap me up in its cozy blanket and take me back into its peaceful serenity.

Chapter Eighteen

Chase

I peer into the surrounding woods, letting my eyes follow the terrain, looking for something, anything, a clue that might tell me where Aaron has gone. My gut tells me he is out there, in the woods and in trouble. I spin around and meet Caleb's panic stricken eyes.

"Go back and tell Brandon to look within the city limits, in alleys, behind buildings, anywhere a person might find seclusion. You and I, we'll search outside the walls."

Caleb nods and flees back around the tower out of sight.

"Wait for me, don't go alone." He calls out as he runs.

"I'll stay close to the tower. Get back here as fast as you can."

While Caleb is gone, I wander a short distance into the forest, letting my eyes scan for any sign of Aaron. Shivers rack my body without mercy and I shake relentlessly. If something has happened to him, I will never forgive myself. I feel utterly horrible about how things went down. I strung him along knowing full well I would cave in to my parents' demands the instant they opened their mouths. To build such an amazing thing with Aaron, then turn around and throw it in his face. Blatantly tell him I want to be with him before walking away. I feel like the cruelest person alive. How could he not feel hurt and confused after the way I treated him. When I think about what Caleb shared with me and what Aaron has endured his whole life, I can't help but feel a little upset that Aaron never shared this with me. We'd spent a fortnight wandering the woods every night talking and sharing about our pasts and yet this never came up. I try to put myself in Aaron's place, imagine what it would be like to have developed these coping mechanisms as a child – knowing they were wrong and unhealthy - to deal with something beyond your ability to control. Maker, the torment he must feel sometimes.

Going farther in the woods than I promised, I keep my eyes to the ground in front of me. Listening to the sounds of the forest, I pray for a clue that might lead me in the right direction. The buzzing of the cicadas in the trees is loud and a few scampering chipmunks run past me through the brush just ahead. Something catches my eye, about thirty paces farther in. On the ground lies something not native to the surrounding forest of greens and browns. A white object. Moving faster, I approach it. The closer I get, the more I see. It is a white cloth material of some kind, crumpled and sitting in a ball at the base of a tree.

Standing over the object, my heart stutters in my chest and I drop to my knees. It's a shirt. Aaron's shirt. I pick it up and hug it to my body. He was here. Burying my face in the material, I inhale the essence of Aaron into my nose and feel tears well up in my eyes. My vision blurs. Where is he? What has he done?

Fear rips through my body and the shakes rattling me are uncontrollable. I need to find him.

Maker help me. Please let him be okay.

"Chase?"

Caleb is back and is standing behind me. I glance up at him and see his wide eyes staring back at me.

"What is it?" He asks, a tremble in his voice as he shifts his gaze to what I'm holding.

"It's his shirt. He was here." I refuse to part with it and hold it tightly wrapped around my hands. "We need to search the area. He's here somewhere."

Caleb and I spread out and walk deeper through the forest. My eyes continue to follow the terrain, but fear of what I may find holds me back and I move slower than I did before.

What if he's dead? What if all we find is Aaron's lifeless body?

I shake my head, trying to rid the awful thoughts from my brain. I hate myself for the coward I've been my whole life, not having the guts to stand up to my parents and putting their wants and demands ahead of my own. It's made my life miserable. The thought of losing Aaron feels like a slap in the face and I swear if I find him alive I will make things right between us…Somehow. I can't continue to deny who I am. I've lived a lie my entire life and left a trail of misery in my wake. No more. I have no idea what I plan to do, I just know I have to do the right thing for once. I need to do what I want. I need to find my happiness, and stop doing solely what's expected of me.

Up ahead, I can hear the flow of the creek rushing past. I'm familiar with the area, having wandered this way before on my own time just needing a quiet walk with my thoughts. I move toward it with measured steps. The terrain drops off about ten paces ahead of me and the creek runs past below. A shiver runs up my spine and over my scalp as I get closer. I stop moving. Instinctively, I know something is wrong up ahead. Numbness covers my body as I force my feet to carry me forward the remaining ten paces. I peer over the edge of the drop off and my knees wobble and buckle as I catch sight of the crumpled body of Aaron lying lifeless and still at the edge of the waters below.

"Caleb…Caleb!" I don't even recognize the shriek of my own voice as it pierces the air.

Before he has caught up, I'm fumbling down the cliff edge to the bottom. It's steep, but manageable if a person is careful; I'm far from careful. I lose my footing a few times, catching myself and setting myself to balance again using the tree roots sticking out precariously from the edge to help me. Caleb is behind me, tearing down the ledge with more skill than I. The blood pounding in my ears is drowning out whatever he is yelling. At the bottom, I drop down at Aaron's side and pray harder than I've ever prayed that he is still alive. His face is drained of color, he is so white it sends terror ripping through my veins. His body is cold to the touch and I lower my head to his bare chest, resting my ear close to his heart. I hold my breath and listen. At first I can't tell if I'm hearing my own blood pounding in my ears or the soft thudding of his heart. I take a few deep breaths and listen again, trying to focus on the sound. It is definitely the soft thump of a heart under my ear. It is a weak bumping, but it's definitely there. I let out a relieved breath. He's alive. My eyes dart to Caleb as he looks to me expectantly.

"He's alive." I say. "Get help, we can't move him alone. I need to get him to the surgery."

Caleb turns and flees faster than I've ever seen him move.

Waiting for Caleb to return feels like the longest wait I've ever had to endure. Aaron is unresponsive to my every attempt to rouse him so I do an inventory of what I can see of his injuries. I'm guessing he fell the twenty feet or so down the slope. His arm across his chest is definitely broken, I can tell right away by the awkward angle of it lying across his body. There is a deep gash off to the side of his abdomen and I have the sinking feeling, he made that mark himself. It looks controlled and much like the other old scars he wears. The blade he no doubt used is lodged in his upper thigh and there is bruising over many parts of his body. He has a nasty, raised, lump on his head, just below his hairline where it looks like he hit it badly in his fall. I trace gentle fingers across his face and call his name, trying to get him to wake up.

"Aaron. Aaron, can you hear me? Open your eyes for me. It's Chase."

The longer he lays unconscious, the more my heart aches. My guilt is overwhelming, almost more than I can bear. I feel like if I hadn't pushed him away, none of this would have happened. I gave him all of me and then I took it back and left him nothing but hurt.

A noise from above makes me lift my head. Caleb is back with Brandon and Alistair in tow. I shouldn't be surprised at Alistair's presence. He always has Brandon's back, no matter what, and if Brandon was instant on helping, Alistair would be nowhere else but at his side, even if it has to do with me.

The men climb down the rough edge of the drop-off and surround Aaron. They look to me in anticipation of some kind of instruction.

"His arm is broken, try not to move it. I can't tell if there are other broken bones, but he's banged up pretty good so we should assume he might have. We need to move him carefully."

Feeling helpless, the weaker man in the group, I watch as the three stronger soldiers take Aaron's body as though he weighs no more than a child and carry him back through the woods to the city. Keeping pace with them, my mind kicks into doctor mode and races to think of everything I will need back at the surgery once we arrive.

* * *

During the rest of the morning, I work over Aaron's unconscious body, mending the wounds I can see and setting the bone in his arm before wrapping it securely. The three other men help me maneuver him when needed; rolling him, propping him on his side, lifting him, so I can work without obstacles. Aaron is still unresponsive which concerns me greatly. I don't know when these injuries took place, but if it was two nights ago, as I suspect, and if he has been unconscious the entire time, I worry he might have seriously injured his head in the fall. I have seen head injuries before, when I was an apprentice in Saldrium, and sometimes, patients just didn't wake up. "Commotion of the brain" I think I remember it being called. I read details about the assumed repercussions somewhere in my studies. I can't remember all the details and it troubles me, but what I do remember isn't promising.

I plop down on the stool beside Aaron. There is nothing more I can do for him. I've removed the dagger from his thigh, suturing the opening after bathing it in warm water to remove the dirt. I applied leeches around the area because it is already an angry red and hot to touch. I fear it will fester. The gash in his abdomen I just bathed in warm water, it is not as deep a cut as I originally thought, and wasn't bleeding any longer, so I left it alone. The scratches have all been cleaned of dirt and I have laid a blanket over Aaron's body because he is still quite cold to the touch and shivers rack him every so often. His head wound is more swollen than anything and aside from a little cleansing of dirt from the abrasion, there is little more I can do for it. I'm exhausted and feel utterly helpless now.

Brandon approaches and lays a hand on my shoulder giving it a gentle squeeze and a pat. My eyes never leave Aaron.

"We are heading back to the castle. Keep us posted on how he's doing, and if you need anything, send for us." He says. "Seriously, Chase. Anything."

I nod.

"Doctor Greaves is in the next room if you need his help again." Brandon continues. "I'm sending Caleb home to rest as well." He gives my shoulder another squeeze and removes his hand.

I nod again. There is no point in everyone standing over Aaron's body. None of it will make him any better. Only time will tell.

Once I'm left alone, the emotions from the last few days overwhelm me and uncontrolled sobs pour from my body. I lay my head on Aaron's chest, listen to his steady heart beating under my ear, and cry even harder.

What kind of a man am I to deny everything I had with Aaron? Yes, it is unconventional and yes it will shame my family and their name, but is living a lie for the rest of my days and dragging emptiness in my wake the way I want to live? No! Why did I run from happiness right into the arms of misery? I don't want to be married. I don't want to leave Ludairium and I don't want to live a day of my life without this man by my side. I know the connection Aaron is talking about, and I'd be lying to everyone if I continued to deny it. The way he warms my heart and makes me feel whole is something I have never felt before. Maker help me, I love him more than I realized.

I don't know for how long I lay softly weeping on the chest of the unconscious man who has stolen my heart, but the soft rap at the door makes me sit up, swipe frantically at my eyes trying to dry my tears, and cover my pain. Doctor Greaves pushes the door open a little, poking his head in.

"Your mother is here to see you, son. Should I tell her it's not a good time?"

I can see the concern in his face. That blasted woman will never let up. I rub at my swollen eyes and straighten my blood stained shirt. I look a wreak and feel even worse.

"Give me moment please."

He nods and ducks back out of the door, latching it behind him. I splash a few handfuls of water over my face and dry off on a clean rag. Fixing my features to something that hopefully hides my hurt proves to be more difficult. I know she will see right through me. She always does. I just hope she doesn't see too much because now is not how I want this to go down. I need more time to think.

Entering the main room, I avoid my mother's gaze and make my way to the herb laden shelf behind the table at the far side, hoping to look busy as I pull down random bottles and peer at them with scrutiny.

"I'm extremely busy, Mother. I don't have time for this right now."

"Chase. Alexander. Schuyler." Wow, I get all three names now, she is really pissed off. "You will come back to the castle with me right now and pay some element of attention to your future wife if I need to drag you there myself."

"Mother, I'm a doctor, as per you and Father's demands. I have a job to do right now and I cannot leave my patient. He is not well."

"This man is a doctor." She points to Doctor Greaves. "He will take care of that boy. You have other responsibilities."

"No." I meet her eyes and the aching I feel in my chest burns inside me. *He is not a boy.* I want to yell. *He is all man and he is my lover. He means more to me than you do.* "I'm not leaving him, Mother. He was close to dead when we found him and my job is to take care of and fix people. I will stay here all night if I have to. Leave me be."

My mother is taken aback with my tone and her momentary, stunned look silences the room.

"You forget yourself, child. You do not speak to your Mother like that. I will send your Father to deal with you."

She spins around in a flurry of skirts and I yell after her in frustration.

"Send Father, but he will get the same response. I'm not leaving."

She slams the door in her wake and only then does Doctor Greaves lift his eyes to meet mine.

"I think you have a decision to make, son. And soon by the look of things."

I know he's right. I don't respond and instead scrub a hand over my face as I return to Aaron's side, closing the door between the two rooms behind me.

Chapter Nineteen

Aaron

As I drift from the dream world back to the surface of consciousness, I recognize something to be different. The noises around me are not the same. I'm no longer cold or wet. The pain is nothing more than a dull throbbing now, much more tolerable than before. My eyes are heavy and I keep them closed, too tired to try opening them. So tired. I can feel the tug of the dream world wanting to draw me back down, and I'm ready to submit and let it take me away when I hear something different. Something new and yet strangely familiar echoing around above me. It keeps me grounded in this place, away from the comforts of the escape I long for. I want to fight against it, but I'm being guided by a soft, intimately recognizable voice calling my name.

"Aaron…Aaron, wake up."

I know this voice, only how, I can't remember. I want to open my eyes, but they are so heavy I can't muster the strength. It's the voice of longing and desire, one that sends a calming over my exhausted limbs. I want to see the face behind it. I try again to open my eyes.

"Aaron, open your eyes." *I'm trying.* "Aaron, it's Chase. Please come back to me."

The light that seeps in past my lids stings a little, but I force them wider, fighting the discomfort. Everything around me is a blur. A shiny, reflective room of bright lights. It's blinding and I blink a few heavy blinks before the fuzziness starts to clear. Coming into focus, is the angelic face belonging to the voice. It's even more beautiful than I remember. The soft green of his eyes are pooled and burdened with grief and sadness. Concern creases his forehead and worries his lip, but regardless, there has never been a face more perfect than the one looking down on me right now. This must be heaven. Something had been terribly wrong, but now I'm filled with such a calming peace, I know I must have passed to the afterlife and am in heaven where the angels all wear the gorgeous face of my sweet Chase.

"Aaron, can you hear me?"

The angel is speaking, but his words are unclear.

"Aaron, please try to look at me. Focus, Aaron. Can you see me?"

The haze around the angel's face begins to soften and edges begin to form. I hear my name falling off the angel's soft lips. His voice is worried. I shift my eyes to the clearing edges and angles of the room that are converging into solid objects. I try to make sense of what I'm seeing. A window; the source of the bright light. A table, laden with vials and a basin off to the side. Shelves with more vials and jars. I know this place. The pieces slowly fall back together as the voice becomes more distinct, clearer.

"Aaron. Can you hear me, Aaron…Please, do you understand what I'm saying?"

The unclouded form of Chase hovers over me. I feel his warm hand tracing my cheek and see soft tears falling from his reddened eyes. This isn't heaven. It's not an angel. It's Chase, my sweet Chase, and this is the surgery. I blink a few more times trying to dispel the remaining bits of fog. I want to stop his tears, they have caused an aching in my heart and I can't stand any more pain. My mind knows what I want to say, but I have to think hard to get the message to reach my mouth.

"I missed you."

My voice doesn't sound like my own, it is gravelly and raspy from not having been used and I have to listen to what I have said to ensure the words I spoke made sense. They must have. The tears falling from Chase's eyes flow with more abundance and his face is on mine, kissing me. Maker, how incredible his lips feel.

"Oh, thank the Maker." He says.

Kisses attack every piece of my face landing on my cheeks, my lips, my nose, and then on my forehead. I feel my body involuntarily flinch as a pain jolts through to my temples. He reels back, regret draining the color from his already pale face.

"I'm so sorry, Aaron. I didn't mean to hurt you."

Pain or not, I'm only sad because the kissing has stopped and Chase has pulled back in alarm.

"It's okay." My voice is clearer than it was a moment ago. "Please kiss me. Don't stop. Just not the head."

Chase's brings him lips to mine and kisses me so tenderly, I reconsider my original thoughts of this being heaven. Nothing has ever felt so amazing and the warmth it brings to my body soothes all my aches and pains. If it's not heaven, then this is what heaven should be like. Pulling back, he looks into my eyes, I already miss his warm mouth.

"How do you feel?" He asks.

I do an inward examination of my body, trying to feel it and answer honestly. There is pain. It's mild, but it's there. My arm has a dull throb, my head is pulsing along with my heartbeat from the recent attack of kisses it underwent. There is still a pressing weight on my body and I feel heavy and tired.

"Rough."

It's the simplest, most encompassing explanation I can offer. My energy is depleting and thinking is wearing me out fast.

"What happened to me?" I ask.

"I was hoping you could tell me. Can you remember anything?"

I squint my eyes at the light shining in the window and think back. There are snippets of information scratching at the surface of my brain, but none of them are clear thoughts and I can't find the answers I'm looking for. I shake my head in defeat, wishing I could force clarity.

"What is the last thing you remember?" He asks.

That answer comes easily and a wave of sadness and guilt overwhelm me. I had tucked that piece of information away inside, trying to forget it. I try to hide the hurt from my face and clear my throat.

"You left me."

I avert my eyes as the ache in my heart grows. How could I let myself forget that? Chase had walked away from me, telling me he didn't want me anymore. Shit, what the hell happened to me? How did I wind up in the surgery? Why do I have this overriding sense of guilt? I squeeze my eyes shut trying to think clearly and remember the circumstances leading up to this.

"Aaron… Stay with me. Look at me."

"I'm just thinking. Trying to remember something." Hesitantly, I open my eyes to look at him again. His expression is that of concern and love and it is leaving me confused. What am I not remembering?

"Listen, Chase." I try to form a proper thought to express myself. I know the man doesn't want a relationship with me. He made it clear and I will have to learn to accept it, but damn it, can we not at least be friends? I want his friendship more than anything. "I get that you don't want to do this with me anymore-"

"Aaron-"

"No, really. Listen. I won't lie, it hurts like hell, but I don't want to lose you as a friend."

"Shut up and listen, Aaron. I was wrong. I never should have left you. What we have is beyond anything I have ever known and I'd be a fool to turn my back on it."

I stare at him a little dumbstruck for a moment while my brain tries to catch up.

"But your parents and you're getting married. It's okay. I won't pretend I understand, but if you have to do this, please don't walk away from our friendship." I say.

Chase's eyes pool up again and I can see him blink the tears away as he places his hands to cradle my head.

"Aaron. You're not hearing me. I'm not going to marry her. I will find some way to tell my parents the truth," he lets out a wobbly breath, "even if they never speak to me again. I don't care. I need to do this for me…For us. I want to be with you. I want us to be together."

Chase pauses, but I can see he is not finished talking. His lips move around unspoken words as he tries to find them.

"Aaron, I love you. I'm not going anywhere, unless it's with you."

His lips are on mine again and I want to touch him and wipe his tears away, but when I make effort to lift my arm a jarring pain makes me gasp.

Chase pulls back and sees the pain in my face.

"Where are you hurting?"

"My arm." I squeeze my eyes shut and grit my teeth. "What's wrong with it?"

"It's broken. I have it wrapped up and flanked with wood to stabilize it. Try not to move it. You knocked your head quite badly too, and you have a really bad lump there, that's why it hurt when I kissed it earlier."

"Geez… Is that all?"

"No." It was meant as a sarcastic comment but I open my eyes again and see Chase's face scrunch up. Worry takes over his delicate features and he looks sadly down at me.

"What? Tell me."

"I need you to think and tell me what you do remember of the last few days."

I let out a frustrated sigh and again try to dig in my brain and come up with answers. Little bits of information come back one at a time as I poke into my memory but none of it makes sense.

"Buzzing. I remember a distinct buzzing…Oh, and water. I was wet."

"We found you at the water's edge, by the creek. Do you remember how you got there?"

"Umm…No…Not really. I remember suffocating. On more than water. It was pain." I shake my head. "I can't describe it better than that. It was like I was being drained of life somehow…" my voice trails off as something trickles back into the front of my mind. A thought wants to reveal itself, but it hasn't quite come into view yet and I concentrate on it in my mind, trying to see it.

"Aaron." Chase takes my hand gently and I feel his warmth wrapping around my fingers. "There are more injuries. You have a gash on your abdomen, and when we found you, your dagger was lodged in your thigh. Do you remember why?"

All is revealed as the elusive thoughts makes themselves visible. It's the trigger I need. As though someone washes away the dirt from a muddy painting, the picture I couldn't see before is now coming back into focus. The whiskey…So much whiskey. The uncontrollable urge to make the pain stop. The guilt slams back into me with full force. *Shit! What have I done?* My mouth falls open and I gape at Chase. *What have I done? What have I done?* I slowly pull my hand free from his grasp and muddle over what to say. I've never told Chase, yet the look on his face right now tells me I don't have to and he knows. I thought I was stronger than it. I thought I had left this in my past. How could I do something so stupid?

"Chase…I don't know what you know but I can see in your eyes you may have pieced together some things about me I haven't told you." I inhale a deep breath, steeling myself to do the right thing. "Once I explain it. I don't want you to feel bad or in any way make this out to be your fault. It's not. This is all on me and it's something I've been battling my entire life-"

"Aaron, look at me."

I look up from where I've been fidgeting with the blanket covering my body. I search deep into his beautiful green eyes staring back at me and wish this had all turned out differently.

"Did you cut yourself, Aaron?" Chase asks saving me breath.

Clenching my teeth tight together, forcing myself to hold his gaze, I nod.

"I'm a broken man, Chase. That's what I'm trying to tell you. I've been fighting this my whole life. I've been so good. It's been years since I acted on it, but I don't know what happened. I got overwhelmed. I didn't know how to stop it. Caleb and I have been working together to try to find other ways for me to manage, but I…I lost the control this time…I…I just…I shouldn't have done it. I should've went to Caleb for help like he told me to."

I want to turn away and hide myself. The shame and guilt of it all is too much. Chase's hand comes up and holds my face firm in place. I'm beyond embarrassed of my actions and curse myself for not handling it better. A child having these issues is understandable, maybe, but I'm a grown man, and to admit the lack of control that overcame me is humiliating. I don't want him to see the broken man that I am. Because that's what I am. No normal man succumbs to weakness like this, yet my whole life has been this awful fight for control I don't know any other way. I want to shrink out of sight, but Chase continues to hold me in place.

"Aaron… We can get through this."

"No! Chase, if you had known the half of it you would never have even tried with me. I wasn't honest with you and I'm too messed up for this…For us. I'm so sorry. I thought I was better…I thought-"

"You're not broken, you just were trying to cope the only way you know how, albeit, there are better ways than sinking blades into your skin, so shut up okay? I want to be with you. I want to be there for you and help you any way I can. Trust me. Believe in me."

"How could you want to be with me after you know what I do to myself?"

"It doesn't exactly come as a huge surprise, Aaron. You are the man who showed up at my door repeatedly to be healed. I questioned it back then. I guess I just didn't realize how deep it went. It doesn't change anything. I still want to be with you. Maybe we can work together and I can help you break this habit for good or at least support you if things get bad again."

I have to fight the overwhelming urge to fall into Chase's arms because I can't let him do this. No matter how badly I want it. I can see the guilt of what has happened all over his face. He blames himself and it's the last thing I need or want. This is my weight to bear not his.

"I can't do this to you, Chase. I can already see you trying to make this," I indicate to my broken body with my good hand, "your fault. It's not and I won't let you blame yourself."

"Aaron."

"What about your parents?"

"Forget them. I need to be a man and stand up to my parents. Take what I want from life and not worry so much about doing things their way anymore. I want this, Aaron. I want you. Let me love you."

Chase's lowers his lips to graze mine and plants soft kisses on the corners of my mouth, teasing his tongue gently on the crease. My willpower is weak. Maker, he feels good.

"I will not let you blame yourself." I say turning to capture his mouth with mine. When I lift my head to join our lips, he dodges my kiss and sends me on a chase after them. Smiling, he keeps them just out of my reach.

"Chase, kiss me." I plead. "Please. Maker help me, I've missed your lips on mine so much."

"You'll let me love you?"

How can I say no? How can I resist my heart's desire? I may be reckless and have a shit load of problems, but I'd like to think I'm not entirely foolish.

"Always."

The love in his eyes sparkles and glints with an emerald shine as his lips reconnect with mine. His kiss is light and I can tell he is afraid of hurting me. I slide my tongue along his mouth, encouraging him to deepen it, showing him I okay with more. Toying with my tongue he finally gives in and grants me the access I seek. His intoxicating taste bursts across my pallet as I explore every inch of his mouth, lifting my head to delve in even further, swirling my tongue with his, feeling the warmth of our bond heat up my entire body. I missed him so much, the euphoria of the kiss makes me forget my pain. I can feel myself growing stiff as he meets my aggression with his own and for an instant I'm thankful beyond measure that my cock is still in one piece. Now, I just need the rest of my body to cooperate so I can claim this man and show him just how much I love him.

I can feel Chase pulling away again, but this time he holds me down with a gentle hand on my chest, not allowing me to continue my pursuit.

"Lay back or you'll hurt yourself."

"I need you, Chase. I need to make love to you and hear my name whispered across your delicious lips as I take you places you have never known."

A smile grows on his face and he traces a hand down my chest, teasing around my growing erection, making me moan.

"I can see your excitement, soldier, but you need your rest. If you even tried that right now, you would probably set yourself back in your healing or cause permanent damage. Besides what kind of doctor would I be to allow that?"

"The merciful kind."

"Forget it. I'd hurt you."

"It would be worth it."

"Besides, I have some things I need to do right now. I have to go let down a sweet young lady and tell her I will not be her future husband. I have a mother to disappoint and a father to disgust with the revelation of my sexuality. If I don't go do this soon, I'm afraid it may all go down right here and you, Mr. Pryor, have no way of defending yourself, and to be honest, I'm a worse bodyguard than I am a swordsman. So I'm going to go let them down as far away from you as I can. It's all the protection I can offer."

"I appreciate that."

"I want you to rest. I have no idea how long I'll be, but I'll come right back, I promise you."

A deep yawn escapes me at the mention of resting and I realize I'm beyond tired. I'm exhausted.

"Good luck, Chase. I love you, truly."

He bends down and plants a soft kiss on my eye lids as I struggle to keep them open.

"I love you too, Mr. Pryor."

Chapter Twenty

Chase

The gates leading up the front of the castle stand open, as always. Since Alistair's coronation seven years ago, he has not allowed them to be shut for any reason. He refuses to close himself off from his people.

There are mountains of things to respect about this man who is our King. Under different circumstances, we may even have been friends. Today, despite our differences, I need him to be aware of my next step as it could swing back on him if I anger my father enough with my revelation. I'm not saying my father will forget himself and who owns the lands he runs, but he has never been one to mince words and his abrupt manor and lack of couth could have a negative affect if Alistair were to be caught off guard. Alistair and I may agree to disagree on most everything, but I know he will have my back today unquestionably.

Moving with measured paces up the front stairs, I speak with the guards and request audience with the King.

A single guard escorts me down a maze of halls and up a winding flight of stairs to a higher level, deep within the castle's heart. Rapping softly on a heavy wooden door, the guard asks me to wait as he enters the room.

I need to make this brief, explain the situation and leave. I can't get tangled into any other conversations, I need to confront my fears and my parents, before I lose my nerve.

Holding the door for me, the guard grants me access.

Alistair is sitting, bent over his desk at the far side of the room, writing; quill in one hand while the other traces methodically across his unshaven scruff. Terrace doors stand open and a warm breeze blows in, billowing the drapes that have been drawn aside and bring with it the telltale smells of fall; rotting leaves and damp earth. The fireplace sits cold; bookcases cover the opposing wall interspersed with paintings.

Alistair places his quill aside, and hides the papers he is busy working on out of my sight. He indicates to a chair against a wall to my right.

"Pull up a seat."

I obey, bringing the chair to sit opposite him at the table and sit awkwardly on the end of the seat. Common cause or not, I still don't feel comfortable being in the same room as this man.

"How's Aaron?" He asks.

"He's awake. Battered, sore, but I think he'll be okay. I don't see signs of permanent damage so far. He won't be able to fight for a while though, not with a broken arm."

"How long do you think until he can be back on the field?"

I shrug. "Hard to say. His arm is going to take some time to heal and it might cause him problems in the long run, but if he works at it, hopefully it won't affect him forever."

Alistair nods his head and leans back in his seat.

"I assume you have an answer for me."

Confusion creases my face and Alistair raises an eyebrow. I completely forgot I have yet to give him an answer about joining the negotiation party. Damn. In light of my decision to come clean to my parents and begin a relationship with Aaron, I'm no longer sure what my answer is any longer. Aaron's ability to go north if the armies should march this winter has now been compromised. What would he think if I up and left to go on what I still see as more or less a suicide mission? Shit. My previous decision to go doesn't feel right anymore and I don't know what to do.

"I don't know yet. It's not why I'm here. But I can have an answer for you tonight, if that's all right?" I just need more time to think.

His stern eyes study me as he picks up a mug and drinks deep. Whiskey no doubt, our King has an inexorable taste for it and I rarely see him without a mug close by.

"I'm here because I'm about to cause some potential hostility inside your castle walls and I thought it only fair to give you some warning."

This softens his feature and brings a smirk to his face.

"Is that so?"

"I'm about to approach the Lord of Saldrium and his wife and tell them I will not be marrying the Lady Maribelle. I'm also about to tell the man that his only son prefers the company of other men and that I'm no different than the sodomite barbarian who runs this realm."

Alistair nearly chokes on his next mouthful of whiskey as he burst out laughing. Not the reaction I was expecting.

"Between you and me, Chase, I never was fond of your father, he's kind of a dick." He says.

I smile. "Well that's a relief, because by the way he talks, he's not very fond of you either. I guarantee he will be abrupt in his departure and with luck he will have nothing to say to you, at least if he knows what's good for him. I just wanted you to know in case I'm wrong."

"I could enjoy a battle of words with him."

"I've had my fair share. The most recent and probably the last one I'll ever have is just moments away."

"I'd love to be a fly on the wall."

Standing, I give him a smirk. "Indeed." Bobbing my head, careful to ensure it doesn't look like a bow, I turn to go.

"Chase." Alistair calls out, stopping me at the door.

I glance over my shoulder.

"If you need to talk with Aaron about going north, I understand. Just have him keep his mouth shut, or he'll end up back in the creek by my own hand."

I turn all the way back to face Alistair. The man never ceases to surprise me. Not the throwing Aaron in the creek part; that I somehow expected from him. But the blatant display of empathy at my situation gives him a little bit of humanity and for the first time I can look past the infuriating negative traits and see the man Brandon sees. I smile warmly at him.

"Thank you. I really appreciate that, Alistair."

"Good Luck."

I let out a heavy sigh. I'll certainly need it.

* * *

Pacing outside the Lords apartments, I play words around in my head, trying to decide how to say what I have to say as quickly and painlessly as possible. The longer I pace, the more the nerves build up inside me. I can feel the internal shaking taking hold and without clenching my teeth together, they chatter uncontrollably. I hug my hands to my body and try to steady my breathing. I think of Aaron and know I'm doing the right thing, as hard as it is. For the first time in my life, I'm going to stand up to my parents and take my life back. It will have devastating consequences, but I can live with that and I'm ready for them. Giving my body a shake, I knock lightly on the door before pushing it open.

My mother and Lady Maribelle are in the next room, cozied up in the upholstered chairs by the window, both reading. My father is stewing over papers at the desk in the corner, drink in hand.

No one notices me until I clear my throat to draw their attention.

My mother looks up and her features turn as icy cold as her stare.

"Well, well, well, look who's here. How can we help you, young man?" She asks.

"Mother." I say with irritation.

"Oh no, you aren't my son. *My* son would not have disrespected his Mother with such harsh words, and in front of other people no less. *He* has more respect than that."

I roll my eyes at the juvenile game she is playing.

"Enough, Mother. I need a word with you and Father in private, if I could."

Lady Maribelle's eyes shift from me to Mother and back. She doesn't rise or make any effort to move.

"Nonsense. Chase Alexander, you can speak in front of your soon to be wife for crying out loud. Maker knows you've gone out of your way to avoid doing so thus far."

"I can't, Mother. I'm asking that she leave us in private. What I have to say is not for her ears."

I didn't notice my father come to stand close by, stern eyes drilling into me from above; at a height I didn't inherit.

"Leave us." He says to Lady Maribelle. His voice is stern, but his penetrating gaze never leaves me.

That gets her moving. She is up and out the door without being told twice. After her exit my Mother is on her feet, hands on her hips, huffing at me.

"What is this notion you have that you must keep your future wife out of this discussion? Honestly, Chase, she is to be married to you, she at least-"

"Stop, Mother." I say, louder than I intend.

"Do not speak to your mother with that tone, young man. I heard all about your little foray in the market and again at the surgery. Quite frankly, I'm disgusted with your behavior."

"Father, I'm trying to explain-"

"Enough. You will listen to what I have to say and stop the drivel from coming out of your mouth this instant." My father growls from above me.

I pull myself to my measly five feet, ten inches and square off with my monstrous looking, stone wall of a Father. I refuse to let him push me around anymore. Although, a little afraid he might throttle me, I keep my momentum going.

"No. No one ever listens to what I have to say and right now, I have something pretty damn important to say. So shut the bloody hell up and listen to me, dammit."

My father is taken aback and for once seems to have lost all ability to speak.

"I'm not marrying Lady Maribelle."

I let the words hang in the air as I catch my breath. My heart pounds harder in my chest as I hear the words leave my lips.

"Excuse me?" My mother asks.

"I'm not marrying her…or any other woman for that matter. I'm not returning to Saldrium either. I'm staying here and continuing my doctoring in Ludairium. The King has special need of me here to assist with the war efforts and the soldiers. I'm not leaving."

My mother's mouth is hanging open and my father's eyes have narrowed at me, but neither speak, so I keep pushing forward. Why stop now? I swallow hard and backtrack a little since I'm falling off course of how I wanted to say things.

"I'm not going to marry who you think I should marry, just because it happens to suit you. I have wants, desires, and needs to think about too. Besides, I'm in a relationship already and I'm not casting it aside because it is one you will not approve of."

"In a relationship. Chase, I had no idea." My mother says.

"Yes." I stutter before continuing. All or nothing. "He's the best thing that has ever happened to me. He is fun and loving and we get along really well. I'm in love with him and-"

"He?" My father's voice booms over top of everything I'm saying.

I swallow the lump in my throat. "Yes. He. I'm not marrying a woman, because I have no desire to. I have no interest in being with a woman, I never have. I have always preferred men and I'm not hiding it anymore, from you or anyone, because I don't have to. Laws were abolished last winter and it is no longer forbidden. I refuse to hide away like a bloody coward any longer."

"Oh, Chase. You are mistaken, honey."

My mother is up at my side, grasping my hand, but I pull away.

"I'm not, Mother. This is who I am, and you can accept me for it or not, but I hope you can accept me."

"Baby, you are just confused."

"Maker help me, Mother, I'm not confused."

My father stands over me, his larger frame dwarfing me.

"No son of mine is a sodomite bastard. You were raised better than that, and you will stop this nonsense coming from your mouth this instance. Do you understand me?"

I turn and look up into my father's dark, angry eyes and for the first time in my life, stand my ground, unafraid.

"I will not. I'm no different than our sovereign ruling this realm, Father, and if you can't handle that then I'm sorry the Maker has made you so close minded that you would rather your son live a lie than be happy."

"That barbarian of a King has done this to you. You have lived in this city too long under his influence. He has spoken poison into your brain. You forget who you are."

I laugh. I actually laugh out loud right in my father's face. "Guess what, Father. I know exactly who I am. Your son has been sharing his bed with men long before ever moving to this city. I've known who I am since I was ten years old, long before that man was ever our King. This has nothing to do with him. It has everything to do with you. Look at me," I hold my hands up, "This is who I am. Accept who your son is or don't, but I can't change it any more than you can."

I can see the fire burning behind his eyes as he leans in close to my face. I don't flinch from him, I stand firm.

"Then you are not my son."

He turns and storms from the room without another word.

I expected that reaction. I planned for that exact thing and worse, yet the stab in my heart at hearing his words hurts me to my core. I meet my mother's eyes; she is struggling to know what to do. Her loyalty to her husband makes her want to take flight, but I can see the pain behind her eyes as she looks at me. Knowing, if she walks out now, she loses her son for good.

Cupping my face in her firm grip, she looks at me with pleading eyes, "Chase, baby, are you speaking truthfully?"

"I am, Mother."

"And this man you are seeing?"

"His name is Aaron and I love him. Nothing you say will change that."

She nods understanding. "I love you, son, but I must stand by your father. You know this."

"I know." And I do. I was prepared for it. "You take care of yourself, Mother. I don't expect he will allow us to see each other again."

My mother places a soft kiss on my forehead.

"Regardless, you will always be *my* son."

I kiss my mother's cheeks before ushering her out the door. I do not want my troubles to become hers and I know my father's stern hand.

Alone in the apartments, I collapse into one of the chairs by the window. I know I should feel relived at having such a weight lifted off my shoulders, but the heaviness I feel contradicts my expectations. Somewhere deep inside I had hoped beyond hope that my parents could love me anyway. It was foolish thinking and the sadness at being without a family hurts like an open wound.

I hope Lady Maribelle isn't too upset. I had hoped I could break the news to her myself. Now, I have no doubt she will hear horrific lies about me instead; in my father's attempt to cover up the atrocity that is, or rather was, his son.

"Am I interrupting?"

The soft, barely there voice startles me from my musing and I look up to see the bluey-purple gaze of the Lady Maribelle.

"My Lady," I say, standing, "I was just thinking of you. I figured you would be with my parents, hearing vicious stories by now, and be halfway back to Saldrium."

She smiles shyly and lowers her gaze.

"They went barreling past me in the deep throws of an intense conversation I did not want to interrupt. I would be surprised if they even noticed me."

"Ah...So you don't know?"

She tilts her head and her smile grows. "Don't know what exactly?"

"Oh...Umm." I'm not sure I know how to start, I abandoned the idea of having this same conversation again after my father stormed out, assuming they would have told her immediately.

"I'm going to wager a guess that you do not want to marry me?" She says smile still steady on her face.

"That is part of it yes." I say, keeping her gaze. I feel it's only fair to be brave and give this woman the truth. "But, if you'll allow me to explain."

She holds a hand up stopping me.

"I'm going to wager another guess and forgive me, Doctor, if I am incorrect, but I think that I am not. This Caleb man's friend, the one who was missing and who is now found, is your lover correct?"

The shock must have been clear on my face.

"I guessed right?" She asks.

"How did you know?"

"My dear Doctor, you cannot hide the love you have for him from your eyes. It is plain as the nose on your face." She tweaks my nose and smirks.

"Please forgive me for misguiding you, it was never my intent. I'm sure you are a lovely woman."

"I'm relieved you decided to let it out. Being married to a man who cannot love me, through no fault of his own, would have made for a sad life for both of us."

"You'll will make someone a wonderful wife someday. You are indeed a lovely woman and very beautiful."

"Thank you, Doctor. I'm sure my father will have more suitors lined up for me once I'm home."

"Indeed." Taking the Lady Maribelle's hands in my own, I kiss both her cheeks. "Safe travels, My Lady. I apologize for what you may have to endure on your journey."

Chapter Twenty-One

Aaron

By the time Chase returns in the early evening, I have convinced Doctor Greaves to assist me in sitting up. I have a dull ache in my head and if I'm not careful how I move my arm, I send sharp pains to shoot down to my fingers; making them numb. The dizziness and nausea have passed and aside from an overall feeling of weakness, coupled with a twinge of hunger, I feel significantly better.

"You're up." Chase says upon seeing me sitting. "Do you feel all right?"

"I've felt better, but I'm okay."

My eyes shift over to the elderly doctor who takes the hint and leaves the room with a smile, closing the door behind him.

"How did it go?" I ask.

Chase pulls up a stool beside me and flops down on it with a sigh. "Well, I'm orphaned, that's for sure. My poor mother will no doubt be getting an earful all the way back to Saldrium. My father will find some way of blaming this all on her. You know, had she raised me differently, I surely wouldn't be like this. Probably needed to be more stern or not let me stir the soup that one time when I was six."

"Right, because that's why." I laugh.

Chase lays his hands on my legs, and rubs them carefully to avoid the fresh wound and sutures where my dagger had lodged itself in my fall.

"I have to talk to you about something, Aaron."

His voice becomes serious and I take his hand in mine and give it a squeeze.

"Is everything okay?" I ask. Chase looks worn out and I'm afraid he's over doing himself.

"I just need to run something by you." He plants a soft kiss on my lips.

I nod. "Okay."

"Alistair has made a request of me and I need to give him an answer this evening sometime, but I can't make a decision without talking to you first. It only seems fair."

His gaze is following his hands as they caress up and down my legs and he can't seem to look at me. I can tell whatever it is, it's important and it's bothering him. I tilt his head up to meet my gaze and let a finger trail down his cheek and across his lips. His eyes are blood shot and swollen. Dark bags hang heavily underneath them giving away his exhaustion.

"You look tired." I say.

Chase tries for a weak smile and drops his gaze again to my lap.

"Look at me, please." I pull his face up again. "What do you need to say?"

"They are trying to avoid going to war. Alistair has set up a negotiation party to cross the border and talk terms with the leader of the Outsiders. He's asked me to join them. I don't know details, but he has assured me every precaution is being taken to ensure the safety of his men. Although, he also warns of the possibility that it could all go downhill. Brandon feels strongly that it will be a successful mission. He's taken over as tactical advisor and he has a good head on his shoulders. I trust his word. Anyhow, I'm not being ordered to go, but asked. Alistair's allowing men to choose if they want to be a part of it or not. I promised him an answer by tonight."

The air in my lung thickens and I hold it there, unable to let it out or draw more in. The aching burn in my chest begs me to breathe, but I can't seem to remember how. I know the seriousness of our cause. I came to Ludairium for that precise reason. I want to fight for our lands and I know the risks it entails. I just never assumed to fall in love and that the man I loved would need to put himself in the same position. How do I tell him to stay? How do I be so selfish as to not want him to put himself in harm's way, when I would expect to be doing the same. Yet, how do I let him go, knowing it's the right thing and that I may never see him again?

"When would you leave?" I ask. My voice breaks and the turmoil I'm feeling is evident in the squeak.

"The intention is early winter and only if we fail in our negotiations would the armies need to march."

"I can't march with them any longer."

"I know." Chase says sympathetically.

"Do you want to go? Do you want to do this?" My heart pounds in my ears.

"It scares me, but I feel like it is where I'm needed and what I'm supposed to do. As much as Alistair and I don't see eye to eye, I trust him and I trust Brandon. If things go wrong, it will be through no fault of theirs."

I nod as I shimmy my body forward on the table and let my feet rest on the floor below. I'm not sure if my legs are strong enough to hold my own weight, but I'm about to find out. Using my unwrapped arm, I take a firm hold of Chase's arm and shift my weight from the table to my legs.

"What are you doing?" Chase's voice is alarmed and he takes tight hold of me, anticipating I may fall.

"We are going back to your place, because it's closer and I know I'll never make it to mine, and I'm going to make love to you before I pass out, which hopefully won't happen before we are finished or I will be seriously embarrassed."

"Like hell you are. Sit down, soldier, and do as you are told."

Leaning hard on Chase, getting my balance, I risk letting go of his arm, and trace a thumb across his lips as I bring my face down, claiming his mouth. He tries to pull away, but I hold his chin firm and pull him closer, pressing my tongue to his opening, demanding access. His willpower weakens and he wraps his arms around me, probably more to ensure my stability then for any other reason, and allows me to deepen the kiss and explore what I want. Releasing his mouth, only for the need to breathe, I lean in to his ear.

"Do not tell me what I can and cannot do, Doctor. If you are leaving me to put your life at risk for our lands, then I will spend every instant of the time I have left with you, claiming this gorgeous body of yours and making you remember that you are mine. I want to give you a reason to fight harder so you will come home again. Now, help me back to your place, and give yourself over to me, or do you intend to make me beg?"

Without another word, Chase wraps an arm around my waist and helps guide me to the door. I'm more stable than I anticipated, but the desire to have the man on my arm is no doubt giving me more strength than I would ordinarily have.

* * *

Sleep and exhaustion pull me down under its great weight and I can feel myself losing my battle with consciousness. A thin sheen of sweat and the gorgeous body of my naked man cover me and I have never felt so at peace. Chase's face is buried in my neck and I can hear the soft sounds of his labored breathing as his body comes down off the high of our love making. I trace my hand up and down his bare back and pull him tighter against me. I never want to leave this glorious moment and fight the sleepiness tugging me down. Chase stirs and buries his head deeper into my neck. His lips move over the soft skin and his teeth take a nibble here and there, causing shivers to course over my body and my cock to reawaken.

"Be careful, Doctor, you will undo me at this rate."

"What happened to spending every moment we have claiming my body? Have you given up already after only one time?" He says between bites.

"Never." I whisper in his ear. I slide my hand lower to cup his firm ass in my hand. "I will make love to you with every ounce of strength I have in me, although I'm afraid it is dwindling faster than I had hoped."

Chase lifts his head to meet my gaze, his eyes are wide and filled with concern.

"Aaron, I'm teasing, are you okay? You really should be resting."

"Nonsense, I said dwindling, not gone."

I lift my head and claim his mouth before he can object, and hold him close to me, my hand never leaving his firm backside. I can feel his desire growing between our close pressed bodies and know I'm in trouble. Strength of body and strength of mind are two different things and right now I can only pray my body can hold up to what my mind has in store.

Chapter Twenty-Two

Chase

Reluctantly, having left Aaron sleeping in my bed, I sit in Alistair's solar for the second time today and await his arrival. The sweet taste of Aaron's lips and the warmth of his touch still linger on my skin. Once my business here is complete, I look forward to rejoining him and spending the rest of the night with our bodies pressed close together. I feel incredibly selfish for not letting my patient rest and feel better, but the desire to be near him is stronger and he's making it really hard to be the stern doctor I know I should be.

The sound of a door opening behind me brings me to my feet, and years of respect having been drilled into me makes me have to consciously stop and think before I bow and insult the man before me. I greet Alistair instead with a nod and lower myself back in my chair as he comes around to sit across from me at the desk.

"I've been informed Lord and Lady Schuyler have vacated the premise. Went well I take it?"

I smile and nod. "It went as expected. I'm glad you didn't have to endure my father's wrath. He was pretty upset."

"I could have handled him."

"I have no doubt you could have."

Alistair leans back in his seat and props his feet up on his desk. "So, I take it you have an answer?"

"I've decided to go with your men beyond the border." I say, getting to the point directly.

Alistair lets out a relieved breath, rubs a hand over his face and through his hair.

"Thank you, Chase. I know it was probably a difficult decision, but I'm truly grateful you have decided to go. I hope there will be no need for your doctoring skills, but sending the men without a healer didn't sit well with me."

"I understand. Do you have any more details you can share with me? Do you have a better idea when this will be happening, when we'll be leaving?"

Alistair drops his feet to the ground and sits more forward at his desk, pursing his lips. Alistair studies me. I hate being in the dark and I'd prefer to be prepared for what I'm facing.

"Well, we've had correspondence from the other side. Their leader, who has remained nameless, has agreed to the meeting, but they've made certain demands before they will agree to a party of my soldiers stepping foot on their grounds for negotiations."

"I'm afraid to ask what those might be."

Alistair lets out a heavy sigh. "They want our men fully escorted while on their lands, which is understandable. They want us to lay down our weapons. The party will be escorted to meet with whoever this is who commands them. This part doesn't sit as well with me, but Brandon seems to think it is a reasonable demand and one that he was expecting. He's not concerned. They have given me their word that our men will not be harmed, provided we cooperate fully. Regardless of the outcome of the negotiations, our men will return unscathed. Lastly," he pauses and drums his fingers over the table, "they want *me* to be the one to hand over my men at the border."

I shuffle in my seat. "You? This sounds sketchy and dangerous. They expect us to just trust them and put you out there in harm's way?"

"Yeah. The council and Brandon don't agree with the last request. They want me nowhere near the border and no part of this at all. I'm to remain in Ludairium."

"So what happens if we don't agree with all their terms? Will it fall through?"

"An alternative is being considered to that particular demand. One I'm not pleased with."

"Should I ask?"

"Hmm." Alistair studies me and strokes a thumb through the scruff on his chin before shaking his head. "I plan to pull the party together in the coming days and go over everything in full detail. You'll know everything you need to know then. You'll have to be satisfied with waiting."

I nod understanding as I rise from my seat. "I should go. I need to keep an eye on my patient. I'm not sure I can trust him to lay still long enough to heal properly without supervision."

Alistair chuckles. "Tell him his King says to behave and listen to his doctor. I need him back on that field."

We share a smile as I head for the door. "I'll pass it on."

* * *

In order to keep an eye on Aaron's healing, I suggested he stay with me for a few days while the worst of his injuries healed - and selfishly because I just didn't want to send him home. I quite like sharing a bed with him, despite having to gear back his eager libido a little bit which evidently remained completely intact after his fall. Every day his injuries are a little better and now, aside from his broken arm, what remains are nothing but minor nuisances.

Doctor Greaves continues to run the surgery, insisting that I take some time to sort myself out and have a break. The man was exceptionally pleased to hear of my decision not to marry the Lady Maribelle. In fact, he beamed like a proud father when I openly decided to tell him that Aaron and I are together. It's freeing to say the words out loud and I can only imagine it will feel even better with every day that I become more comfortable accepting this new life.

This morning I suggested we head for a walk around the outskirts of the city so Aaron can get some exercise and fresh air. Hand in hand we make our way through the thick forest toward the pond where - what now feels like a lifetime ago - three bears sent us scurrying away in fear. The fall air is cooler today and when we sit back in the same spot by the water's edge we don't dip our feet in but instead curl up into each other's arms for some added warmth.

"Winter's coming on quick this year." Aaron says as he pulls me in tight against him and kisses the top of my head.

"It is." I let out a sigh. "Why do I always end up on the damn road in the winter time? I hate the cold."

Aaron chuckles. "All the more reason to get this business done quickly and get back here. I'll keep you warm every night if you'll let me."

"Nothing would make me happier." I let my fingers trail along Aaron's thigh as I listen to his heart under my ear. "You'll take care of yourself while I'm gone, won't you?"

"I will."

"No picking up a sword until Doctor Greaves gives you the okay."

"Yes, Doc. Don't worry, I'll behave."

We rest quietly for a long while simply sharing the moment, neither of us feeling a necessity for words. As the afternoon sun begins its decent in the sky, I shuffle around so I can look more directly into Aaron eyes. "Aaron...You're doing a lot better now and I know you were kinda staying with me while you recovered from the worst of your injuries-"

His eyes sadden. "Have I overstayed my welcome?"

"No!" I jump in, "Not at all. I was just going to ask…I mean if you wanted to… Will you stay?"

"You mean room with you?"

"Yes… If you want to."

A warm smile fills Aaron's face and a shine radiates from his eyes as he brings his thumb up to trace it across my bottom lip. "I can't think of anything I'd want more." He leans in capturing my mouth in a kiss, softly and sweetly, pouring all his heart into me in the one simple gesture. "I love you, Chase." He whispers against my lips.

"I love you, Aaron."

Cradling my head back against his shoulder he removes my tie to stroke his fingers through my hair in that all too familiar way. Silence grows between us and I know we are both thinking of the near future and what it might bring. It seems so unfair that I finally find the strength to walk my own path in life and I'm forced to take a detour. But that's all it is, I remind myself, a detour. Aaron will be here. Aaron will wait for me.

"I will miss you." I say.

He squeezes me a little tighter against his chest. "I'll be right here waiting for you when you get back, because you *are* coming home, Chase. You are. I refuse to see it any other way."

"I'm coming home," I affirm, "and we'll be together."

"Always."

Epilogue

Chase

The buzz of voices in the Great Hall give off an aura of trepidation and nerves on edge. There are about twenty-five soldiers gathered alongside myself and a few councilmen waiting for the promised address regarding our trip north.

I can still feel the warmth of Aaron's breath where he whispered in my ear on my way out this morning - from our home, our together spot, our beginning - *Don't be afraid, handsome. This war will not be forever. You and I, however, will be. I promise you.* I smile at the memory and bring a hand to my heart as I wedge myself between a few soldiers and make my way to the front of the bustle so I can see better.

Alistair is upfront in the deep throws of a conversation with Brandon, the tension between them a near palpable thing; thick and icy cold. Brandon arms are crossed over his chest, eyes like stone, with an expression that is less than readable. Alistair, however, is speaking intently to him, touching him frequently; the vision of a pleading, desperate man who is on the verge of losing his control. Alistair never was very good at masking his emotions and right now he clearly doesn't give a shit who's watching him. He's animating his point with failing arms and gestures, and as I watch them escalate, I try to get a reading for what's going on. Alistair finishes saying whatever he is saying and looks to Brandon expectantly with wide eyed uncertainty. Brandon finally meets his gaze, but his expression remains firm and impenetrable. He simply shakes his head with finality and I see Alistair's shoulders slump as he looks up at the ceiling, rolling his head on his shoulders in defeat. It's only then that Brandon's face softens slightly and he reaches out to squeeze Alistair arm. I see the forming of the words "I'm sorry" pass over Brandon's lips. Alistair shakes his head and pulls back, gesturing to the crowded room before he walks away with what looks like a mixture of frustration and hurt. Brandon's eyes follow him a moment before he sets his jaw and walks forward toward the waiting assemblage.

"All right men. If we can gather around, we'll get this ball rolling."

A hush falls over the room as all eyes turn toward Brandon. Alistair has planted himself on the far wall with his head down as he chews his thumb. Something isn't right. The chill coursing over my body makes me shiver as I turn my attention back to Brandon.

"Firstly, I'd like to thank each and every one of you for choosing to take part in what will hopefully be the final step to end a war. Through correspondence with the Outsiders we have finalized the plans for crossing the border and I'd like to ask everyone to be prepared to ride by the new moon. That's fourteen days from now. Pack light. Pack warm. You will be on a tight schedule."

The hum in the room elevates slightly and Brandon needs to raise his hand to settle the men.

"There are certain stipulation that have been agreed upon for these negotiations and I'd like to share these with you so you are prepared for what you will be facing once you reach the border." Brandon pauses and steals a glance over to Alistair who still refuses to look up at him. I see a flick of something pass over Brandon's face but when he turns back to continue his speech he is as firm as ever and whatever was there is now gone. "When you reach the border you will ride through to the midway point of the pass in the mountains. You will be met there by an escort of Outsiders to take you on the final leg of your journey to meet with their leader. It is at this point that it has been agreed upon that you will lay down your weapons and cross the border unarmed." Brandon takes a deep breath before continuing and I see the first signs of worry crinkle his forehead ever so slightly. "The Outsiders have demanded that our King be present at the border for the exchange." The men stir again and a wave of opinions flow through the crowd as murmurs and whispers.

"I can hear you admonishing the idea before I'm even finished speaking and I agree with you. The council agrees with you. Our King should be nowhere near the border and it is a risk we are not willing to take."

I dart my eyes back to Alistair. Still the man remains with a bowed head, chewing his thumb raw and bloody.

"The council and I have come up with an alternative to this demand that we feel will be effective."

"The Outsiders have been poking our borders continually for the past two years, yet there has never been an attack as far south as here in Ludairium. There is no reason to believe that these men have any knowledge of who our King is or what he looks like. For this reason, we have decided that *I* will ride with the party, along with an additional five men to be responsible for my safety and *I* will take the responsibility of impersonating our King at the border for the exchange."

My jaw hangs slack as his words and their understanding become clear. I shift my eyes frantically between Alistair and Brandon, the pieces to their mysterious conversation a moment ago falling into place. Brandon continues to speak, but his words fade into the background as I tune him out. I watch Alistair shove off the wall and stumble away to the back of the room looking as though he is carrying the weight of the world on his shoulders. He walks out the doors at the far end and I hesitate a moment, glancing back to Brandon as he continues to update the men.

Bloody hell.

For reasons I can't piece together or understand, I spin around and shove past a few men to follow Alistair out the doors.

I find him halfway down the hall sitting on the ground with his head in his hands. Having approached him cautiously, I slide down the wall opposite him. He glances up and looks unsettled to find me there. Ignoring his discomfort, figuring it is better not to draw attention to the awkwardness between us, I simply move the conversation forward.

"This sounds dangerous. You're letting him go?" I ask.

"I can't convince him to change his mind, Chase. He's stubborn." He sighs and leans his head back against the wall behind him. "He wants to go and the blasted council agree with him. They think he'd be the ideal person because he knows me best. The fact that he can strategize on the spot and deals well under pressure only solidifies his case. He's confident and determined…and…I just can't…" Threading a hand through his hair he shakes his head. He looks worn out. The coming war is stacking years on his life mercilessly. "I can't say no to him. I want to, but I can't. Not when he wants it this badly. Shit. How the hell am I supposed to be okay with this? Huh?"

I understand fully. How can you send the man you love more than life itself into such a dangerous situation with no guarantees? It's the same thing Aaron is doing with me…Letting go, knowing it's what has to be done. Trusting in fate to bring me home again.

"Brandon is wise beyond his years, Alistair, but you already know that. His mind works far beyond yours or mine and if he thinks this is how it should happen, he's probably right."

"That's just it. I know that… I know."

I don't know what else to say. The reality of this looming war has pressed down on the people of Ludairium for years. It's coming to a head. Our future will be determined soon. Everyone will do their part because it's what's right. It's what's expected. But the outcome has always been hidden behind a thick fog, unseen and unknown.

Alistair meets my eyes and for once there is no jealousy or hostility toward me, only a pleading look. Desperation. Fear.

"Please watch out for him. Please don't let him do anything stupid."

Something changes between us in that moment, in that single request as we sit across from each other. A new found respect forms and I find myself nodding, agreeing to his wishes, knowing full well if I fail and any harm comes to this man's lover that I will have an even worse fate to come home to.

The End...For now.

Coming Soon

August 2016

"Secrets Best Untold"

Nothing goes as expected. Nothing is as it seems.

The final book in the Tales from Edovia series will revisit Alistair and Brandon as they try to save the realm from the Outsiders.

The stakes are high. The price is steep.

Can true love survive?

About the Author

I live in the small town of Petrolia, Ontario, Canada and I am a mother to a wonderful teenage boy (didn't think those words could be typed together...surprise) and wife to a truly supportive and understanding husband, who thankfully doesn't think I'm crazy...yet.

I have always had two profound dreams in life. To fall back hundreds of years in time and live in a simpler world not bogged down by technology, and to write novels. Since only one of these was a possibility I decided to make the other come alive on paper.
I write mm romance novels that take place in fantastical, medieval type settings and love to use the challenges of the times to give my stories and characters life.

You can find me on Facebook and twitter.

Reviews are the best way to thank an author. Consider leaving a review on Amazon or Goodreads. Thanks!

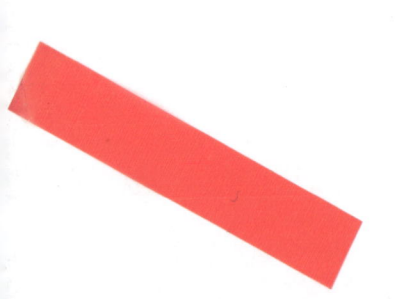

Made in the USA
Lexington, KY
20 August 2016